W9-BZD-779

The Vampire

A. M. Milnige 8·2011

Edited by Alan Dundes

The Vampire

A Casebook

The University of Wisconsin Press

The University of Wisconsin Press
1930 Monroe Street, 3rd floor
Madison, Wisconsin 53711-2059

3 Henrietta Street
London WC2E 8LU, England

www.wisc.edu/wisconsinpress

Copyright © 1998
The Board of Regents of the University of Wisconsin System
All rights reserved. No part of this publication may be reproduced,
stored in a retrieval system, or transmitted, in any format or by any
means, digital, electronic, mechanical, photocopying, recording, or
otherwise, or conveyed via the Internet or a Web site without written
permission of the University of Wisconsin Press, except in the case of
brief quotations embedded in critical articles and reviews.

4   6   8   7   5

Printed in the United States of America

Library of Congress Cataloging-in-Publication Data

The vampire: a casebook / edited by Alan Dundes.
190 pp.   cm.
Includes bibliographical references and index.
ISBN 0-299-15920-5 (cloth: alk. paper).
ISBN 0-299-15924-8 (pbk.: alk. paper)
1. Vampires.   I. Dundes, Alan.
GR830.V3V33   1998
398.21—DC21   98-10399

ISBN-13: 978-0-299-15924-5 (pbk.: alk. paper)

Contents

Preface

The vampire is one of the most fascinating but at the same time fearsome of all the creatures of folklore. Most people are familiar with the vampire through literary novels and short stories as well as a host of films featuring this frightening and loathsome revenant who returns at night from his grave to suck the blood of his hapless victims. But the fact is that the vampire did not originate in literature or popular culture. Literary and motion picture vampires are secondary, deriving from a long history of traditional legends found especially prominently in eastern Europe. It is these legends or folklore of the vampire which are the basic source of the endless series of literary and film depictions of this representation of the "living dead."

Unfortunately the bulk of the voluminous scholarship devoted to the vampire has tended to concentrate on the literary and the popular cultural manifestations of the vampire, often giving scant attention to their folkloristic underpinnings. The present casebook is an attempt to redress this imbalance. Literary vampires such as the celebrated Dracula of Bram Stoker's 1897 novel will be mentioned only in passing; there are plenty of books and essays devoted to that one novel alone. This set of essays is specifically designed to treat the traditional, not the literary, vampire.

We begin with Katharina Wilson's essay on the history of the term *vampire*, including a discussion of the various theories of the word's possible etymology. Then we have selected from the numerous ethnographic accounts of the vampire in various east European countries one of the most comprehensive and detailed of these, namely, Agnes Murgoci's "The Vampire in Roumania." This is followed by a more sophisticated consideration of the Romanian vampire by one of the leading contemporary students of the vampire, Professor Jan Louis Perkowski of the University of Virginia. Since the vampire is also reported in many other east European and Slavic cultures, we selected a representative survey of such instances by Professor Felix Oinas of Indiana University, the doyen of scholars in the United States concerned with Slavic folklore.

The next three essays refer to the vampire in the former Yugoslavia with references to Serbia and Bosnia. Professor John V. A. Fine, Jr., of the University of Michigan offers a fascinating glimpse of early nineteenth-century Serbian cases of the state and church trying in vain to halt vampire-hunters from unearthing and desecrating the graves of suspected vampires. Friedrich S. Krauss, one of the leading folklorists at the begin-

[handwritten margin note:] Tired of people looking at the end result of vampires instead of the genesis of them.

[handwritten margin note:] 2 U.S. Scholars on the Folklore.

vii

ning of the twentieth century, wrote a brief note on countermeasures employed to ward off vampires, a note which is rarely cited. Krauss's note is followed by a most interesting discussion by Veselin Čajkanović, a professor of classics at Belgrade University in the 1920s. Stimulated by a newspaper report of a Bosnian vampire, he tries to determine whether the custom of burning a vampire arose earlier or later than the custom of driving a stake through its body to neutralize it.

From Serbia, we move next to Greece. Juliette du Boulay, a British social anthropologist, not only provides excellent ethnographic detail about the vampire in modern Greece, but also attempts to delineate an ambitious structural model to explicate that detail. Because her study is limited to Greek data, it is not clear whether her analysis of the Greek vampire does or does not apply to vampires in other cultures.

The last three essays are not so much concerned with the vampire in a particular cultural setting as with seeking to understand the vampire phenomenon in general. The first of the three is a remarkable erudite study by historian Paul Barber, who proposes a novel approach to the vampire. He believes that most if not all of the beliefs surrounding the vampire can be explained in terms of the *folk* perception or misperception of what happens to a cadaver after death. The second of the three final essays represents the clinical and criminological approaches to vampires. There seem to be individuals who act out vampirelike behavior; that is, they ingest the blood of their victims. Whether this bizarre behavior is *caused by* vampire folklore or whether it is a possible original *cause of* vampire folklore is not altogether certain. In any case, Professor Philip Jaffé of the University of Geneva and Frank DiCataldo of the Bridgewater State Hospital in Bridgewater, Massachusetts offer quite a different perspective on the vampire or vampirism. The last essay, by the editor, tries to achieve a combined folkloristic and psychoanalytic approach to bring the volume to a close.

The reader may or may not find persuasive any of the various theoretical attempts to illuminate the vampire of tradition. But at the very least, the reader may come to understand that the vampire is much more than simply a scary creature of the human imagination. The vampire has been and continues to be a factor in the lives of all those who encounter it—in reality or in fiction. It is truly a matter of life and death!

The Vampire

The History of the Word *Vampire*

Where does the word vampire *come from? How old is it? Is it of Turkish origin? Serbian origin? Bulgarian origin? Hungarian origin? There has been considerable discussion among scholars about when and where the term may have originated. Professor Katharina M. Wilson of the University of Georgia reviews the competing theories and tries to track the first appearances of the word in French, German, English, and other languages.*

For other considerations of the possible etymology of vampire, *see Hans Holm Bielfeldt, "Die Wortgeschichte von deutsch* 'Vampir' *und* 'vamp' " *in* Serta Slavica in Memoriam Aloisii Schmaus *(Munich: Rudolf Trofenik, 1971): 42–47; and Kenneth E. Naylor, "The Source of the Word* Vampir *in* Slavic," *Southeastern Europe 10 (1983): 93–98. Both of these studies argue for a Slavic origin of the word.*

Like the legend of the living dead, so the origin of the word *vampire* is clouded in mystery. For most readers and authors alike, the vampire is a dark and ominous creature of the woods of Hungary or Transylvania. His name is often believed to be of the same national origin.[1] However, both linguistic studies concerning the etymology of the term *vampire* and the first recorded occurrences of the word in major European languages indicate that the word is neither Hungarian nor Romanian.

There are four clearly discernible schools of thought on the etymology of *vampire*, advocating Turkish, Greek, Slavic, and Hungarian roots for the term. The four groups are, respectively, chronological and geographic entities: the first group is represented by a nineteenth-century Austrian linguist and his followers; the second consists of scholars who were the German contemporaries of the early eighteenth-century vampire craze; the third comprises recent linguistic authorities; and the last is almost entirely limited to recent English and American writers.

The first group of etymological theorists on the word *vampire* consists of Franz Miklosich and many followers, Montague Summers and Stephan

Reprinted from the *Journal of the History of Ideas* 46 (1985): 577–583.

3

Hock among them, who use him as their authority.[2] Miklosich, a late nineteenth-century Austrian linguist, suggests in his influential work *Etymologie der slavischen Sprachen* that the word *vampire* and its Slavic synonyms *upior, uper,* and *upyr* are all derivatives of the Turkish *uber* (witch).

The second theory subscribes to the classical origins of the term. Summers, for instance, refers to an unidentified authority claiming the Greek verb πι (to drink) as a possible source for *vampire*.[3] Another etymological explanation along this line was proposed by Harenberg in the eighteenth century. S. Hock quotes the German scholar as saying, "Es läst sich vermuten dass das Wort zusammen gesetzet sey aus Bluht draus Vam geworden, und piren, das ist begierig nach einer Sache trachten."[4]

The third theory, which advocates the Slavic origin of the word, has now gained almost universal acceptance, and the root noun underlying the term is considered to be the Serbian word *BAMITUP*. Kluge, Falk-Torp, the Grimm brothers, Wick, and Vaillant all point to the Serbian origin of the word as do, for example, the *OED* (London, 1903), the German *Brockhaus,* the Spanish *Encyclopedia Universal Illustrada* (Madrid, 1930–33), and the *Swensk Etymologisk Ordbok* (Lund, 1934–54).[5] Vasmer mentions the 1074 *Liber Prophetarum* as a possible source for the term, but this suggestion is refuted by A. Brückner on the grounds that in the *Liber Prophetarum* the word *upir* appears as a proper name.[6] Other sporadic attempts to explain the Slavic etymology of the word include Sobolevskij's theory that *vampire* derives from an old Polish or Polabic root and Maszynski's suggestion that the Serbo-Croatian verb *pirati* (to blow) contains the stem for *vampire*.[7] A. N. Afanas'ev lists several possible theories, among them the Lithuanian *wempti* (to drink).[8]

A quite convincing case for the Bulgarian origin of the word is made by A. Brückner in his 1934 article "Etymologien."[9] He contends the Serbian term *vampir* is only a borrowing from Bulgarian via Greek. Thus, the Serbian *BAMITUP* appears to have served merely as a transmitter, but is not the root of the term.

The fourth school of writers, notably English and American, contend that the belief in vampires has its roots in ancient superstition but that the word itself is of recent and Hungarian origin. In a recent publication on vampires, for example, Raymond McNally says:

> Linguistic authorities differ over the origin of the word. For example, F. Miklosich, an eminent scholar of Slavic languages, claims that "vampire" derives from uber, the Turkish word for witch. But undoubtedly the source of "vampire" is the Hungarian word vampir.[10]

4

Similar statements are made by Summers and Wolf, just to name a few.[11] Their speculations, however, seem utterly unfounded, for the first appearance of the word *vampir* in Hungarian postdates the first use of the term in most Western languages by more than a century.

Just as the etymology of *vampire* is subject to controversy, so is the history of the introduction of the word into the recorded vocabulary of major European languages and literatures, and the way of transmission is not always clear.

In France, according to most dictionaries, the word *vampire* was introduced in 1737 through the *Lettres Juives*, the ninth chapter of which recounts two incidents of vampirism in the village of Kisilova near Graditz.[12] But the *Mercure Galant* reported already in 1693 and 1694 cases of vampirism in Poland and Russia.[13] Also, in 1693 a Polish clergyman asked the Sorbonne how one is to deal with vampires or corpses believed to be vampires. Calmet records that the doctors Fromageau, de Precelles, and Durieroz unanimously condemned the cruel treatment.[14] The term, however, became a household word in French only after Dom Calmet's 1746 publication of his *Dissertations sur les apparitions et sur les revenants et les vampires*.

In French belles lettres the vampire theme appears first as a reaction to the popularity of Polidori's story *The Vampire* and its dramatic versions in England. *The Vampire* was translated into French in 1819 by Henry Faber, and it was followed by more or less obvious imitations and continuations by Cyprien Bernard (1819), Charles Nodier (1820), and others.

The German fortunes of the word are strikingly similar to those in France, even though a cognate of the term *vampire* was already introduced to the German scholarly audience in 1721, when Gabriel Rzazynsky published his work *Historia naturalis curiosa regni Poloniae*.[15] Rzazynski recounts several seventeenth-century stories of Polish, Russian, and Lithuanian vampires, which he calls by their Polish name (*upior*). In the vernacular, however, the term first appeared in newspaper reports of the *Wiener Diarium* and other Viennese papers that published, as in France, the results of an official investigation concerning vampirism in the Graditz district which took place in 1725. Some of the pamphlets identified the Serbian district Graditz as a place in Hungary (rather than a province of Hungary); this reference may underlie the popular belief that Hungary is the homeland of vampires. Six years later even greater attention was given to an incident in the winter of 1731–32, when a vampire epidemic was reported in Medvegya, Serbia. The incident involved Arnold Paul, and the case, reported in the *Visum et Repertum* of the investigating commission, was reprinted in Nuremberg in 1732 in the *Commercium litterarium ad rei medicae et scientiae naturalis incrementum institutum*.[16] The official reports were followed in Ger-

5

many and Austria by a burst of medical and philosophic treatises by anonymous authors and by scholars such as C. F. Demelius (1732), G. Gengell (1732), J. C. Pohlius (1732), J. C. Meinig (1732), J. H. Voigt (1733), J. C. Fritch (1732), J. H. Zopf (1733), J. C. Harenberg (1733), J. C. Stock (1732), and G. B. Bilfinger (1742).[17]

The first use of vampires in German belles lettres occurred in 1748, when August Ossenfelder's poem "Der Vampyr" appeared as the appendix to Christlob Mylius' article about vampires in the *Naturforscher*. The vampire theme received the first truly memorable treatment in 1797, when Goethe composed his "vampirisches Gedicht" entitled "Die Braut von Corinth," but the actual wide-scale popularity of the vampire theme was occasioned, as in France, through the translations and adaptations of Polidori's *The Vampire* in the 1820s.

In England, the term first appeared in the seventeenth century. According to Todd and Skeat, Paul Ricaut (Rycaut) introduced the term in his *State of the Greek and Armenian Churches*, published in 1679.[18] Todd quotes Ricaut as saying: "[The vampire is] . . . a pretended demon, said to delight in sucking human blood, and to animate the bodies of dead persons, which when dug up, are said to be found florid and full of blood." The reference, however, is misleading, as Ricaut does not mention vampires by name here; he only describes the phenomenon as a superstition resulting from the reproachable overuse of excommunications in the Greek church. Ten years later, in 1688, the term must have been fairly well known, because Forman, in his *Observations on the Revolution in 1688*, written in the same year and published in 1741, used the term in a footnote metaphorically without attaching any explanation to it. He says:

> Our Merchants, indeed, bring money into their country, but it is said, there is another Set of Men amongst us who have as great an Address in sending out again to foreign Countries without any Returns for it, which defeats the Industry of the Merchant. These are the Vampires of the Publick, and Riflers of the Kingdom.[19]

The *OED* mistakenly refers to the *Travels of 3 English Gentlemen from Venice to Hamburg, Being the Grand Tour of Germany in the Year 1734*, as the first use of the word in English. The composition of the *Travels* postdates both Ricaut and Forman by half a century, and the work was not published until 1810, when the earl of Oxford's library was printed in the *Harleian Miscellany*. The description of vampires in the *Travels* is nevertheless the first serious English explanation of the phenomenon and will therefore be considered here.

The anonymous author of the *Travels* was a member of the Royal Society and of the University of Oxford, and this description of vampires is contained in the description of Lubiana in the duchy of Carniola, Serbia. Usually, only the first sentence of the two very informative pages dealing with vampires is given, so it will be quoted more fully here. It reads:

These Vampyres are supposed to be the bodies of decreased persons, animated by evil spirits, which come out of the graves, in the night time, suck the blood of many of the living, and thereby destroy them. Such a notion will, probably, be looked upon as fabulous and exploded, by many people in England; however, it is not only countenanced by Baron Valvasor, and many Carnioleze noblemen, gentlemen, etc., as we were informed, but likewise actually embraced by some writers of good authority. M. Jo. Henr. Zopfius, director of the Gymnasium of Essen, a person of great erudition, has published a dissertation upon them, which is extremely learned and curious, from whence we shall beg leave to transcribe the following paragraph: "The Vampyres, which come out of the graves in the night-time, rush upon people sleeping in their beds, suck out all their blood, and destroy them. They attack men, women, and children, sparing neither age nor sex. The people attacked by them complain of suffocation, and a great interception of spirits; after which, they soon expire. Some of them, asked at the point of death, what is the matter with them, say they suffer in the manner just related from people lately dead, or rather the spectres of those people; upon which, their bodies, from the description given of them, by the sick person, being dug out of the graves, appear in all parts, as the nostrils, cheeks, breast, mouth, etc. turgid and full of blood. Their countenances are fresh and ruddy; and their nails, as well as hair, very much grown. And, though they have been much longer dead than many other bodies, which are perfectly putrified, not the least mark of corruption is visible upon them. Those who are destroyed by them, after their death, become Vampyres; so that, to prevent so spreading an evil, it is found requisite to drive a stake through the dead body, from whence, on this occasion, the blood flows as if the person was alive. Sometimes the body is dug out of the grave, and burnt to ashes; upon which, all disturbances cease. The Hungarians call these spectres Pamgri, and the Serbians Vampyres; but the etymon, or reason of these names, is not known. . . .

These spectres are reported to have infested several districts of Serbia, and the *bannat* of Temeswaer, in the year 1725, and for seven or eight years afterwards, particularly those of Mevedia, or Meadia, and Parakin, near the Morava. In 1732, we had a relation of some of the feats in the neighborhood of Cassovia; and the publick prints took notice of the tragedies they acted in the bannat of Temeswaer, in the year 1738. Father Gabriel Rzaczynski, in his natural history of the kingdom of Poland, and the great duchy of Lithuania, published at Sendomir, in 1732, affirms, that in Russia, Poland, and the great duchy of Lithuania, dead bodies, actuated by infernal spirits, sometimes enter people's houses in the night, fall upon men, women, and children, and attempt to suffocate them; and that of such diabolical facts his countrymen have several very authentic relations. The Poles call a man's body thus informed Upier, and that of a woman Upierzyca, i.e., a winged or feathered creature; which seems to be deduced from the surprising lightness and activity of these incarnate demons.[20]

does this relate back to the myth of the succubus/incubus.

The appearance of the *Travels* in the *Harleian Miscellany* was followed by extremely popular works on the vampire theme, such as Byron's "The Giaur," Southey's "Thalaba," and Polidori's *The Vampire.*

In Italy, the Latin use of the word precedes its use in the vernacular. Pope Benedict XIV responded to a question similar to the one asked at the Sorbonne. Unlike the learned doctors, however, Pope Benedict realized that the belief in vampires was firmly rooted in ancient superstition and was not easy to extirpate. He considered the subject in Chapter 4 of the second edition of his work *De Servorum Dei Beatificatione et de Beatorum Canonizatione,* published in Rome in 1749. In the chapter entitled "De vanitate vampyrorum," the pope takes issue with the cruel maltreatment and mutilation of corpses believed to be vampires. In the vernacular, the term *vampiro* first appeared in Davanzati's *Dissertazione sopra i vampiri* in 1789.

In Russian, *vampir* is said to be a recent borrowing from either German or French, while the Russian cognates of *vampire, upir* and *upyr,* were shown by Brückner to be of Bulgarian origin.[21] Kayimierz Moszyinsk, on the other hand, argues that the term *upire* has been known for a long time among the East Slavs, for written sources of the years 1047, 1495, 1600 mention the word either as a proper name (of a Novgorodian prince) or as place names.

Finally, in Hungary and Transylvania, the supposed homeland of vampires, the term *vampire* exists only as a neologism and was never as popular as in the West. In Hungarian, the word *vampir* first appeared in 1786 in an article of the *Nyelvtudományi Értekletek:* "Vampirok . . . living people").[22] Thus, the term postdates the English and French use by a century and the German use by half a century. According to Benkő Lóránd, the word was introduced in Hungary through the German press.[23] Mór Jókai introduced the term into Hungarian belles lettres in 1874. In Transylvania, on the other hand, the term is even more recent and is included in the *Dictioner de Neulogisme.* Nandris points out that "for vampire the Slavs had a word, which does not exist as a loan word in Rumanian, and the Russian word of which is *upyr.*"[24] In an article on Romanian vampires, Agnes Murgoci notes several vampire-related superstitions and says, "As regards the names used for vampires, dead and alive, *strigoi* (fem. *strigoica*) is the most common Roumanian term, and *moroii* is perhaps the next most usual."[25] The term *vampire* is little used, but Ms. Murgoci has found a reference to vampires in the *Biserica Orthodoxa Romana:* "The Archbishop Nectarie (1813–19) sent round a circular to his higher clergy (protopopes) exhorting them to find out in what districts it was thought that the dead became vampires."[26]

In sum, the earliest recorded uses of the term *vampire* appear in French, English, and Latin, and they refer to vampirism in Poland, Russia, and Macedonia (southern Yugoslavia). The second and more sweeping introduction of the word occurs in German, French, and English, and records the Serbian vampire epidemic of 1725–32.

Thus, the historical data appear to complement the linguistic studies, for the first occurrences of the term *vampire* in European languages all refer to the Slavic superstitions; the wide dissemination of the term and its extensive use in the vernacular follows the outburst of vampirism in Serbia. Paradoxically, although the superstition of vampirism seems to have developed in eastern Europe, the word *vampire* (for which the Slavic cognate is *upir*), which is now universally used to describe the phenomenon, seemed to have gained popularity in the West.

Notes

1. A great many of the vampire novels and plays are set either in Hungary or in Transylvania as, for example, Bram Stoker's *Dracula* and Melesville's play *Le Vampire.* I am grateful to Prof. A. O. Aldridge of the University of Illinois for his helpful suggestions.

2. Franz Miklosich, *Etymologischen Wörterbuch der slavischen Sprachen* (Vienna: Wilhelm Braumüller, 1886).

3. Montague Summers, *The Vampire, His Kith and Kin* (London, 1928), 18.

4. Stephen Hock, "Die Vampyrsagen und ihre Verwertung in der deutschen Literatur," in *Forschungen zur neueren Litteraturgeschichte* 17 (1900): 1–133.

5. Kluge, *Etymologisches Wörterbuch der deutschen Sprache* (Berlin, 1975); Falk-Torp, *Norwegisch-Dänisches etymologisches Wörterbuch*, 12th ed. (Leipzig, 1956); Wick, *Die Slawischen Lehnowörter in der neuhochdeutschen Schriftsprache* (Marburg, 1939).

6. Max Vasmer, *Russisches etymologisches Wörterbuch* (Heidelberg, 1953); and A. Brückner, "Etymologien," *Slavia Casopis pro Slovanskon Filologii,* 13 (1934): 272–280.

7. Quoted from Vasmer, *Russisches Etymologisches Wörterbuch.*

8. A. N. Afanas'ev, "Poetic Views of the Slavs regarding Nature," in *Vampires of the Slavs,* ed. Jan L. Perkowski (Cambridge, Mass., 1976), 164.

9. Brückner refutes earlier and contemporary attempts to assign a Serbian origin to the term, and he proposes that the Bulgarian word *upir* lies at the root of the word *vampir.* He defines *upir* by saying, "Es nannten so Bulgaren die den Alten

bekannten Nachtvögel mit ehernem Schnabel welche Schlafenden das Blut aussaugen" (279). He also explains the gradual change in meaning from one mythological monster to another: " . . . die Nachtvögel sind zu Nachtwandlern, zu Nachtmenschen geworden, die nunmehr aus dem Grabe steigen und vom Blute der lebenden zehren" (279). Incidentally, the Slavic word *strigoi*, which now means "monsters" or "werewolves," originally referred to night-birds that sucked the blood of children as well. Brückner suggests that the term *upir* was borrowed by the Greeks from Bulgarian, just as the Greek word for werewolf, *strigoi*, is also a Bulgarian borrowing, and acquired the nasal "am" in Greek. He says: "Das 'am' vom heutigen Vampir ist somit neugriechisch, der Name selbst bulgarische Benennung der strigae, die sich erst im Christlichen Aberglauben aus Nachtvögeln zu eigenen Vampiren verwandelten . . ." (279).

10. Raymond I. McNally, *A Clutch of Vampires* (Greenwich: New York Graphic Society, 1974), 10.

11. Summers, *The Vampire*, 18. Leonard Wolf, *The Annotated Dracula* (New York, 1975).

12. Yovanovitch, *La Guzla de Prosper Mérimée* (Paris, 1911), 310.

13. Quoted by Dom Calmet, *Traité sur les apparitions des esprits, et sur les vampires, ou les revanans de Hongrie, de Moravia* (Paris, 1751), Vol. 2, 60: "Ils paroissent depuis midi jusqu'à minuit, et viennent sucer le sang des hommes au des animaux vivans en si grande abondance, que quelquefois il leur sort par la bouches, par le nez et principalement par les oreilles, et que quelquefois le cadavre nage dans son sang répandu dans son cercueil. On dit que le Vampire a une espèce de faim, qui lui fait manger le linge qu'il trouve autour de lui."

14. Ibid., Vol. 2, 65ff.

15. Gabriel Rzazynsky, *Historia naturalis curiosa regni Poloniae* (Sendomir, 1721), is credited by Hock with introducing vampires to the German scholarly audience.

16. Interestingly (at least to readers of Bram Stoker's *Dracula*), Gypsies were used as experts for destroying the Serbian vampires. Prof. Vukanović quoting Rauft says: "In the year 1731 vampires disturbed the village of Medvedja. The High Command from Belgrade immediately sent a commission of German officers and others to the spot. They excavated the whole cemetery and found that there were really vampires there, and all those dead found to be vampires were decapitated by the Gypsies, their bodies cremated and the ashes thrown into the river Morsira," T. P. Vukanović, "The Vampire," in *Vampires of the Slavs*, ed. Perkowski, 205.

17. C. F. Demelius, *Philosophischer Versuch, ob nicht die merckwurdige Begebenheit derer Blutsauger in Niederungarn, anno 1732 geschehen, aus denen principiis naturae könne erleuchtet werden* (Vinariensi, 1732); G. Gengell, *Evers Atheism* (quoted by the *Travels of 3 English Gentlemen*); J. C. Pohlius, *Dissertatio de hominibus post mortem sanguisugis, vulgo sic dictus vampyren* (Leipzig, 1732); J. C. Meinig, *Besondere Nachricht von denen Vampyren oder so genannten Blut-Saugern* (Leipzig, 1732); J. H. Voigt, *Kurtzers Bedencken von denen Acten-Mässigen Relationen wegen derer Vampiren, oder Menschen- und Vieh-Aussaugern* (Leipzig, 1732); J. C. Fritch, *Eines Weimarischen Medici muthmassliche Gedanken von denen Vampyren, oder sog. Blutsangern* (Leipzig, 1732);

J. H. Zopf, *Dissert. de. Vampyris Serviensibus* (Duisburg, 1733); J. C. Harenberg, *Vernünftige und Christliche Gedanken über die Vampirs oder Bluhtsaugende Todten* (Wolffenbüttel, 1733); J. C. Stock, *Dissertatio Physica de Cadaveribus Sanguisugia* (Jena, 1732); G. B. Bilfinger, *Elements Physices cum Disquisitione de Vampyris* (Leipzig, 1742).

18. Todd's augmented edition of Dr. Johnson's *English Dictionary* (1827); and W. Skeat's *Etymological Dictionary of the English Language* (1884).

19. Charles Forman, *Observations on the Revolution in 1668* (London, 1741), 11.

20. *Travels of 3 English Gentlemen*, in *Harleian Miscellany* (London, 1810).

21. The recent introduction of the term *vampir* from German or French into Russian is attested by Vasmer (see n. 6 above) and by Preobrazhensky, *Etymological Dictionary of the Russian Language* (New York, 1951).

22. Quoted from Benkö Lóránd et al., *A Magyar Nyelv Történeti Etimologiai Szótará* (Budapest: Akadémiai Kiadó, 1976). The same is said in *Révai Nagy Lexikona*.

23. Ibid.

24. Grigore Nandris, "The Historical Dracula: The Theme of His Legend in the Western and in the Eastern Literatures of Europe," in *Comparative Literature: Matter and Method*, ed. A. O. Aldridge (Urbana, 1969), 124.

25. Agnes Murgoci, "The Vampire in Roumania," in *Folklore* 37 (Dec. 1926): 321. [Ed. note: See also herein, pp. 12–34.]

26. Ibid., 323–324.

a duplicate of the article it printed up before reading this collection!

AGNES MURGOCI

The Vampire In Roumania

Nowhere in the world is the vampire more prevalent than in Romania. Although other eastern European countries may contest this dubious honor, certainly the Romanian vampire has been described in great detail. Of the many accounts of the presence of the vampire in Romania, there seems to be consensus that one of the very best is that penned by Agnes Murgoci, who read a paper on the subject at a meeting of the English Folklore Society in May of 1927. That paper formed the basis of her essay "The Vampire in Roumania," which continues to be cited by almost all serious scholars studying the vampire. It is noteworthy for its raw data extrapolated from the author's intimate knowledge of Romanian sources. Her translations of legends, for example, make such data accessible to those who cannot read Romanian.

For other considerations of the Romanian vampire, see Elias Weslowski, "Die Vampirsage im rumänischen Volksglauben," Zeitschrift für österreichische Volkskunde 16 (1910): 209–216; Dorothy Nixon, "Vampire Lore and Alleged Cases: The 'Undead' as Believed in by East Europeans in General and Romanians in Particular," Miorita 6 (1979): 14–28; Adrien Cremene, La Mythologie du vampire en Roumanie (Monaco: Éditions du Rocher, 1981); and Harry A. Senn, Were-Wolf and Vampire in Romania (Boulder: East European Quarterly, 1982).

The folklore of vampires is of special interest from the light it throws on primitive ideas about body and soul, and about the relation of the body and soul after death.

In Russia, Roumania, and the Balkan states there is an idea—sometimes vague, sometimes fairly definite—that the soul does not finally leave the body and enter into Paradise until forty days after death. It is supposed that it may even linger for years, and when this is the case decomposition is delayed. In Roumania, bodies are disinterred at an interval of three years after death in the case of a child, of four or five years in the case of young folk, and of seven years in the case of elderly people. If decomposition is not then complete, it is supposed that the corpse is a vampire; if it is complete,

Reprinted from *Folklore* 37 (1926): 320–349.

and the bones are white and clean, it is a sign that the soul has entered into eternal rest. The bones are washed in water and wine and put in clean linen, a religious service is held, and they are reinterred.

In Bukovina and the surrounding districts there was an orgy of burials and reburials in the years 1919 and 1920, for not only were people dying of epidemics and hardships, but also the people who had died in the early years of the war had to be disinterred.

It is now considered to be exceptional that a spirit should reanimate its body and walk as a vampire, but, in a vampire story quoted below, it is said that they were once as common as blades of grass. It would seem that the most primitive phase of the vampire belief was that all departed spirits wished evil to those left, and that special means had to be taken in all cases to prevent their return. The most typical vampire is therefore the reanimated corpse. We may call this the dead-vampire type.

People destined to become vampires after death may be able in life to send out their souls, and even their bodies, to wander at crossroads with reanimated corpses. This type may be called the live-vampire type. It merges into the ordinary witch or wizard, who can meet other witches or wizards either in the body or as a spirit.

A third type of vampire is the *vârcolac*, which eats the sun and moon during eclipses.

A typical vampire of the reanimated-corpse type may have the attributes of a lover, as in Scott's William and Helen. The *zmeu* may also be such a lover.

The *strigele* (sing. *striga*) are not really vampires, but are sometimes confused with them. They are spirits either of living witches, which these send out as a little light, or of dead witches who can find no resting place. These *strigele* come together in uneven numbers, seven or nine. They meet on rocky mountains, and dance and say:

Nup, Cuisnup,
In casa cu ustoroi nu ma duc.

[Nup, Cuisnup, I won't enter
any house where there is garlic.]

They are seen as little points of light floating in the air. Their dances are exquisitely beautiful. Seven or nine lights start in a line, and then form into various figures, ending up in a circle. After they break off their dance, they may do mischief to human beings.

As regards the names used for vampires, dead and alive, *strigoi* (fem.

13

strigoica) is the most common Roumanian term, and *moroii* is perhaps the next most usual. *Moroii* is less often used alone than *strigoi*. Usually we have *strigoi* and *moroii* consorting together, but the *moroii* are subject to the *strigoi*. We find also *strigoi*, *moroii*, and *vârcolaci*, and *strigoi* and *pricolici* used as if all were birds of the same feather. A Transilvanian term is *şişcoi*. *Vârcolaci* (*svârcolaci*) and *pricolici* are sometimes dead vampires, and sometimes animals which eat the moon. *Oper* is the Ruthenian word for dead vampire. In Bukovina, *vidme* is used for a witch; it covers much the same ground as *strigoi* (used for a live vampire), but it is never used for a dead vampire. *Diavoloace*, beings with two horns and spurs on their sides and feet, are much the same as *vidme*.

As Dr. Gaster* reminds me, in many disenchantments we find phrases such as:

> De strigoaica, de strigoi,
> Şi de case cu moroi.

> [From vampires (male and female),
> and from a home with vampires.]

> De deochetori şi de deochetoare,
> De moroi, cu moroaiça,
> De strigoi cu strigoaica.

> [From those who cast the evil eye
> (male or female), from vampires
> (male and female).]

> Ci, íi dracul cu drácoaica, striga cu strigoiul,
> Deochiu cu deochitorul, pociturá cu pocitorul,
> Potca cu potcoiul.

* Ed. note: This is no doubt Moses Gaster (1856–1939), a Romanian Jew and distinguished scholar who came to England after being expelled from Romania in 1885. A prolific writer on Jewish folklore, he joined the English Folklore Society, serving as president from 1907 to 1908. His son Theodor (1906–1992) was also an important contributor to folklore study. For details about Moses Gaster's life and publications, see the various essays in his festschrift, Bruno Schindler and Arthur Marmorstein, eds., *Occident and Orient* (London: Taylor's Foreign Press, 1936) and in Bruno Schindler, ed., *Gaster Centenary Publication* (London: P. Lund Humphries, 1958), and especially Venetia Newall, "The English Folklore Society under the Presidency of Haham Dr. Moses Gaster," in *Studies in the Cultural Life of the Jews in England*, ed. Dov Noy and Issachar Ben-Ami (Jerusalem: Magnes Press, 1975), 197–225.

[The devil with the female devil, the spirit of
the dead witch with the vampire (male), the evil eye
with the caster of the evil eye, the bewitchment with the
bewitcher, the quarrel with the mischief-maker.]

Ciuma, the plague, is occasionally one of the party. The *strigoi* and *moroi* are almost inseparable, hunting, however, with witches, wizards, and devils.

The nature spirits (*ielele* and *dánsele*) usually have disenchantments of their own, for they work apart from vampires and wizards, who are beings of human origin. While the peasant groups nature spirits apart from the more human workers of evil, he groups the living and the dead together, for the caster of the evil eye and the bewitcher are living men, though prospective vampires. The vampire, in fact, forms a convenient transition between human workers of evil and the devil, who resembles the dead vampire in not being alive in the flesh.

The vampire (a reanimated corpse) and the devil (a spirit) ought not, strictly speaking, to be alike, but the peasant, finding it difficult to imagine a spirit without a body, thinks of the devil in the form of a crow or a cat, or even in a quasi-human form. The devil is a target for the thunderbolts of St. Elijah, and can be transfixed by one. Even the spirit of a living man, if separated from his body, must have some body or form. In Transilvania it is thought that many people can project their soul as a butterfly. In Vâlcea souls of vampires are considered to be incarnated in death's-head moths, which, when caught, should be impaled on a pin and stuck to a wall to prevent their flying further. A small, graceful thing which flutters in the air like a butterfly or a moth is as near as these peasants can get to the idea of pure spirit. The peasant in Siret goes a step further when he conceives of the soul as a little light. He has got beyond what is tangible.

The belief in vampires has often caused trouble to the rulers of Roumania. Ureche, in his *History of Roumania*, quotes the following:

In 1801, on July the 12th, the Bishop of Siges sends a petition to the ruler of Wallachia, that he should order his rulers of provinces to permit no longer that the peasants of Stroesti should dig up dead people, who had already been dug up twice under the idea that they were *vârcolaci* [term here used instead of *strigoi*].

In the *Biserica Orthodoxa Romana* (an 28) there is the following:

15

The Archbishop Nectarie (1813–19) sent round a circular to his higher clergy (protopopes) exhorting them to find out in what districts it was thought that the dead became vampires. If they came on a case of vampirism they were not to take it upon themselves to burn the corpse, but to teach the people how to proceed according to the written roll of the church.

The following accounts of vampires are taken from the Roumanian periodical of peasant art and literature, *Ion Creanga*. It was edited by my late friend, Tudor Pamfile, one of the most competent and industrious folklorists Roumania has ever had. The stories in *Ion Creanga* were taken down by careful observers, and published as nearly as possible in the exact words of the peasants.

N. I. Dumitrascu is responsible for the following, printed in *Ion Creanga:*[1]

Some twenty or thirty years ago (from 1914) in the commune Afumati in Dolj, a certain peasant, Mărin Mirea Ociocioc, died. It was noticed that his relations also died, one after the other. A certain Badea Vrajitor (Badea the wizard) dug him up. Badea himself, going later into the forest up to the frontier on a cold wintry night, was eaten by wolves. The bones of Mărin were sprinkled with wine, a church service read over them, and replaced in the grave. From that time there were no more deaths in the family.

Some fifteen years ago, in Amărăşti in the north of Dolj, an old woman, the mother of the peasant Dinu Gheorghiţa, died. After some months the children of her eldest son began to die, one after the other, and, after that, the children of her youngest son. The sons became anxious, dug her up one night, cut her in two, and buried her again. Still the deaths did not cease. They dug her up a second time, and what did they see? The body whole without a wound. It was a great marvel. They took her and carried her into the forest, and put her under a great tree in a remote part of the forest. There they disembowelled her, took out her heart, from which blood was flowing, cut it in four, put it on hot cinders, and burnt it. They took the ashes and gave them to children to drink with water. They threw the body on the fire, burnt it, and buried the ashes of the body. Then the deaths ceased.

Some twenty or thirty years ago, a cripple, an unmarried man, of Cuşmir, in the south of Mehedinţi, died. A little time after, his relations began to die, or to fall ill. They complained that a leg was drying up. This happened in several places. What could it be? "Perhaps it is the cripple; let us dig him up." They dug him up on Saturday night, and found him as red as red, and all drawn up into a corner of the grave. They cut him open, and took the customary measures. They took out the heart and liver, burnt them on red-hot cinders, and gave the ashes to his sister and other relations, who were ill. They drank them with water, and regained their health.

16

In the Cuşmir, another family began to show very frequent deaths, and suspicion fell on a certain old man, dead long ago. When they dug him up, they found him sitting up like a Turk, and as red as red, just like fire; for had he not eaten up nearly the whole of a family of strong, young men. When they tried to get him out he resisted, unclean and horrible. They gave him some blows with an axe, they got him out, but they could not cut him with a knife. They took a scythe and an axe, cut out his heart and liver, burnt them, and gave them to the sick folk to drink. They drank, and regained their health. The old man was reburied, and the deaths ceased.

In Văguileşti, in Mehedinţi, there was a peasant Dimitriu Vaideanu, of Transilvanian origin, who had married a wife in Văguileşti and settled there. His children died one after the other; seven died within a few months of birth, and some bigger children had died as well. People began to wonder what the cause of all this could be. They took council together, and resolved to take a white horse to the cemetery one night, and see if it would pass over all the graves of the wife's relations. This they did, and the horse jumped over all the graves, until it came to the grave of the mother-in-law, Joana Marta, who had been a witch, renowned far and wide. Then the horse stood still, beating the earth with its feet, neighing, and snorting, unable to step over the grave. Probably there was something unholy there. At night Dimitriu and his son took candles and went to dig up the grave. They were seized with horror at what they saw. There she was, sitting like a Turk, with long hair falling over her face, with all her skin red, and with finger nails frightfully long. They got together brushwood, shavings, and bits of old crosses, they poured wine on her, they put in straw, and set fire to the whole. Then they shovelled the earth back and went home.

Slightly different methods are described by other observers as employed in other districts:

In Romanaţi the vampire was disinterred, undressed, and put in a bag. The clothes were put back into the coffin and sprinkled with holy water, the coffin put back into the grave, and the grave closed. A strong man carried the body to the forest. The heart was cut out, and the body cut up and one piece after another burnt. Last of all the heart was burnt, and those present came near so that the smoke passed over them, and protected them from evil. Here, as elsewhere, it is emphasized that the burning must be complete. If the smallest piece of bone remains unburnt, the vampire can grow up again from it.

In Zârneşti, when the vampire is dug up, iron forks are put into her heart, eyes, and breast, and she is reburied with her face downwards.

In Mehedinţi it is sometimes considered sufficient to take the corpse far away to the mountains and leave it there. This is comparable with, but

[Handwritten margin note, left top:] sitting like a Turk: sitting cross-legged — this would be analogous to the American saying "sitting Indian style"

[Handwritten margin note, left bottom:] 28) Same folklore — Vampires have regenerative abilities

would not appear to be so efficient as, the Greek plan of taking the body of a vampire over the sea to an island.

The most general method for dealing with a vampire is as follows: It must be exhumed on a Saturday, as on all other days it will be wandering away from the grave. Either put a stake through the navel or take out the heart. The heart may be burnt on charcoal, or in a fire; it may be boiled, or cut into bits with a scythe. If the heart is burnt, the ashes must be collected. Sometimes they are got rid of by throwing into a river, but usually they are mixed with water and given to sick people to drink. They may also be used to anoint children and animals as a means of warding off anything unclean. Sometimes, however, the curse of a priest is sufficient to seal a vampire in its tomb.

The tests to determine whether any dead man is a vampire, or not, are as follows:

1. His household, his family, and his live stock, and possibly even the live stock of the whole village, die off rapidly.
2. He comes back in the night and speaks with the family. He may eat what he finds in dishes and knock things about, or he may help with the housework and cut wood. Female vampires also come back to their children. There was a Hungarian vampire which could not be kept away, even by the priest and holy water.
3. The priest reads a service at the grave. If the evil which is occurring does not cease, it is a bad sign.
4. A hole about the size of a serpent may be found near the tombstone of the dead man. If so, it is a sign of a vampire, because vampires come out of graves by just such holes.
5. Even in the daytime a white horse will not walk over the grave of a vampire, but stands still and snorts and neighs.
6. A gander, similarly, will not walk over the grave of a vampire.
7. On exhuming the corpse, if it is a vampire it will be found to be:
   (a) red in the face, even for months and years after burial,
   (b) with the face turned downwards,
   (c) with a foot retracted and forced into a corner of the grave or coffin.
   (d) If relations have died, the mouth will be red with blood. If it has only spoilt and ruined things at home, and eaten what it could find, the mouth will be covered with maize meal.

If the vampire is not recognized as such, and rendered innocuous, it goes on with its evil ways for seven years. First it destroys its relations, then it destroys men and animals in its village and in its country, next it passes into another country, or to where another language is spoken, and becomes a man again. He marries, and has children, and the children, after they die, all

18

become vampires and eat the relations of their mother. As Miss Durham*
says, this action of a vampire is probably suggested by the epidemics which
wipe out families and indeed villages in the countries of southeastern Europe. If, however, we assume a vampire for every epidemic, they would
certainly be only less plentiful than leaves of grass.

In case it is feared that any man may become a vampire, precautions must
be taken at burial or soon after. As suicides are potential vampires, they
should be dug up at once from their graves, and put into running water. A
man may know that he was born with a caul, and leave word what is to be
done to save his family from disaster. Or his relations may know of the
danger and guard against it. There are various methods of avoiding this
danger, and several may be used at the same time. The commonest method
is to drive a stake through the heart or navel. In Vălcea, it is sufficient to put a
needle into the heart, but in Bulgaria it is a red-hot iron which is driven
through the heart. Small stones and incense should be put in the mouth,
nose, ears, and navel, and under the finger nails, "so that the vampire may
have something to gnaw." Garlic may also be placed in the mouth. Millet
may be put in the coffin, or in the mouth and nose, so that the vampire will
delay many days till it has eaten the millet. The body should be placed face
downwards in the coffin. If it is a case of reburial, the corpse should be
turned head to foot.

A nail may be put under the tongue. The coffin should be bound with
trailers of wild roses, or other bands of wood. In Teleorman, when people go
to the house of death on the third day in order to burn incense, they take
nine distaffs, which they stick into the grave. If the corpse should rise, it
would be pierced by them. They also take tow, strew it on the grave, and set
fire to it, so that it shall singe the vampire.

Although in Roumanian folklore vampires and devils are fairly nearly
akin, I have found so far no instance in which the dead corpse is supposed to
be reanimated by a devil and not by its own soul. This, however, is what is
described as happening in Ralston's *Russian Folk Tales*.[2] In Serbia and Bulgaria a nail should be put in the back of the neck, as well as a stake through
the heart, so that the devil who means to use the body as a vampire may not
be able to distend the skin.

The causes of vampirism are various. Roumanians think that a man born

---

* Ed. note: This refers to Mary Edith Durham (1863–1944), an amateur-traveler who became quite a sophisticated ethnographer in the Balkans, particularly Albania. Murgoci is
probably alluding to Durham's short essay "Of Magic, Witches and Vampires in the Balkans," *Man* 23 (1923): 189–192, where she suggests the connection between a belief in
vampires and the fear of epidemics.

with a caul becomes a vampire within six weeks after his death; similarly people who were bad and had done evil deeds in their lifetime, and more especially women who have had to do with the evil one and with spells and incantations. It is known that a man is a vampire if he does not eat garlic; this idea is also found among the South Slavs. When a child dies before it is baptized, it becomes a vampire at seven years of age, and the place where it was buried is unholy. Men who swear falsely for money become vampires six months after death. If a vampire casts its eye on a pregnant woman, and she is not disenchanted, her child will be a vampire. If a pregnant woman does not eat salt, her child will be a vampire. When there are seven children of the same sex, the seventh will have a little tail and be a vampire. A dead man becomes a vampire, if a cat jumps over him, if a man steps over him, or even if the shadow of a man falls over him. Some Roumanians think that, if people are fated to be vampires, they will become one whether they wish it or not. Then during their lifetime, when they sleep, their soul comes out of their mouth like a little fly. If, during sleep, the body is turned round so that the head is where the feet were before, the man dies.

Other Roumanians think that even if a child is born with a caul, i.e., is born to be a vampire, something can be done to mend matters. In the first place, the caul must be broken at once, so that the child may not swallow it and remain an evil vampire, casting the evil eye all its life, and eating its relations after death. The midwife should go outside with the baby, after it is washed and wrapped up. If it is a dug-out house, half underground, she should go onto the top of it; otherwise she goes to the back, and calls out with the baby in her arms, "Hear, everyone, a wolf is born onto the earth. It is not a wolf that will eat people, but a wolf that will work and bring luck." In this way, the power of the vampire is broken, and evil turns to good. For vampires who are no longer vampires bring luck.

If a dead man, supposed to be a vampire, has a brother born on the same day of the year, or month of the year, as himself, there is great danger of the dead vampire causing the living brother to become a vampire. This must be prevented by a process called "taking out of iron." An iron chain, the one used for hanging the pot over the fire, or one used in bullock carts, is taken and put round the two brothers. The ends are solemnly closed and opened three times, and usually the priest reads a religious service. When the iron is opened for the last time, the living brother is free—he is no longer in danger of becoming a vampire.

There are various characters which distinguish the dead-vampire type only, others common to both types, and a great many which belong to live vampires and witches only. It is said that *strigoi* meet *moroii* and *vârcolaci* at the boundaries, and decide on their program of evil for the coming year—

Witch folklore in America & England run parallel to the Romanian folklore of the meetings of strigoii, moroii, & varcolaci.

who is to be killed and by whom. Elsewhere it is said that at these same boundaries, where neither the cuckoo sings nor the dog barks, the dead vampires meet the living ones, and teach them all sorts of incantations and spells. They meet also in churchyards, in ruined or deserted houses, or in the forest. They may quarrel among themselves, and fight, using the tongues of hemp brakes,[3] or more rarely swords, as weapons. Once a man, who was walking round a cemetery, met a vampire, who forced him to carry his hemp brake for him. The man was hardly able to get home, and was ill in bed for many months after. Another man saw a female vampire near a cemetery, and threw a stone at her. She caused an evil wind to blow on him, and it blew him down and took away his senses. He never regained his reason. Apoplexy is also caused by bewitchment by a dead vampire.

Peasants who are thinking of live rather than dead vampires tell us that they walk out to the boundaries of villages, the women together with their head, and the men with their head. They have signs that enable them to bewitch all living things and do what they like with them. Thinking only of live vampires, peasants from Mihalcea and the neighborhood tell us that it is chiefly women who are vampires. One may be specially for hens, another for ducks, and another for lizards. They take the "power" (Roum. *mana*) of these animals for themselves. Some take the milk and "power" of women. Some have special power over bread, others over rain, over hens, or over bees. They take the "power" of bees and bring it to their mistress. If bees lose their "power," they no longer collect honey, and they have nothing to eat even for themselves. There was once a woman who made bread that was so good that half the village ate it. No one else could get such a pleasing taste as she did. This was because she knew how to take the "power" of bread from other women.

It is more especially on St. George's Eve that these vampires go to the boundaries to take rain and the "power" of animals, so as to have enough for the whole year. If they do not take "power" for themselves, they take it for those who pay them. They bring "power" and beauty to women who pay; also they cause men to hate the rivals of those who hire them. They can take "power" from women, and thus take milk away from nursing mothers. They can turn themselves into horses, dogs, or cats, so as to frighten people. The female vampires are dry in the body and are red in the face both before and after death. They go out on St. Andrew's Eve to the boundaries even if they have just borne children. They get out by the chimney, and come back worn out and in rags. The male vampires are bald, and after death grow a tail and hooves.

When a vampire washes itself, rain will fall from heaven. Thus, when a drought occurs, nobles send all their men to wash, because any of them may

21

be a vampire. The moment any vampire wets its tail, there is rain. Vampires never drown, they always float on top. It is usually special vampires (live) who have power over rain; however, heavy rains in Zârneşti were supposed to be caused by a recently buried girl, thought to be a vampire.

Vampires, whether live or dead, are generally born rather than made. However, a peasant from Strojineţi said that there is a class of female vampires which are really only half vampire; that is to say, they are not vampires by birth, but have been taught to be vampires by the real ones, and shown how to do things. They put enchantments on cows, take on the form of a girls' lover, and so kill her. They are helped by St. Andrew, so that the priest conceals from them the time that St. Andrew's Day comes. Such vampires are alive, but after they die they walk.

There is a character by which a live vampire can infallibly be distinguished. It is known that vampires fight with hemp brakes. Now if anyone comes to a house and asks for a hemp brake, say, "Come tomorrow for the stand and the H-axle of the hemp brake." The next day she will come. Then put three needles on the threshold with their points upwards and some bits of garlic. She will not be able to get out of the house until she gets out the needles and removes the garlic, so she will go to the door, and return and again go to the door, thus proving that she is a vampire (*strigoica*).

In general dead vampires come out every night except Saturday, when they are to be found in their graves. The vampires that are reanimated corpses or spirits of the dead disappear, like all evil spirits, at cockcrow. Vampires that are nothing else than witches or wizards can come out in the daytime all the year round, just like other human beings. Their power is greatest at new moon, and weakens as the moon grows old. The two periods in the course of the year when vampires are generally considered to be most active are St. Andrew's Eve and St. George's Eve. In Roşa, it is said that vampires begin to walk on St. Andrew's Eve, and separate after St. George's Day, after which they have no power, because flowers and the holy sweet basil begin to grow, and this shows that the power of God is increasing. This statement is interesting, as it shows that the peasant conceives of God as a god of fertility, and of vampires as inhabitants of the underworld. In Popeca, vampires are said to be at their worst before Easter. This would also bear out the idea of their being subdued by a rising God. In Mihalcea, they are said to walk only from St. Andrew's Eve to Epiphany. When the priest sings *Kyrie eleison* all evil spirits perish till next St. Andrew's Eve. In Siret they are said to be free from St. Andrew's Day till Transfiguration, and from St. George's Day till St. John's.

The precautions against visits from vampires are taken more especially before St. Andrew's Day and St. George's Day, but also before Easter

Sunday and on the last day of the year. Garlic keeps off vampires, wolves, and evil spirits, and millet has a similar action. On St. Andrew's Eve and St. George's Eve, and before Easter and the New Year, windows should be anointed with garlic in the form of a cross, garlic put on the door and everything in the house, and all the cows in the cowshed should be rubbed with garlic. When vampires do enter, they enter by the chimney or by the keyhole, so these orifices call for special attention when garlic is being rubbed in. Even though the window is anointed with garlic, it is wisest to keep it shut. Especially on St. Andrew's Eve, all lamps may be put out and everything in the house turned upside down, so that if a vampire does come, it will not be able to ask any of the objects in the house to open the door. It is just as well for people not to sleep at all, but to tell stories right up to cockcrow. If you are telling stories, vampires cannot approach. Women should keep on saying their prayers. They may also beat on the hemp brakes to keep the vampires away. It is unwise to leave hemp brakes or shovels where vampires can get hold of them, for they like to ride on them. Vampires also like to take the tongues of hemp brakes as weapons and fight with them, till the sparks fly; hence the tongues should never be left fixed in the hemp brakes. Especially on St. George's Eve, it is a wise precaution to put on your shirt inside out, and to put a knife or scythe under your head when you sleep, turning the cutting edge outwards. It may also be as well to sleep with the feet where the head usually is, so that, if a vampire does enter, it will not find you.

At any time of the year it is well, especially at night-time, never to answer until anyone calls you three times, for vampires can ask a question twice but not three times. If you reply when they speak to you, they may turn your mouth skew, make you dumb, cut off your foot, or kill you.

There is a special kind of witch, *vidme*, who differs in her attributes from the witch that is called a vampire. The *vidme* are evil, bewitch people, and steal children. God said to them, "God will not help you in what you are doing." They replied, "And we will not help you to ascend." So God could not ascend to heaven. Elsewhere we are told that Christ reproved them, and they answered, "But you will not ascend where you thought you would, for we will cut your wings, so that you will remain down here." In a third variant, this discussion comes in connection with the Ascension. It is only after Christ has come to an understanding with these witches that he can ascend to heaven.

The following account of *vârcolaci*, considered to be the creatures which eat the sun and moon and thus cause eclipses, is taken from the Roumanian Academy's pamphlet *Credinţele Ţăranului Român despre Cer şi Stele* (Beliefs of the Roumanian Peasant concerning the Sky and the Stars), by I. Otescu.

23

Vârcolaci are supposed to be different from any beings on the earth. They cause eclipses of the moon, and even of the sun, by mounting up to heaven and eating the moon or sun. Some think that they are animals smaller than dogs. Others that they are dogs, two in number. Others again think that they are dragons, or some kind of animal with many mouths, which suck like an octopus, others that they are spirits and can also be called *pricolici*. They have different origins; some say that they are the souls of unbaptised children, or of children of unmarried parents, cursed by God and turned into *vârcolaci*. Others say that they take rise if, when anyone is making maize porridge, they put the porridge stick into the fire, or if, when anyone is sweeping out the house at sunset, they sweep out the dust in the direction of the sun. Others again say that *vârcolaci* originate from the air of heaven, when women spin at night, especially at midnight, without a candle, especially if they cast spells with the thread they spin. Hence it is never good to spin by moonlight, for vampires and *vârcolaci* get up to the sky by the thread and eat the sun and moon. They fasten themselves to the thread, and the thread makes itself into a road for them. As long as the thread does not break the *vârcolaci* have power, and can go wherever they wish. They attack the heavenly bodies, they bite the moon, so that she appears covered with blood, or till none of her is left. But if the thread is broken their power is broken and they go to another part of the sky.

How is it that the moon comes out whole after an eclipse if it has been eaten up? Some people say that, as the moon is really stronger than the *vârcolaci*, they are just able to bite it, but in the end the moon conquers, for the world would come to an end if the moon were really eaten up.

G. F. Ciauşanu, in his *Superstitüle poporului Român*, reports that in Vâlcea there are said to be beings who are called *vârcolaci*, because their spirit is *vârcolaci*. They are recognised by their pale faces and dry skin, and by the deep sleep into which they fall when they go to the moon to eat it. But they eat it only during an eclipse, and when the disc of the moon is red or copper coloured. The redness is the blood of the moon, escaping from the mouths of the *vârcolaci* and spreading over the moon.

When the spirit of the *vârcolac* wants to eat the moon, the man to whom the spirit belong begins to nod, falls into a deep sleep as if he had not slept for weeks, and remains as if dead. If he is roused or moved the sleep becomes eternal, for, when the spirit returns from its journey, it cannot find the mouth out of which it came, and so cannot go in.

During an eclipse the peasants in Vâlcea beat on fire shovels to frighten away the *vârcolaci* from the moon. In Putna they toll the church bells. Elsewhere they make noises with tongs, gridirons, and irons of all sorts, beat trays, and let off guns. Gipsies play on the fiddle and lute,—anything to make a noise.

Some people think that the *vârcolaci* pull at the moon and drop off when tired, others that the moon gets away very quickly from them, and they are just able to nip off a bit as she passes. The sun escapes, because the lion on which it

24

Interesting folkloric attitude toward lunar eclipses

rides fights with the *vârcolaci*. Some say that God orders the *vârcolaci* to eat the moon, so that men may repent and turn from evil.

It is curious that the word *vârcolac*, or *vrykolaka*, which is the general name for a vampire in Macedonia and Greece, is only exceptionally used to mean a vampire in Roumania, and usually means an animal which eats the moon. *Vârcolac* means "werewolf," and in Roumania it is the wolf or animal significance which predominates; in Macedonia, the human significance, the idea of devouring not being lost in either country.

A considerable number of vampire stories are of the type of Scott's William and Helen; the vampire comes to fetch his lady love, and takes her with him to his tomb.

In the first series of these stories, he loves one girl only, and seeks her out when she is alone; in the second series he chooses her out from other maidens at an evening gathering, and may destroy all other people present at the gathering.

The Girl and the Vampire.[4] (Story from Râmnic Sârat.) Once in a village there were a girl and a youth who were deeply in love, their parents did not know, and when the relations of the youth approached the parents of the girl with a proposal of marriage they were repulsed because the youth was poor. So the young man hanged himself on a tree, and became a vampire. As such he was able to come and visit the girl. But, although the girl had loved the man, she did not much like to have to do with an evil spirit. What could she do to escape from danger and sin? She went to a wise woman, and this wise woman advised her what to do. The vampire came one evening to make love to the girl and stayed late. When he knew that it was about time to leave, he said,— "Good night," and made ready to go. The girl, following the advice of the wise old woman, fixed into the back of his coat a needle, to which was attached one end of the thread from a large ball of thread. The vampire went away, and the ball unrolled and unrolled for some time and then, all at once, it stopped. The girl understood what had happened, and followed the clue given by the thread. She traced it along the road, and found that it entered into the churchyard, and went straight to a grave. There it entered the earth, and that was the end. She came home, but the next night, as twilight came on, she hastened to the churchyard, and stood some distance from the grave to see what would happen. It was not long before she saw the vampire coming out, going to another grave, opening it, eating the heart of the dead man buried there, and then setting out towards the village to visit her. She followed him as he left the churchyard.

"Where were you this evening, and what did you see?" asked the vampire after he had greeted her. "Where was I? Nowhere, I saw nothing," said the girl. The vampire continued,—"I warn you that, if you do not tell me, your

25

father will die." "Let him die, I know nothing, I've seen nothing, and I can say nothing." "Very well," said the vampire, and indeed in two days the girl's father was dead. He was buried with all due rites, and it was some time before the vampire again came to the girl.

One night, however, he came and made love to her as usual, but before leaving he said,—"Tell me where you were that evening, because, if you will not, your mother will die." "She may die nine times. How can I speak when I know nothing?" answered the girl.

After two days the mother died. She was duly buried. Again some time passed, and the vampire reappeared, and now he said,—"If you do not tell me what you saw that evening, you shall die too." "What if I do?" said she, "it will be no great loss. How can I invent a story, if I know nothing and have seen nothing?" "That is all very well, but what are you going to do now, for you are about to die?" replied the vampire.

On the advice of the wise old woman the girl called all her relations together and told them that she was going to die soon. When she was dead they were not to take her out by the door or by the window, but to break an opening in the walls of the house. They were not to bury her in the churchyard, but in the forest, and they were not to take her by the road but to go right across the fields until they came to a little hollow among the trees of the forest and here her grave was to be. And so it happened. The girl died, the wall of the house was broken down, and she was carried out on a bier across the fields to the margin of the forest.

After some time a wonderful flower, such as has never been seen, either before or after, grew up on her grave. One day the son of the emperor passed by and saw this flower, and immediately gave orders that it should be dug up well below the roots, brought to the castle, and put by his window. The flower flourished, and was more beautiful than ever, but the son of the emperor pined. He himself did not know what was the matter, he could neither eat nor drink. What was the matter? At night the flower became again the maiden, as beautiful as before. She entered in at the window, and passed the night with the emperor's son without his knowing it. However, one night she could contain herself no longer, and kissed him, and he awoke and saw her. After that, they pledged troth to each other, they told the emperor and empress, they were married, and they lived very happily together. There was only one drawback to their happiness. The wife would never go out of the house. She was afraid of the vampire.

One day, however, her husband took her with him in a carriage to go to church, when there, at a corner, who should there be but the vampire. She jumped out of the carriage and rushed to the church. She ran, the vampire ran, and just had his hand on her as they both reached the church together. She hid behind a holy picture. The vampire stretched out his hand to seize her, when all at once the holy picture fell on his head, and he disappeared in smoke. And the wife lived with the emperor's son free from all danger and sin for the rest of her life.

A variant of this story is given by Afanas'ev in his *Russian Popular Tales*, and is quoted by Ralston in his *Russian Folk Tales*. The main points of difference between the Russian and the Roumanian story are that, in the Russian tale the following occurs:

1. The first meeting of the lover and the girl was at an evening gathering on St. Andrew's Eve.
2. He asked the girl to see him on his way home, and proposed marriage to her.
3. The girl's mother advised fastening the thread to his coat; the next night she fastened it to him, followed him to the churchyard, and saw him eating the dead. He is, however, live, not dead.
4. They met again at the gathering. Questions, answers, the death of the girl's parents and herself, and the digging of the flower by the emperor's son are similar in both versions. The girl makes it a condition of marriage that she does not go to church for four years.
5. Going to church earlier, she sees the lover at the window, still refuses to answer, and her husband and son die.
6. The grandmother gives her holy water and water of life. The lover again asks his question. The girl tells him that she saw him eating corpses, and then, by sprinkling water on him, turns him into ashes. With the water of life, she brings back to life her husband and son.

Vampire Story from Botoşani.[5] A girl and a young man were once in love, but the youth died and became a vampire. The girl knew nothing of this. She happened to be alone in her parents' house, and she put out all the lights and went to bed as usual. Now vampires can enter into empty houses or into unclean houses, but the girl's house was clean and holy, so he could not come in. Instead of coming in he called at the window, speaking in the same tone and using the same words as he did when alive. "Stupid girl, come with me," he said, and took her hand and led her, undressed as she was, to his tomb. "Go in," he said. "No, friend, I'm afraid," she said. He went in first, and called, "Come quicker." "Wait," she said, "I've lost my beads. They must have fallen hereabouts." And she ran and ran until she saw a house with a light. She went in and found a dead man called Avram on a bench. She drew the bolts of the door and lay down in hiding behind the oven. The vampire came after her with true vampire persistency. He knocked at the window, saying, "Avram, open the door." Avram was himself a vampire, and was going to obey and open the door. But the hen saw what was happening, and said to the cock,—"Crow, so as to save the poor girl." "No, you crow. It is not my turn." So the hen crowed quickly before Avram could get to the door, and the girl escaped, because she was clean and holy, and vampires do not easily get hold of clean souls.

In a variant of this story the vampire comes to his sweetheart, and takes her away with him to his grave. She is able, however, to escape by stopping up the entrance to the grave with woven linen, and running away. It has been suggested that the idea behind the stopping of the path of the vampire with linen is the same as that when millet seed is put in his way; he is obliged to disentangle and straighten out the threads of the linen in the one case, or count the millet seed in the other.

A simpler variant, in which the hero is a dragon (*zmeu*) and not a vampire, is as follows:—A soldier relates how a dragon in the form of a tongue of fire entered into a woman's house by either the door or the window. It became a man, made love to her, and then again became a flame and disappeared. As the hero is a *zmeu* and not a vampire, the "grave" motive is wanting.

In the following lover stories, the action begins in a crowded evening gathering:

A Story from Botoşani.[6] There was once a time when vampires were as common as leaves of grass, or berries in a pail, and they never kept still, but wandered round at night among the people. They walked about and joined the evening gatherings in the villages, and, when there were many young people together, the vampires could carry out their habit of inspiring fear, and sucking human blood like leeches. Once, when an evening gathering was in full swing, in came an uninvited guest, the vampire. But no one knew that he was a vampire. He was in the form of a handsome youth, full of fun. He said "Good day" very politely, sat down on a bank beside the girls, and began to talk, and all the girls imagined that he was a youth from another part of the village. Then the vampire began to tell stories and jokes, so that the girls did not know what to do for laughter. He played and jested and bandied words with them without ceasing. But there was one girl to whom he paid special attention, and teased unmercifully. "Keep still, friend. Have I done anything to annoy you?" said she. But he still kept on pinching her, till she was black and blue. "What is it, friend? You go too far with your joke. Do you want to make an end of me?" said the poor girl. At the moment her distaff fell. When she stooped to pick it up, what did she see? The tail of the vampire. Then she said to the girl next to her,—"Let's go. Run away. The creature is a vampire." The other girl was laughing so much that she did not understand. So the girl who knew the dreadful secret went out alone into the

28

yard, on the pretext that she had to take some lengths of woven linen to the attic. Frightened out of her wits, she ran away with the linen, she ran into a forest, old as the world and black as her fear.

Her companions at the gathering awaited her return. They looked and waited until they saw that she was not coming back. Where could she be? "You must fetch her wherever she is," roared the vampire, with bloodshot eyes and hair standing on end. As the girl could not be found, the vampire killed all the rest of the merrymakers. He sucked their blood, he threw their flesh and bones under the bed, cut off their lips, and put their heads in a row in the window. They looked as if they were laughing. He strung up their intestines on a nail, saying they were strings of beads, and then he fled away. He arrived at the forest where the girl had taken refuge, and found her under a beech-tree. "Why did you come here, little girl? Why did you run away from the gathering?" The girl, poor thing, was so frightened that her tongue clove to her mouth, and she could say nothing. "You are afraid, little girl. Come home with me. You will feel better there." Then, involuntarily, she asked,—"Where?" "Here in the forest. Come quicker," said the vampire.

They arrived at a hole in the depth of the forest, and she saw that this was the home of the vampire. He pressed her to enter first. "No, no. I don't want to. You go first." So the vampire went in, and began to sweep and clear up. The girl, however, stopped up the hole with the lengths of linen, and fled quickly towards the east. In her flight she saw a little light a long way off. She ran towards the light, came to a house, and found it empty, except for a dead man, who was lying stretched out on a table, with a torch at his head, and his hands crossed on his breast. What was she to do? She entered the house, climbed up on to the stove, and went to sleep, worn out by suffering and fear. And she would have rested well, had not the terrible vampire pursued her. He had thrown aside the linen, and rushed after her, mad with rage. He came into the house, and the dead man rose, and they fought and wrestled till the cock crew and the girl awoke. Now the light was out, the dead man was gone, and the only sound was the song of the little cricket. The girl was left alone with her guardian angel. The dead man and the vampire both vanished at cock-crow, for both were vampires. Waking up in the darkness, the girl looked round the house three times, thought she was at home and had had a horrible dream, and then fell asleep again calmly and fearlessly. When she woke again, and saw all the beauties of the forest, and heard all the songs of the birds, she was amazed and thought herself in heaven. She did not stop long in wonder, but set out for her parents' house, hoping to bring them back with her.

She reached her home, and began to tell about the vampire and how he had gone, and what beautiful things she had seen in the woods of paradise. The parents looked at her, and, full of amazement and doubt, made the sign of the cross. The girl sank into the ground, deeper and deeper, for she too had become a vampire, poor thing. The vampire had bewitched her, and the beauty of the dwelling in the wood had enchanted her too much.

29

Another variant of the story[7] is as follows:

There was an evening gathering in the village, as is the custom. But the youths and maidens present were not the children of well-to-do peasants. The gathering was held in a deserted house; the youths were a noisy, laughing, mocking crowd who made themselves heard from one end of the village to the other, and the girls were just like them. They made a great fire, the girls started spinning, the boys told all kinds of jokes, and the girls shook with laughter. After it had grown late, three young men, unknown to the company, entered the house. "Good evening, good evening," was said, and they joined in the general conversation. While everyone was talking, one of the girls dropped her distaff. The distaff fell under the strangers' feet, and the girl stooped to pick it up. When she went back to her seat she was as white as chalk. "What is it?" asked one of those near her. And the girl murmured that the three strangers had horses' hooves instead of feet. What was to be done? They whispered to one another, and to the boys, that the three strangers were vampires, not men. Then one by one, one by one, they slipped out of the door, and wended their ways homewards. The three vampires remained as vampires, but they did not remain alone in the house, for there was a girl asleep on the oven.

With the dawn of the next day, the sister of the sleeping girl, together with some friends, came to see what had happened to her. When they were still some distance from the house they saw a grinning face looking out of the window—"Oh, oh," they said, "our sister is laughing." They drew nearer, and, entering into the house, were horror-struck and made the sign of the cross. It was the head only which was in the window; the lips were cut off, and so the face seemed to smile. Her intestines were stretched out on the nails and on shelves, and the whole house was stained with blood. Poor girl![8]

In the two following vampire stories from Siret, vampires are thought of as wizardlike beings, being men or women capable of projecting their soul from their body at will:

A woman from Siret[9] tells the following:—Vampires are just like other folk, only that God has ordained that they should wander over the country and kill people. There was one that wandered through ten villages, killing their inhabitants. He had a little house in the plain, which was always empty except when he himself was there. One day he thought of going on a journey, and baked bread in preparation. He made ten loaves and put them on the table. Twelve men who were going to work passed the cottage, and noticed that there was a light. One of the men said,—"I'll just go in and light my pipe." They all entered, and the vampire became a cat. The men saw that there was no human being in the house, so they took all the loaves, except one, which they left

30

because they had seen the cat. This was lucky for them, for otherwise they would all have been bewitched and died.

The vampire went round the villages, taking with him the one loaf.

When the men returned from work, they again passed the cottage and again saw a light. They entered, and this time saw the vampire, who told them of their escape. Their luck was great, for in all the villages where the vampire had wandered he had killed men and torn them to bits.

Vampire Story from Siret.[10] An old man with some soldiers was driving in a cart in Transilvania, trying to find where he could get some hay. Night came on during their journey, so they stopped at a lonely house in a plain. The woman of the house received them, put maize porridge (*mămăligă*) and milk on the table for them, and then went away. The soldiers ate the maize porridge, and after their meal looked for the old woman to thank her, but were unable to find her. Climbing up to the attic to see if she was there, they found seven bodies lying down, one of which was the woman's. They were frightened and fled, and, as they looked back, they saw seven little lights descending on the house. These were the souls of the vampires. Had the soldiers turned the bodies with their faces downwards, the souls would never have been able to enter the bodies again.

In the following stories vampires are witches (in one case a wizard) pure and simple. In the first two we have them joining in witches' revels; in the others they get hold of the "power" of cows for their own ends:

There was a lady of the highest society in Botoşani who was dressed up in beautiful Paris clothes for a party on Dec. 31st; she went into her nursery, got out by the chimney, and came back all in rags, and exhausted.[11]

A lad who was in service with a female vampire noticed once that she was covered with blood during the day-time. He watched her closely, and saw that she anointed herself with something, and went out by the chimney. The lad also anointed himself with the ointment in the box, and went out of the chimney after his mistress. He arrived at a far off desert region, where the vampires fought. He watched them stabbing one another and fighting. The vampires go with their bodies, not their souls only. The ointment with which the vampires anoint themselves is made of the grease of serpents, hedgehogs, and badgers.[12]

One of the main characters of the live (witchlike) vampires is that they can take the "power" of cows.

There was once a female vampire (*strigoica*) who had no cow of her own. However, she kept a wooden cow in her attic, and milked it day and night

31

continually. She had taken all the milk of other people's cows, and brought it to her own wooden cow.[13]

A woman who was a vampire (*strigoica*) went to confession and told the priest that she had taken the "power" of other people's cows (*i.e.* got more milk from her own cow at their expense). The priest said to her,—"Take the butter from this milk, go into the forest, anoint a tree with it, and then, after three days, go back and see what happens." She did this and found a great number of serpents and other horrible creatures in the butter. "You must know," said the priest, "that these will suck your blood in the next world, because you have taken "power" from everything in this world."[14]

In the variant given below, the woman is not called a vampire, but just a *baba* or old wife:

An old woman in Strojineți got as much milk from her cow as one usually gets from ten cows. A poor woman, who was getting very little milk from her cow, asked the old wife to cure it. The old wife took butter from her cow, and butter from the poor woman's cow, and put both lots into water. In the old wife's butter there were numbers of serpents, lizards, worms, and other horrible creatures; in that of the woman, there were only little fishes. "Look," said the old wife. "In the other world these serpents will suck from me. If you wish to share my fate I will arrange that your cow shall give much milk also." But the poor woman did not wish this. When the old wife died, a light was seen from time to time going to her house. It was seen chiefly by rather dull people.[15]

In the following story we have a contest of strength between a witch and a vampire, two beings that seem of exactly the same nature, the witch being the more admirable only in that she takes the side of the human beings.

The Witch versus the Vampire.[16] A lady in Siret had a cow, and a vampire had taken away its "power." But she found a wise woman, named Hartopanița, who knew how to break the power of the vampire. She saw him once in the house. She made a sign with her finger, screwed up her mouth, and said a word which bound the vampire to the spot. He remained as if frozen, and could not move a step. But he caused the wise woman to come out in sores, and she could not get rid of them till she had asked him to forgive her.

In the following three accounts the vampire has the character of a devil, and the word *strigoi* could be replaced by *drac*:

Vampires wander at the cross-roads. If anyone has a great wish, and is entirely fearless, there is the means to attain the wish. Go to the cross-roads at night. Take a large vessel with water. Make a fire, and, when the water boils, take a black cat, without one white hair, and drop her into the pot. A black cat is supposed to represent the soul of the devil. After it is quite dark, when the pot with the cat in it is boiling vigorously, devils begin to come to ask you to stop boiling the cat. You must not speak a word. You must wait until the chief of all the devils comes, for he will come last of all. He will ask you to stop boiling the cat, just as the other devils did; but he will also promise you everything you wish. Then you will let him take the cat, and in exchange you will receive whatever you most desire.[17]

The next two stories are about the danger of sneezing.

The Thief and the Vampire.[18] There were once two partners, a thief and a vampire. "Where are you going this evening?" said the thief to the vampire. "I am going to bewitch the son of Ion," said the vampire. "Don't go there. It is there that I want to go this evening to steal oxen. You can go somewhere else." "Go somewhere else yourself," said the vampire. "Why should you go to Ion's house of all places? He has only one son, and there are heaps of other houses you could go to," said the thief. "No, I'm going to Ion's," said the vampire. "Well, I'm going there too," said the thief. Both of them went. The vampire went to the door, and the thief to the window. Ion's son inside sneezed, and the thief said quickly,—"Long life." This took away the vampire's power. He was able to make the boy's nose bleed, but he did not die. The thief then went in and told the parents what had happened, and they gave him some oxen as a reward. It is always well to say "Long life" when anyone sneezes.

Sneezing.[19] A young noble was about to start on a journey, and his horse was waiting saddled and bridled. There was a thief creeping up to steal the horse. As he came near he saw a vampire just under the window, waiting for an opportunity to put a spell on the noble. The noble sneezed, and quickly the thief said,—"Good health," for if he had not done so the vampire would have seized the occasion to bewitch the noble, and he would have died. It was, however, the vampire who burst with anger at missing his chance. People came out to see what was the matter. The thief showed them the burst body of the vampire, and explained what had happened. The parents were so glad that their son had escaped that they gave the horse to the thief as a reward. This shows us that we must always say "Good health" when anyone sneezes.

It is clear that the idea behind the word *strigoi* varies from one account to another. While the word *strigoi* generally denotes a reanimated corpse like

33

the *vrykolaka* of Greece and Macedonia, its use to denote a witch or wizard who can project body or soul is common in Roumania, and especially in Moldavia. Its significance has become less terrible. Witches in Roumania are often little more than wise old women, or *babas*, who in their turn are only less common than leaves of grass; they also attempt good deeds as well as evil.

Notes

1. *Ion Creanga*, 7 (1914): 165.
2. W. R. S. Ralston, *Russian Folk Tales* (London, 1873), 318.
3. The hemp brake used by the Roumanian peasant consists of a narrowish, trestlelike table or stand. At one end an H-axle is fixed. Jointed to this is the tongue, an object like a T-shaped hammer with the horizontal part of the T very flat and broad, and often made of iron. The stalks of the hemp are laid on the table in the direction of its length, and the head of the hammer is brought down on them again and again till they are thoroughly crushed. Sometimes the H-axle of the hemp brake is in the center of the table, and there is a tongue at either end. When this is so, two women can work at their hemp crushing at the same time.
4. *Ion Creanga* 7 (1914): 82.
5. Ibid., 5 (1912): 11.
6. Ibid., 4 (1911): 202.
7. Ibid., 6 (1913): 237.
8. This delightful habit of cutting off the lips of their victims is not peculiar to vampires. It is the way Montenegrins, Turks, and others occasionally treat their defeated enemies.
9. *Ion Creanga* 6 (1913): 80.
10. Ibid., 17.
11. Ibid., 7 (1914): 24.
12. Ibid., 6 (1913): 306.
13. Ibid., 18.
14. Ibid., 105.
15. Ibid., 108.
16. Ibid., 18.
17. Ibid., 5 (1912): 244.
18. Ibid., 6 (1913): 51.
19. Ibid.

The Romanian Folkloric Vampire

Among the numerous scholars who have studied the vampire, there are only a handful who have achieved eminence. One of these is Jan Louis Perkowski, a professor of slavic languages and literatures at the University of Virginia. Not only has he written a great deal on the subject, but he has also regularly offered a popular college course, "Vampires of the Slavs," which attracts hundreds of interested students.

An important contribution to vampirology is his Vampires of the Slavs *(Cambridge, Mass.: Slavica Publishers, 1976), which consists of a dozen essays or extracts, several of which were translated by Professor Perkowski and three of which were written by him. (None of the essays in that volume have been included in this one, because they are readily available to readers with access to major libraries.) But perhaps his major work is* The Darkling: A Treatise on Slavic Vampirism *(Columbus, Ohio: Slavica Publishers, 1989).*

Although most of Professor Perkowski's published investigations of vampires concern Slavic data, the following essay analyzing Romanian reports was chosen for this volume because of its obvious advance over the earlier anecdotal treatment of the Romanian vampire. After presenting translations of nineteen authentic field-collected texts, he classifies the elements of the texts in an orderly way, thereby facilitating the formulation of hypotheses and the articulation of tentative generalizations or conclusions about the nature of the Romanian vampire.

For the reader of English literature even a passing reference to the Romanian province of Transylvania is sure to evoke frightening images of vampirism, but most especially Bram Stoker's literary vampire, Count Dracula. Stoker's hero is not solely a creature of his imagination. In fact, he patterned Count Dracula after an actual fifteenth-century Romanian prince, known variously as Voivode Dracula and Vlad Țepeș. Essential to keep in mind, however, is the fact that there is no historical evidence of any sort to support the notion that Vlad Țepeș was a vampire. Without any doubt this imputation originated in Stoker's creative imagination.[1]

Reprinted from *East European Quarterly* 16 (1982): 311–322.

He melded history & folklore.

The fact that Vlad Țepeș was not a vampire does not mean, however, that vampire cult practices have never existed in Romania. Over the years various Romanian folklorists have collected bits and pieces of vampire data. During the early 1930s Emil Petrovici, the eminent Romanian linguist, collected dialect samples throughout Romania in preparation for a Romanian dialect atlas. A selection of these texts was eventually published in 1943 as a supplement to the atlas.[2] Among them are several texts dealing with vampire beliefs. With the assistance of Professor Emil Vrabie, professor of Romance and Slavic linguistics at the University of Bucharest, I have been able to translate these dialect vampire accounts, which I will attempt to classify and analyze.

An interesting introduction to the study of Romanian vampires is Agnes Murgoci's article "The Vampire in Roumania."[3] She states, "The most typical vampire is therefore the reanimated corpse. We may call this the dead-vampire type." Further on she says, "As regards the names used for vampires, dead and alive, *strigoi* (fem. *strigoica*) is the most common Roumanian term, and *moroii* is perhaps the next most usual. *Moroii* is less often used than *strigoi*. Usually we have *strigoi* and *moroii* consorting together, but the *moroii* are subject to the *strigoi*. We find also *strigoi*, *moroii*, and *vârcolaci*, and *strigoi* and *pricolici* used as if all were birds of the same feather."[4]

Professor Petrovici's vampire texts, which were collected from the four corners of Romania, and, in one case (Text XVI), from across the border in Yugoslavia, are nineteen in number, fifteen of which concern the *strigoi*, three the *moroi*, and one the *pricolici*, thereby affirming Dr. Murgoci's observation that *strigoi* is the most common vampire designation.

The following are English translations of these nineteen dialect texts:

TEXT I

Strigoi—pp. 18–19
(village of Ohabă, Severin District)

A man died and he turned into a *strigoi*. Now he comes to torment the women in the house where he used to live. The police even went to his grave. They dug him up and saw that he was bloated and ruddy. They tried to impale him with a pitchfork through the stomach, but they could not implant it. Then a soldier tried to strike him with his rifle, but he could not do it. He struck himself instead. So it was necessary to summon a special woman who knew incantations, but she would perform them only when she was alone with the dead body. Afterwards she stuck a knife into the stomach of the corpse. I do not know what has happened since then. I have not heard anything for about two weeks. (recorded 8/3/1932)

36

TEXT II
Strigoi—p. 19
(village of Glimboca, Severin District)
When a corpse is placed into its coffin, it is rubbed with garlic and *leoștean* [a parsley-like herb called lovage]. This is important, because the dead person otherwise would become a *strigoi*. (recorded 8/3/1932)

TEXT III
Strigoi—p. 27
(village of Secășeni, Caraș District)
They put some whiskey [*rachia*] into a bottle and buried it with the corpse, so that the *strigoi* would drink it and not return home. His relatives say to him, "Peter or John [his name] drink rachia and go to Vărădia [a village name] and don't come home!" If you do this the *strigoi* won't come home, but will go to Vărădia to drink *rachia*. After returning home from the grave they must remain silent, because, if they break silence the ceremony will have no effect. (recorded 7/3/1932)

TEXT IV
Strigoi—p. 62
(village of Scărișoara, Turda District)
Unmarried persons run a greater risk of becoming a *strigoi* at death, so measures must be taken. You have to stick a sickle into the corpse's heart in order to protect yourself and your relatives. If not, the *strigoi* draws his relatives to the grave. (recorded 7/27/1937)

TEXT V
Strigoi—p. 65
(village of Feneș, Alba District)
Every person is a *strigoi*. A person can be rain, hail, wood, a tree, cow, or an ox, sheep or a pig. When that person dies, the one who was rain brings on torrents when he dies. The one who was hail brings on a hail storm. The one who was a cow causes the cows to die, etc. (recorded 9/23/1931)

TEXT VI
Strigoi—p. 139
(village of Roșia, Bihor District)
You put a candle, coin, and towel into the hand of a dead person, so that he won't turn into a *strigoi*. It is also a good idea to pierce the dead man's skin with a needle. If a corpse has even a small hole in its skin, it cannot become a *strigoi*. (recorded 3/27/1937)

TEXT VII
Strigoi—p. 198
(village of Coropceni, Vaslui District)
On the Feast of St. Andrew (November 30th) it is useful to rub garlic on the doors and windows to protect yourself against *strigoi*. (recorded 7/26/1934)

TEXT VIII
Strigoi—p. 230
(village of Somova, Tulcea District)
People who die unforgiven by their parents are in danger of becoming *strigoi*. In order to remove this type of *strigoi* a priest is called to read from the Gospels. Then the corpse is exhumed, cremated, and the ashes are thrown to the winds. After this the *strigoi* will never again return. (recorded 8/26/1935)

TEXT IX
Strigoi—p. 239
(village of Căzăneşti, Lalomiţa District)
If a cat or dog walks over or under a body while it is still at home awaiting burial, the corpse will become a *strigoi*. In order to be rid of such a *strigoi* you must bury a bottle of wine near the grave of the dead person and after six weeks dig it up and share it with your relatives. Whoever drinks the wine is protected from the *strigoi*, who will not return. (recorded 5/12/1937)

TEXT X
Strigoi—p. 242
(village of Gura-Sărăţii, Buzău District)
If a cat walks over or under a dead person before he is buried, he will become a *strigoi*. (recorded 6/11/1937)

TEXT XI
Strigoi—p. 247
(village of Ştefăneşti, Ilfov District)
The old people say that if a cat walks over or under a body it will turn into a *strigoi!* The antidote is to exhume the body and shoot it. (recorded 9/7/1935)

TEXT XII
Strigoi
(village of Nucşoara, Muscel District)
Once a *strigoi* turned into a handsome young man and a young girl fell in love with him. They were married, but the girl also wanted a religious wedding. He rejected this idea. Her parents insisted, so he agreed to go to the church, but when they emerged from the church he looked at his wife in a strange way, baring his teeth. She became frightened and told her mother about it. Her mother said, "Don't be afraid. He loves you. That's why he bared

his teeth." When their parents came to visit them, they couldn't find them. They had locked themselves in, but the people could see them through the window. He was sucking her blood. When the people saw it, they shot him through the window. (recorded 6/21/1936)

TEXT XIII
Strigoi—p. 269
(village of Petrila, Hunedoara District)
   Anyone who, at night, sees a dead person becomes ill because of a *strigoi*. (recorded 10/6/1931)

TEXT XIV
Strigoi—p. 286
(village of Măceşul-de-Jos, Dolj District)
   It's important to make a small hole in the skin on the stomach of a dead person to prevent him from becoming a *strigoi*. (recorded 6/6/1936)

TEXT XV
Strigoi—p. 301
(village of Zimnicea, Teleorman District)
   A person who was born with pain and regret when he dies turns into a cat or dog and torments his relatives during the night. The solution is to exhume him and pierce his body with a needle or a nail. Another solution is to walk around the grave with burning hemp [a type of marijuana]. The hemp smoke renders the *strigoi* harmless. (recorded 6/15/1935)

TEXT XVI
Moroi—p. 8
(village of Ždrelo, Moravska Banovina in Yugoslavia)
   If a *moroi* comes, you can get rid of it by burning resin [incense] twice a week on Saturday night and on Tuesday night and it will not come anymore.
   When a *moroi* comes, it drinks blood from the cattle and they die.
   A dead person can turn into a *moroi* in the form of a dog, horse, sheep, or man. In order to get rid of it you burn his clothes. If this is done, he will no longer return.
   In order to prevent transformation into a *moroi* the relatives and friends who attend the burial ceremony have to walk around the grave three times and one of the relatives has to carry the candle last used by the deceased. If this is done the corpse will not become a *moroi*. (recorded 9/17/1937)

TEXT XVII
Moroi—p. 259
(Village of Grădiştea, Vâlcea District)
   If a bad person dies, he turns into a *moroi*. He tries to feed on his relatives, to draw them to the grave. The solution is to exhume him and return him to

those of his relatives who are being attacked by the *moroi*. Then the body is reburied and it is a good idea to put millet seeds and stones into the grave. (recorded 6/13/1936)

TEXT XVIII
Moroi—p. 292
(village of Balş, Romanaţi District)
They say that a corpse leaves his grave as a *moroi* and feeds on his relatives. He prefers their hearts. The solution is to exhume him and if he is ruddy in the face, you have to stab his heart with something sharp like a needle, a pin, or a nail. (recorded 6/21/1933)

TEXT XIX
Pricolici—p. 297
(village of Isbiceni, Romanaţi District)
A dead person becomes a *pricolici* and he feeds on his relatives. When he is exhumed his rump is pointing upwards and he has blood on his lips. You have to take some of that blood and feed it to the person at home who is suffering from the *pricolici*. In this way the relative regains his health.
If a baby steals milk from his mother's breast after having been weaned at one year or more, he will become a *pricolici* if he dies. He then tries to return to his mother or to other relatives to torment them. (recorded 6/19/1935)

In an article entitled "A Recent Vampire Death" I proposed a ten-item analysis outline, which is designed to classify vampire data in such a way as to allow fruitful comparison with similarly derived sets.[5] It is this outline which I will employ in the classification and analysis of Professor Petrovici's data.

1. *Information Source:* Professor Petrovici gathered the data during the course of Romanian dialectological fieldwork within the time span 9/23/1931 to 9/17/1937. Each text was transcribed by hand in a narrow phonetic transcription. They were then published photomechanically in 1943. Professor Petrovici, with whom I was personally acquainted, was an accomplished fieldworker and expert phonetician.

2. *Country and Region:* The texts were gathered throughout Romania from the following districts: Alba, Bihor, Buzău, Caraş, Dolj, Hunedoara, Ilfov, Lalomiţa, Muscel, Romanaţi, Severin, Teleorman, Tulcea, Turda, Vaslui, and Vâlcea. One Text (XVI) was gathered in a Romanian village in Yugoslavia: Ždrelo in Moravska Banovina. The following map gives a schematic representation of the distribution of these regions.

3. *Name:* There are three: *strigoi* (fifteen texts), *moroi* (three texts) and

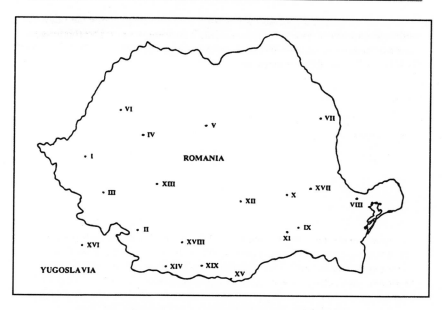

Districts of Romania Serving as Sources of Vampire Data

pricolici (one text). The etymology of the first of these terms is quite clear. *Strigoi* is from the Latin *strix* (nominative plural: *striges*) and in Classical times referred to a screech-owl. In its extended meaning it referred to a vampirelike creature which attacked infants. It was frequently synonymous to the more common Latin term *lamia*.[6]

Moroi may or may not have entered Romanian via Latin. It is found in Slavic *mora*, Germanic (cf. English "night*mare*"), Albanian *morë*, and Modern Greek μόρα.[7] My best guess is that it entered Romanian via Slavic, although this root appears to be common to several Indo-European language families. According to Max Vasmer, in Russian Church Slavonic *mara* was used to translate Greek ἔχσταοις in the sense of "loss of consciousness." In later Slavic it took on the meaning of "succubus," a female night demon which tries to suffocate her sleeping victim. The origin of *pricolici* is unclear, but Cioranescu derives the second part of the word (-*lici*)[8] from Modern Greek λύκος,[9] meaning "wolf." The earliest mention of *pricolici* in regard to the Romanians occurs in Demetrius Cantemirius' Latin manuscript of 1716 concerning the history of Moldavia, in which he says:

41

Tricolicz: The same as French Loup garou [werewolf]—the people believe that it is possible to change themselves by magic into wolves and other voracious animals who assume this role to such a degree that they attack both men and cattle and tear them apart.[10]

4. *Origin* (How do they become one?):
   a. *Strigoi*
      Text I—at death
      Text II—at death
      Text III—at death
      Text IV—unmarried at death
      Text V—every person at death
      Text VI—at death
      Text VIII—at death when unforgiven by parents
      Text IX—cat or dog walks over or under corpse before burial
      Text X—cat or dog walks over or under corpse before burial
      Text XI—cat walks over or under a body
      Text XV—person born with pain and regret at death (becomes a cat or dog)
   b. *Moroi*
      Text XVI—at death (turns into a dog, horse, sheep, or man)
      Text XVII—bad person at death
      Text XVIII—at death
   c. *Pricolici*
      Text XIX—at death of child who drinks mother's milk after weaning
5. *Detection* (How do people know there is one?):
   a. *Strigoi*
      Text I—presence of victim
      Text IV—relatives of deceased die
      Text V—excessive rain or hail or death of livestock
      Text XII—human victim is drained of blood
      Text XIII—victim becomes ill
      Text XV—relatives of deceased are tormented
   b. *Moroi*
      Text XVI—cattle die by loss of blood
      Text XVII—relatives of deceased sicken
      Text XVIII—hearts of relatives of deceased eaten
   c. *Pricolici*
      Text XIX—relatives fed upon or tormented

6. *Attributes* (How is its presence perceived?):
   a. *Strigoi*
      Text I—ruddy and bloated in grave
      Text VI—corpse cannot have a hole in its skin
      Text XII—bare his teeth
   b. *Moroi*
      Text XVI—revenant in the form of a dog, horse, sheep, or man
      Text XVIII—ruddy face in the grave
   c. *Pricolici*
      Text XIX—corpse is upside down in grave; has blood on lips; weaned
         child takes milk from breast of mother
7. *Activity Pattern* (What does it do?):
   a. *Strigoi*
      Text I—torments women where he lived
      Text III—returns home from the grave
      Text IV—kills his relatives
      Text V—causes excessive rain or hail or kills livestock
      Text VIII—returns from the grave
      Text IX—returns from the grave
      Text XII—marries and sucks the blood of his wife
      Text XIII—causes illness in victim by appearing to him at night
      Text XV—torments relatives in form of cat or dog
   b. *Moroi*
      Text XVI—kills cattle by drinking their blood
      Text XVII—feeds on his relatives and tries to kill them
      Text XVIII—feeds on his relatives, especially their hearts
   c. *Pricolici*
      Text XIX—feeds on his relatives; infant *pricolici* torments its mother
         or other relatives
8. *Precautions* (How do they protect themselves against one?):
   a. *Strigoi*
      Text II—rub corpse with garlic and *leoştan*
      Text III—bury a bottle of whiskey (*rachia*) with corpse and exhort
         him to drink it and go to Vărădia; maintain silence at home
         after the ceremony
      Text IV—insert sickle into corpse's heart
      Text VI—place candle, coin, and towel into corpse's hand; pierce
         corpse's skin with a needle
      Text VII—rub garlic on doors and windows on St. Andrew's Day
      Text XIV—pierce skin on stomach of corpse

b. *Moroi*

    Text XVI—at burial relatives and friends walk around grave three times while a relative carries the candle last used by the deceased

9. *Cures* (How do they remove the threat?):

  a. *Strigoi*

    Text I—special woman performs incantation alone and then sticks a knife into the corpse's stomach

    Text VIII—priest reads from the Gospels, the body is exhumed, cremated, and the ashes thrown to the winds

    Text IX—bury a bottle of wine near the grave and then retrieve it and drink its contents with your relatives six weeks later

    Text XI—exhume the body and shoot it

    Text XII—shoot it

    Text XV—exhume the body and pierce it with a needle or a nail; walk around the grave with burning hemp

  b. *Moroi*

    Text XVI—burn resin twice a week on Saturday and Tuesday nights; burn its clothes

    Text XVII—exhume the body and have its victims (relatives of the corpse) rebury it with millet seeds and stones

    Text XVIII—exhume the body and pierce its heart with a sharp object: needle, pin, or nail

  c. *Pricolici*

    Text XIX—exhume the body, take some blood that is on its lips and feed it to the victim

10. *Social/Psychological Role:* Even a cursory glance at the foregoing componential analysis reveals striking similarities among the nineteen texts. Although they were gathered from widely separated villages—ranging from the Danube Delta to the Moldavian, Yugoslav, and Bulgarian borders—the underlying concept is virtually constant: The dead return from the grave to prey on their relatives and on livestock. This is indeed the phenomenon of the revenant, the undead, the vampire.

    It is unfortunate that the corpus of material is sparse and incomplete, that not one single text provides us with data for every element in the analysis outline. It is also unfortunate that not one text is a firsthand, participatory account. Text I comes closest, yet it is more in the nature of a tale, as is Text XII. All of the texts are general and instructive. They tell what must be done to escape from a dire and terrifying situation. Even Texts I and XII are didactic in a parabolic sense.

    On the psychological level, illness and death of unknown origin, or

Problem with the motive body of evidence.

even just the fear of them, evoke a condition of panic through frustration. The situation is hopeless. You cannot comprehend it and there is nothing you can do to help. The actual cause of the illness or death can be a contagious disease, hence relatives as the first victims, or perhaps mental illness caused by morbid grief or feelings of guilt or anger toward the deceased. There are other possibilities, which have been explained elsewhere, but important here is how the social unit, the given village, copes with the problem.[11]

On the sociological level, we find that the precautions and cures in their variety tend to be village specific. Each community establishes its own meaningful ceremony, choosing from its own stock of symbols to perform anxiety-relieving physical acts. The ill may not be cured nor the dead resurrected, but the anxiety, panic, and fear of the victims' relatives can be allayed through these community rituals and life can revert to its normal course.[12] The corpse is a handy scapegoat.

Notes

1. For a discussion of the historical figure Vlad Ţepeş and his characterization in Stoker's novel *Dracula* see: Radu Florescu and Raymond T. McNally, *Dracula* (New York, 1973), 162–181; Nicolae Stoicescu, *Vlad Ţepeş* (Bucharest, 1976), 231–238; and JA. S. Lur'e, *Povest' o Drakule* (Moscow, 1964), 3–13.

2. Emil Petrovici, *Texte dialectale* (Sibiu-Leipzig, 1943).

3. Agnes Murgoci, "The Vampire in Roumania," *Folklore* (London) 37, 4 (Dec. 31, 1926): 320–349. [Ed. note: See also herein, pp. 12–34.] To my knowledge no thorough study of the subject has yet appeared in Romanian, though the vampire theme is usually broached in general works on Romanian folk beliefs. Typical examples are: I. A. Cândrea, *Iarba fiarelor: Studii de folclor* (Bucharest, 1928); Artur Gorovei, *Credinte şi superstiţii ale poporului român* (Bucharest, 1915); and Tudor Pamfile, *Mitologie românească*, I: *Duşmani şi prieteni ai omului* (Bucharest, 1915). Though it is based on Dr. Murgoci's article, Montague Summers' short section on the Romanian vampire is still worthy of mention: *The Vampire in Europe* (London, 1929), 301–315.

4. Murgoci, "The Vampire in Roumania," 321.

5. Jan L. Perkowski, *Vampires of the Slavs* (Cambridge, Mass., 1976), 156–159.

6. Rossell Hope Robbins, *The Encyclopedia of Witchcraft and Demonology* (New York, 1959), 295–296; and Alejandro Cioranescu, *Diccionario etimológico rumano* (Tenerife, 1960), fasc. 5, p. 800.

7. Cioranescu, *Diccionario*, fasc. 4, p. 539; *Dicţionarul limbii române*, eds. Iorgu Iordan and Ion Coteanu (Bucharest, 1965), vol. 6, 878–879; and Max Vasmer, *Ètimologičeskij slovar' russkogo jazyka* (Moscow, 1967), vol. 2, 571.

8. Cioranescu, *Diccionario*, fasc. 5, p. 664.

9. It is interesting to note that Tache Papahagi lists both *strigă* (981) and *moră* (702) in his *Dicţionarul dialectului Aromîn* (Bucharest, 1963), but does not list a cognate for Romanian *pricolici*. This absence argues against the connection with Greek λύϰος, since it is Aromîn speakers who are in closest contact with the Greeks.

10. Demetrius Cantemirius, *Descriptio antiqui et hodierni Statue Moldaviae* (translated and published in Bucharest, 1973), 344. In the same text he says of the *strigoi*,

Striga: From the Greek word στρίγλη. The same meaning which it had among the Romans has been preserved among today's Moldavians—namely, an old sorceress, who kills newborn children with her evil power, but no one knows how. The superstition is quite prevalent among the Transylvanians. So they say that if the striga comes the children are found suffocated in their cradles without having suffered any previous illness. If they suspect some old woman of such an evil act, they bind her hand and foot and dunk her in a river. If she sinks, she is innocent. But if she floats, then that is sufficient proof of guilt and they burn her alive. In vain the old woman proclaims her innocence to the last breath.

11. See Ernest Jones, *On the Nightmare* (New York, 1951), for a Freudian interpretation; and Jan L. Perkowski, "On the Origin of the Kashubian Succuba," *Journal of Vampirism* (Oak Lawn, Ill.) 1, 2 (Nov. 1977–Dec. 1978): 10–11, for a non-Freudian interpretation of the clinical nightmare.

12. Specific analysis of the various symbols which appear in these texts is beyond the scope of this paper, but one or two brief interpretations are in order: the whiskey (*rachia*) in Text III and hemp (marijuana) in Text XV were surely chosen for their soporific qualities.

✻ Problem with pagination
Next page is page 50(but 48 is this page)
Three pages after 49 that
this [47] page + that precedes it.
is on this page

All pages are there.

FELIX OINAS

East European Vampires

Although most scholars tend to be limited to one particular culture or linguistic group, there are some whose breadth of knowledge allows them to encompass a cross-cultural perspective. For example, two of the most comprehensive surveys of the vampire were written by Montague Summers. The Vampire *(London: Kegan Paul, Trench, Trubner and Co., 1928) and* The Vampire in Europe, *published by the same publisher in 1929, are still well worth reading, although one must keep in mind that Summers himself believed in the actual existence of vampires.*

Felix Oinas, professor emeritus of Slavic languages and literatures and of Uralic and Altaic studies at Indiana University, certainly qualifies as such a broad scholar. An Estonian by birth, Professor Oinas' expertise includes Estonian, Finnish, Russian, and east European folklore. The following brief survey draws on traditions from a variety of such cultures. For a sample of his research in Baltic folklore, see Studies in Finnic Folklore *(Helsinki: Suomalaisen Kirjallisuuden Seura, 1985). For a more extensive survey of east European vampire folklore, see Dagmar Burkhart, "Vampirglaube und Vampirsage auf dem Balkan," in* Beiträge zur Südosteuropa-Forschung, *ed. Alois Schmaus (Munich: Rudolf Trofenik, 1966), 211–252.*

The vampire is defined by Jan Perkowski as "a being which derives sustenance from a victim, who is weakened by the experience. The sustenance may be physical or emotional in nature."[1] More commonly, however, the term *vampire* is used in a more restricted sense to denote a type of the dead or, actually, undead. It is a living corpse or soulless body that emerges from its grave and drinks the blood of the living. Belief in vampires is found all over the world, in India, China, Malaya, Indonesia, and elsewhere, but especially in eastern Europe—among the Slavs and their neighbors: the Greeks, Romanians, Albanians, and others.

Among the East Slavs, the vampire is well known to the Ukrainians. The Russians knew it by its name in former times (from the eleventh to the fifteenth century). The vampire tradition is well documented among the West

Reprinted from the *Journal of Popular Culture* 16 (1982): 108–114.

cut the tendons under the knees. In more serious cases it is desirable to strike off the head with a single stroke and to place it between the legs, or to hack the body to pieces. Some of these measures are, however, not completely foolproof; cases have been reported of an exhumed vampire who had been pierced by a stake, but had pulled the stake out. The surest method of disposing of vampires is to completely annihilate the body by burning it and scattering the ashes.

Some of these acts correspond closely to the punishments meted out, especially in the Orient, for particularly heinous murders.[7] The killing of a vampire or any other dangerous person is accomplished in such a way as to make it impossible for the soul to avenge itself.

During the vampire epidemic in Europe, and even in the United States, from the eighteenth to well into the nineteenth century, numerous cases of the mishandling of corpses believed to be vampires have become known.[8] In 1889 in Russia, the corpse of an old man who was suspected of being a vampire was dug up, and many of those present maintained that they saw a tail attached to its back. In Rhode Island, a father in 1874 exhumed the body of his own daughter and burned her heart, in the belief that she was endangering the lives of the other members of the family. In 1899, Romanian peasants in Krasova dug up no fewer than thirty corpses and tore them to pieces, expecting to stop an epidemic of diphtheria. Further instances have been reported from Hungary, Bucharest, Transylvania, and so on.

A tragic event, entitled "Immigrant's Fears of Vampires Led to Death,"[9] was reported in the *Times* of London as late as January 9, 1973. Mr. Myiciura, a Polish immigrant in Stoke on Trent, sixty-eight years of age, a retired pottery worker who had lived twenty-five years in England, was found dead in his bed. He had died from choking on a piece of garlic, which he had placed in his mouth before going to bed. The police officer explained at the inquest: "In his room was a ritual distribution of objects as antidotes to vampires. There was a bag of salt at the dead man's face, one between his legs and other containers scattered around the room. Salt was also sprinkled on his blankets. Outside his window was a washing-up-bowl containing cloves of garlic. There was garlic even in the keyhole of his lodgings."

The dead man's landlady testified: "He thought vampires were everywhere. He used salt, pepper and garlic to keep them away." And the city coroner said: "This is a strange case. This man took precautions against vampires he thought were in his neighborhood. He had a superstitious fear of vampires and choked on a clove of garlic used to ward them off." A verdict of accidental death was recorded.

Perkowski, who analyzed this case, points out that the precautions taken by Mr. Myiciura were those used in Poland to ward off vampires. "The clove

[handwritten margin notes: "Is the death instantaneous or do those who hear the bell fall ill first?"]

[handwritten margin notes: "This transcends the vampire targeting for physical attacks — everyone can hear the bell."]

goes to visit his kinsfolk, first the near relatives and then the more distant ones, and sucks the blood from their bodies, so that they die. If all his blood-relatives have died, he rings the church bell, and, as far as the sound reaches, all who hear it must die."[4]

Vampires are occasionally considered responsible for hardships that befall households and even whole villages: bringing on a drought, causing storms, crop failures, livestock plagues, and diseases. These beliefs are identical with those connected with the "unclean dead" (those who have died unnatural deaths) and have been carried over to vampires.

Vampires appear among the Slavs also as bats.[5] The bat form was added to vampirism in Europe rather late—after the return of Cortez's followers from the New World in the sixteenth century, with tales of blood-sucking bats. Only one type of sanguineous bat, Desmodontidae, exists, which is found in the former Mayan area of habitation in the South American tropics—Panama, the West Indies, and their neighborhood. This so-called vampire bat does not suck blood from its victim, but licks it. Meticulous observations have revealed that the lips of this creature are never near the initial wound, but by moving its long tongue quickly, the bat causes a pulsating ribbon of blood to flow freely into its mouth. In about twenty minutes it consumes the amount of a fair-sized wineglass. In the tropics of the New World, this curious creature had a strong effect on people's beliefs—even a blood-sucking bat god was created. When the Spaniards returned to Europe, their stories of the blood-sucking bat strengthened the superstitions already present. In about 1730 a real "vampire epidemic" broke out in Europe, especially in the Slavic countries. There was a flood of works relating cases about alleged vampires that sucked the blood of people and animals. Plague and other epidemics were attributed either to the stench of the vampires or to their attacks.

What are the ways of rendering a vampire harmless? After the diagnosis of vampirism has been made, there are numerous ways to treat the dead.[6] The simplest consist of measures calculated to afford the dead a peaceful rest, such as placing miniature poplar crosses in the coffin. One may also offer the dead a peaceful occupation by putting quantities of sand and poppy seed into the coffin. The sand and poppy seed must be counted grain by grain before the vampire can leave its coffin. The dead can be kept from leaving the grave by piling a heap of stones onto it. Sterner measures to render harmless a person judged to be a potential vampire are to pierce the body with a sharpened stake (hawthorn or aspen) by beating it into the chest or back, between the shoulder blades, or to drive a stake or nail into the head; to place thorns under the tongue to keep the vampire from sucking blood; to bind the hands of the corpse behind its back; to maim the heels and

49

[handwritten note: "— so the dead literally cannot walk."]

Slavs—the Czechs, Poles, and particularly the Kashubs, who live at the mouth of the Vistula River—and among the South Slavs—Macedonians, Bulgarians, Serbs, Croats, and Slovenes. *Vampire* in Russian is *upyr*, Ukrainian *upýr'*, Bulgarian *vъpir*, Czech and Slovak *upír*, Polish *upiór* (East Slavic), Kashub *wupi, lupi;* the origin of this term is uncertain. Among the South Slavs, the vampire is called by the name of the werewolf, *vukodlak* (in Serbian), *volkodlak* (Slovene), and *vъrkolak* (Bulgarian).[2] In the following essay we shall discuss the vampire primarily among the Slavs, with some references to their neighbors.

There is a host of ideas about the origin of vampires. The most common is that sorcerers, witches, werewolves, excommunicates, and those who died unnatural deaths (such as suicides and drunkards) become vampires at their deaths. People can, however, be destined from birth to become vampires. The union of a werewolf or the devil and a witch is believed to produce a vampire. Likewise, children born with a caul on their head, or with their teeth showing, or with contiguous eyebrows are expected to become vampires. There are antidotes for some of these signs, but not for all. For example, the caul has to be burned and its ashes fed to the child when it is seven years old. Some Greeks believe that children born on Christmas Day are doomed to become vampires. This is a punishment for the presumptuousness of their mothers in having conceived on the same day as the Virgin Mary. People can be made vampires even after death. This happens if a human or unclean animal (cat or dog) steps over a body or a bird flies over it. These acts are evidently connected with the idea that insufficient respect or care for the dead is shown. In order to avoid this, relatives of the deceased keep constant vigil by the corpse as long as it is at home.

Ernest Jones, in his psychoanalytical study of vampires,[3] distinguishes two basic emotions—love and hatred—as motives which are projected to the dead and urge reunion and return from the grave. Love motivates vampires to always visit relatives first, particularly their marital partners. On the other hand, an unconscious feeling of guilt causes people to fear being the targets of a vampire's hatred and revenge.

Vampires are believed to lie in their graves as undecayed corpses, leaving at midnight to go to houses and have sexual relations with or suck the blood of those sleeping, or to devour their flesh, sometimes causing the death of the victims. If the grave is opened, the presence of a vampire can be recognized by finding the body in a state of disorder, with red cheeks, tense skin, charged blood vessels, warm blood and growing hair and nails; in some cases the grave itself is bespattered with blood, doubtless from the latest victim.

A memorat recorded from a Kashub tells that "at midnight the [vampire] awakens and first eats his own dress and flesh, and then leaves the tomb and

48

in his mouth complemented by the salt near his head and between his legs effectively sealed off the portals of his body, just as the portals of his room had been sealed."[10] He might have sealed himself off either to keep the vampire from entering, or, if he was a vampire himself, then to keep his soul from leaving to wreak havoc. However, the first possibility is more plausible, considering especially the landlady's testimony.

In Yugoslavia, the vampire has merged with the werewolf (usually called *vukodlak,* and only occasionally *vampir*). The term *vukodlak* means "wolf's hair" and originally denoted "werewolf"—a man turned into a wolf. There are only traces of the *vukodlak's* werewolfism (lycanthropy) in Yugoslavia. Thus it was told, for example, that a woman changed herself into a wolf and killed forty sheep near Trebinja in about 1880. Her transformation was achieved by making a circle with a rope and—after she had disrobed—turning somersaults in it. Most often, however, the *vukodlak* appears as a vampire. As such, it comes out of the grave at night and visits people at home or in the neighborhood. He either drinks their blood or has amorous relations with his former wife, or his former girlfriends or young widows.

Since the people of Yugoslavia were very much afraid of vampires in former times, there were numerous instances of frauds and tricks played by living persons who presented themselves as vampires.[11] During periods of hunger, vampire impersonators were frequently seen at water mills and granaries. Gangs of young people clothed as vampires vandalized the villages. More frequent were cases where men used a vampire cloak for love trysts with young women. There were even accounts of women who had children by "vampires." These women were visited by other men, in the guise of their "vampire" husbands, and the frightened villagers did not dare to interfere. Joakim Vujic in his travelogue of Serbia relates that in a village near Baja a vampire appeared around midnight, creating a great din and wearing a white shroud, to visit a young widow whose husband had recently died. The frightened people ran out of the house, except for the beautiful widow, who remained in her bed. The vampire stayed with her for an hour, after which he left with much clanking and rattling. This affair continued for three months, until a bold lad with his comrades managed to capture the vampire despite his most desperate resistance. He turned out to be a neighbor of the widow. An investigation revealed that the widow, together with the "vampire," had killed her husband so as to carry on their illicit love affair. Both were sentenced to death.

The tendency to confuse vampires with werewolves is noticeable also in Russia, as indicated by a curious piece of information pertaining to vampires: "More frequently encountered was the belief in Russia that while a dead vampire destroyed people, a live one, on the contrary, defended them.

it is interesting that people would impersonate vampires.

51

According to this belief, each village had its own vampire, as if it were a guard, protecting the inhabitants from his dead comrades. But if he lost his strength and perished in the fight, he himself became an evil and dangerous destroyer."[12]

This information about the "live vampires" as the protectors of villages can hardly be correct, since it defies the basic notions about vampires. This latter role is, however, fitting for werewolves. Among various peoples, werewolves (like shamans) appear as protectors against various hostile powers. According to Serbian beliefs, certain demonic beings (related to werewolves), appearing in the shape of beasts, are benevolent to people and fight against evil spirits. A seventeenth-century report from Latvia relates that werewolves work on the side of God against sorcerers, who are on the Devil's team.[13] If the sorcerers take fertility away into hell, the werewolves bring it back. There are competitions between Latvian and Russian werewolves; if the Latvian werewolves win, the Latvian people will then have a good crop. Considering these data, we come to the conclusion that the live vampire reported in Russia cannot be a vampire but must be a werewolf functioning as the protector of the villagers against evil spirits. The Slavic werewolves are believed to become vampires after death. This is what happened to the so-called good vampire in the report: it becomes an evil and dangerous destroyer. A mix-up between vampires and werewolves in Russia is understandable, in light of the blurring of the notion of the vampire during recent centuries.

Among the Russians, especially in the north, numerous vampiristic traits have been transferred to heretics. The beliefs in heretics show them to be a conglomerate of sectarians, witches, *rusalkas*, and vampires (known by the names *eretik, eretnik, eretitsa, eretnitsa, erestun*). Various episodes among heretics betray their vampiristic essence.[14]

A. Zvonkov reports from Elatomsk District (east-central Russia) the following:

I was told that a peasant's daughter died; the peasant invited his godfather to his house, treated him with food and drink, and asked him to dig the grave. Being drunk, the godfather, who had taken a spade along, strolled directly to the cemetery. He found a fallen-in grave, descended into it and began to dig. The spade hit a coffin, and, all of a sudden, through a rotten branch he saw an *eretitsa*'s eye. The peasant jumped out quickly and ran home without looking back. When he arrived, he climbed onto the stove, but the *eretitsa* was lying there and was looking at him with the same evil eye. The man ran to the yard and then to the manger, but the accursed *eretitsa* had anticipated him: she was lying in the manger, shaking with demonic laughter. From that time on the godfather began to wither and wither. They held services to Zosima and Savvatii, besprinkled him with holy water, but whatever they did, nothing helped, and the godfather died.

In this description, special attention should be given to the detail concerning the *eretitsa's* eye. In Russia and Germany there is a belief that the open eyes of a corpse can draw someone into the grave; for this reason, the eyes of the deceased are closed at the time of death. The Kashubs believe that when a vampire (*vieszcy*) dies, his left eye remains open. Zvonkov's story is an indication that the Russians, like the Kashubs, were familiar with the tradition about the vampire's open eye. According to the Gypsies of Yugoslavia, some parts of the human body, such as the eye, can become vampires. The godfather is constantly followed by the *eretitsa's* eye in the story recorded by Zvonkov. Here the eye seems to function as a full-fledged vampire that draws out the godfather's life substance and causes him to wither away.

In northern Russia, heretics appear after their deaths as evil, bloodthirsty vampires. A report given by Rybnikov from Olonets illustrates this:

> Evil sorcerers don't give peace to the Christians even after their deaths and become *erestuny;* they seize the moment when a neighbor is near his end and, as soon as the soul has left the body, they enter the deceased. After that, unpleasant things happen to the family. There are *erestuny* who 'transform themselves,' i.e., acquire another person's face and endeavor to sneak into their own or into another family. Such an *erestun* lives, it seems, as is fitting for a good peasant, but soon people in the family or in the village begin to disappear one after the other; the *erestun* eats them up. In order to destroy the transformed sorcerer, it is necessary to take the whip used for a heavily loaded horse and give him a thorough thrashing. Then he will fall down and give up his ghost. In order to prevent him from coming to life in the grave, it is necessary to drive an aspen stake into his back between the shoulders.

There is another piece of information about heretics from northern Russia that is similar to this one. Efimenko reports that in the Shenkursk district of Karelia the same person who in his lifetime is called *koldun* (sorcerer) is called *eretik* after his death if he roams around at night in villages, captures people, and eats them. If people "get tired of him," they gather at the grave of the one who was known as a sorcerer during his lifetime, take him out of the grave, and burn him in a bonfire or pierce his back with an aspen stick; the stick prevents any further emergence from the grave.

The *eretik* as vampire appears in Russian literature as well. In M. D.

[handwritten marginal note:] So the heretic does not necessarily become a full vampire — but a single body part can.

Chulkov's *The Mocker, or Slavic Tales* (*Peresmeshnik, ili slavenskie skazki*) a rich peasant, a practitioner of black magic, picks a fight immediately after his death with a dog next to his coffin. The priest at first refuses to bury him or to read the burial service "over such a heretic (*eretik*), who has the devil within him." After he is finally buried, the corpse does not stay in the grave at night, but strolls about the village, catches people by the back of their heads, throws them out the window, and drags them by their beards along the street. People leave the village. They dare to come back only after a hunter has killed the corpse with a hatchet.

Zelenin suggests that "the idea of the bloodthirsty vampire has penetrated from Western Europe to the Ukraine and Belorussia; to the Great Russians it is unknown."[15] Zelenin's position is hardly tenable. There are clear indications that the beliefs in vampires have deep roots among the Slavs and obviously go back to the Proto-Slavic period. These beliefs are also well documented among the early Russians. The term *vampire* (*upyr'*) appears as the name of a Novgorodian prince (Upir Likhyi) as early as 1047 and resurfaces in 1495 as a peasant name. This term has also been recorded in western Russia as both a personal and a place name. The previous existence in Russia of a vampire cult is illustrated by the fight clerics waged in encyclicals against sacrifices made to them.

It is true that the term *upyr'* has been almost unknown in Russia during the last centuries. But the absence of this term does not preclude the presence of the notion of the vampire. As our examples given above show, beliefs pertaining to the vampire were transferred to the heretics. In the heretics' garb, the vampire has continued to live vigorously in the Russian north.

In Estonia, beliefs in vampires are rather undeveloped. The term for vampire in Estonia is *vampiir* (vampire), *vere-imeja* (blood-sucker), or *veripard* (blood-beard). There are numerous stories about revenants who visit people in the night and press down upon them. However, the vampire as a blood-sucking and killing revenant is little known by the people, and the idea may have been taken from their neighbors.[16]

In Hungary the vampire per se is almost unknown in folk religion. However, there are some figures that closely resemble the vampire. The *ludverc* or *luderc* is a burning shaft or star which flies through the air and enters the house through the chimney. A malevolent revenant, it takes on the appearance of the dead marriage partner of the victim and sleeps with her or him, making the person pale and drained. It is exorcised by magic. The belief in *ludverc* is known particularly in Transylvania and is probably a borrowing from Romania.[17] The belief in the living dead, too, is well known to Hungarian peasants all over the country. Though this creature scares people by

[handwritten note: Some folktales do Not have the blood-thirst aspect, but most of folklore does show vampires as figures that harm the living]

its appearance, it does not suck blood, and should not be classed with the vampire.

There is also information about the presence of full-fledged vampires from Hungary. The close examination of the names of those accused in vampirism in court proceedings shows (as Linda Dégh informs me) that they were not Hungarians, but members of some minorities, especially Slavs. Since Hungary before 1918 included vast tracts with non-Hungarian population, the stories about vampires obviously came from those areas. The Hungarians, on the whole, seem to have been reluctant to assimilate these beliefs. It is of course possible that the belief in vampires may have found acceptance among the Hungarians in some restricted localities. It cannot be ascertained with certainty whether the much publicized vampire story in 1912 involves a Hungarian or a person of a national minority. According to this story a farmer in Hungary who suffered from ghostly visitations went to the cemetery one night, stuffed three pieces of garlic and three stones into his mouth, and fixed a corpse to the ground by thrusting a stake through it.[18]

Notes

1. Jan L. Perkowski, *Vampires of the Slavs* (Cambridge, Mass.: Slavica, 1976), 136. Perkowski's work has been used extensively for this article.

2. Kazimierz Moszyński, quoted by Perkowski, *Vampires of the Slavs*, 184–186.

3. Ernest Jones, *On the Nightmare* (New York: Grove Press, 1959), 99ff.

4. Perkowski, *Vampires of the Slavs*, 191.

5. Raymond L. Ditmars and Arthur M. Greenhall, quoted by Perkowski, ibid., 272ff.

6. Aleksandr N. Afanas'ev, quoted by Perkowski, ibid., 171–176; Moszyński, quoted by Perkowski, ibid., 182–184.

7. Jones, *On the Nightmare*, 116.

8. Ibid., 121–124.

9. Perkowski, *Vampires of the Slavs*, 156ff.

10. Ibid., 159.

11. Tihomir R. Djordjevic, *Veštica i vila. Vampir i druga bića* (Belgrade: Naučna knjiga, 1953), p. 185.

12. S. A. Tokarev, *Religioznye verovaniya vostochnoslavyanskikh narodov* (Moscow and Leningrad: Akademiya nauk, 1957), 41–42.

13. For details see Felix J. Oinas, "Introduction to Werewolf," in *The Golden Steed: Seven Baltic Plays*, ed. Alfreds Straumanis (Prospect Heights, Ill.: Waveland Press, 1979), 226–227.

Look up Felix Oinas

14. See Felix J. Oinas, "Heretics as Vampires and Demons in Russia," *Slavic and East European Journal* 22 (1978): 433–438.

15. Dmitrii Zelenin, *Russische (ostslavische) Volkskunde* (Berlin and Leipzig: Walter de Gruyter, 1927), 373.

16. Oskar Loorits, *Grundzüge des estnischen Volksglaubens*, 1 (Lund: Kungl. Gustav Adolfs Akademi, 1949), 100, 563.

17. Linda Dégh, *Folktales of Hungary* (Chicago: University of Chicago Press, 1965), 349, and personal communications.

18. Jones, *On the Nightmare*, 124.

What about this book?

JOHN V. A. FINE, JR.

In Defense of Vampires

Rampant in Romania, the vampire also surfaced in Serbia. It is important for twenty-first-century readers to realize that the vampire in earlier times was no mere fictitious figment of the folk imagination. Vampires were believed to exist and in some instances were thought to be responsible for local outbreaks of disease or other community calamities.

In Serbia in the early nineteenth century, vampire belief was so entrenched that it led to actions not altogether approved by either the governing authorities or the Church. Specifically, the act of one or more individuals digging up a corpse in order to prevent that corpse from indulging in its various nefarious vampiristic activities contravened accepted social norms. A body once buried was in theory not to be disturbed in its final resting place.

Historian John V. A. Fine, Jr., of the University of Michigan, has provided a vivid vignette from the early nineteenth century of documented cases of attempts to curtail the unearthing of suspected vampires in Serbia. Originally his essay carried the subtitle "Church/State Efforts to Stop Vigilante Action against Vampires in Serbia during the First Reign of Miloš Obrenović." Among the fascinating texts translated by Professor Fine is a remarkable dialogue written in 1826 which presents a skeptic questioning two monks, one of whom claims to have actually seen a vampire with his own eyes.

For other works of Fine's, see The Bosnian Church: A New Interpretation *(Boulder, 1975);* The Early Medieval Balkans *(Ann Arbor, 1983);* The Late Medieval Balkans *(Ann Arbor, 1987); and his co-authored book with Robert J. Donia,* Bosnia and Hercegovina: A Tradition Betrayed *(New York, 1994).*

To start a discussion of vampires in Serbia during the first reign of Prince Miloš Obrenović (1815–39) it makes sense to describe how the Serbs of the time saw them. This can best be done by quoting the description of vampires presented by a contemporary Serb, who among his varied talents was a fine ethnographer, Vuk Karadžić:[1]

Reprinted from *East European Quarterly* 21 (1987): 15–23.

A man into whom (according to popular tales) forty days after death a devilish spirit enters and enlivens (making him vampirized) is called a vukodlak. Then the vukodlak comes out at night from his grave and strangles people in their houses and drinks their blood. An honest man cannot vampirize, unless some bird or other living creature flies or jumps across his dead body. Thus everywhere people guard their dead [preburial] to see that nothing jumps over them. Vukodlaks most often appear in the winter (particularly between Christmas and Spasovdan [a moveable feast, forty days after Easter]). When a large number of people begin to die in a village, then people begin to blame a vukodlak from the grave (and in some places begin to say that he was seen at night with his shroud over his shoulders) and begin to guess who it might be. Then they take a black stallion without any spots or marks to the graveyard and lead it among the graves where it is suspected there are vukodlaks, for they say that such a stallion does not dare to step over a vukodlak. When they find the grave of someone they believe or guess to be a vukodlak, then they collect all the peasants and, taking with them a white thorn (or hawthorn) stake (because he fears only a white thorn stake . . .), dig up the grave; and if they find in it a man who has not disintegrated, then they pierce it with that stake and throw it on a fire to be burned. They say that when they find such a vukodlak in a grave, he is fat, swollen and red with human blood ("red as a vampire"). A vukodlak sometimes returns to his wife (especially if she is young and pretty) and sleeps with her, and they say a child born of such a union has no bones. And in times of hunger vampires often gather near mills and around granaries. They say that all of them go with their shrouds over their shoulders. A vampire can also pass through the smallest hole, that is why it does not help to lock a door against them any more than it does against a witch.

Other collections of folk beliefs show variations. Evil people may turn into vampires as a result of their evil lives. Usually vampirization occurs forty days after death, but in certain places the transformation occurs immediately. In some places a child of a vampire and a human woman appears normal; however, he has special talents, one of which often is the ability to be a *vampirdžije*, or vampire-finder.

Now having seen how the Serbs viewed vampires, let us turn to the sources and see the creatures in action and the responses they elicited.

On March 8, 1820, various *kmetovi* (local elders) and other merchants of Ub wrote Prince Miloš that over the last few days people had begun to die off like flies owing to a vampire; as a result people were gathering three to one house, not daring to go out at night owing to fear. So they begged the *vladika* (bishop), who had come to collect Church taxes [*mirija*], to allow them to dig up the graveyard, but he had not allowed them to do this. So they went to [the local governor, Miloš' brother] Lord Jevrem, but he without the *vladika*'s approval was not able to give them permission. So now they begged Prince Miloš either to allow them to dig up the graveyard or to move, because they could no longer endure it.[2]

On March 10 Miloš replied to the *obština* of Ub that they might open the graves, which they suspected had vampires, to seek confirmation of their suspicions [he uses the negative term *superstition* here], but they were forbidden to inflict any injury on the corpses; rather they were to summon the parish priest or the *vladika* to then read over them the prayers for the dead according to the [Church] law.[3]

This halfway permission was sufficient for the peasants to follow their own bent, as is seen from a letter of April 7, 1820, that Jevrem wrote to his brother Miloš. Jevrem reports that he summoned the people of Ub and inquired how things were going with the vampire that had appeared among them; he learned that they had acted on their own without any cleric present. Instead they had called an elder from Panjuha who had taught them how to deal with vampires. Under his guidance they had excavated the suspect graves, piercing one body with a stake and chopping off its head, which was then placed at its feet; and now the graves stood open. In one case dogs had dragged out one woman's corpse, eating it.[4]

This was not Miloš' only vampire concern of that time. For on April 5, 1820, he expelled from Požarevac a *vampirdžije* (a vampire-finder) who had been familiar with vampires in Smederevo.[5] And on April 20 he released from jail a certain *vampirdžije* named Ilija from village Duaka with a warning that if in the future he dug up any more vampires in any village he would be sentenced to a separation from his family and would remain in jail for good.[6] The prince's actions against vampire-finders show that, as he had done in Ub, in regard to them, he tried to follow Church law and use prayers rather than mutilation techniques.

After this promising beginning, if we exclude a case reported by Joakim Vujić that did not involve Miloš, which we shall present below, nothing more is heard about vampires until the 1830s, when we find several other cases. It probably would be safe to assume that they remained active, being dealt with on a local level, through the rest of the 1820s and into the 1830s.

In any case on August 15, 1836, Jovan Obrenović informed his brother Miloš that the peasants of village Svojdrug, without the knowledge of the authorities, that July, had got together and declared Miloš Raković from their village, who had died on the last Little Spasovdan [a moveable feast, falling on the first Thursday after Spasovdan], a vampire; they had dug him up, verified their beliefs in some way, and had reburied him. A short time later they informed their priest, Zaharija, about it, and he, like the rest, superstitious, went with them to Miloš' grave, where for a second time they dug him up. The priest poured holy water on him and they buried him again. Three days later the villagers again gathered and together with the village elder [*kmet*] Aćim Milošević, went to Miloš' grave and for a third time dug it up; they shot the corpse through, cut off his head, and again buried him.[7]

On March 28, 1838, Timok Bishop Dositej Novaković wrote the *prota* [first priest] of Negotin that he had sent the *protojerej* of his diocese, Paun Radosavljević, and the priest of the village of Radujevac, Joan Matejić, to the monastery of St. Roman for a time—a common penalty for ecclesiastical misdemeanors—because they had allowed the villagers of Radujevac to dig up a corpse they believed to be a vampire.[8] The first of April he wrote again to the *prota* of Negotin saying that he had learned that some *protojerej* in Negotin [surely the *protojerej* accused in the first letter] through the local priest had authorized the local villagers to dig up the grave of a man they had declared a vampire and to pour holy oil on him. With this permission the villagers, led by their priests, openly dug up a corpse which had died a short time before. After the priests said their prayers over the dead man, they went home, and then the villagers cut up the dead body and poured barley and boiled wine into its intestines so it would no longer vampirize and then reburied it.[9] The bishop called on the prince to take strict action against priests participating in such affairs in order to eliminate such superstitions.

On June 1, 1839, the Timok consistory under the same bishop wrote the court of the district of Poreč about the villagers of Šarbanovac. They had become upset over nine (whose names are given) who had become vampires, and who, by the testimony of their relatives, had strangled several men, women, and children (who are named) and six little children and a certain number of animals. They had turned to their priest, who had forbidden them to do anything. Not convinced, the villagers waited until the priest was called out of town. Then to investigate the vampirism the peasants dug up the nine dead bodies. The leader of this venture was Novak Mikov, who had made an agreement with the villagers to carry out the work for ten *groša*, market rates. This Novak Mikov, according to information from the villagers, being paid ten *groša*, dug up eight vampires, extracted their hearts, cooked them [the hearts] in boiled wine, thrust them back in their places, and reburied the bodies. The ninth was Jona, spouse of Vinulov. But when they dug her up, they realized she had not suffocated people and children like the other eight vampires, and thus they reburied her whole. The consistory carried out an investigation, interviewing a variety of villagers, and then, having determined the facts of the case, passed it on to the secular district court.[10] On the eighth of July 1839 [the published text says 1838, surely a typo] the *okružni sud* (district court) of Zaječar found Novak and Radovan Petrov—one of four villagers who had taken a leading role in helping Novak—guilty of digging up the dead vampires of Šarbanovac and sentenced them to seven days in jail and thirty strokes of a cane.[11]

An extremely interesting case occurred shortly after Miloš' abdication. On March 9, 1844, the district court of Požarevac charged and on the 15th found guilty Spasoje Petrinog and Dema Jovanović from the village Manastirica, who in the company of Dema's wife, Kalina, and Stana Mijailova from superstition had dug up Spasoje's wife and damaged her body. They believed that the deceased had become a vampire, for some sheep had disappeared. The court found that they had done the action, condemned it as a violation of Christian law, and decided that Spasoje as the husband of the dead lady should receive forty strokes of the cane, Dema twenty-five, and the other two twenty-five strokes of the *kamidžija* (a whip), with the sentence to be carried out at the graveyard where the woman was buried.[12]

On June 6, 1844, the Požarevac district court also sentenced some men from Krepoljin who, holding it was a vampire, had dug up the body of one old lady, piercing it with knives and pistol shots. The leaders of the God-hated affair, Matije Ljubenović and Stojan Dunić, were to receive forty strokes and their three companions (Petar Nikolić, Todor Mijajlović, and Janko Djordjević) twenty-five.[13]

On September 22, 1844, the Požarevac district court sentenced Milić Stojadinović from the village of Šapina to five days in jail and twenty-five strokes for digging his deceased wife up from her grave, where she had lain two years, placing the part of her shroud that had covered her head over her feet, pouring wine over her, and reburying her. He had so acted because he believed she was making it impossible for him to remarry. We are not told how she prevented him from doing this.[14]

One final event of interest, occurring during Miloš' reign, but in territory to the south of his principality and still under the Turks, near Monastery Dečani, is described by Joakim Vujić. The conversation between himself and two monks, which he presents in dialogue form, occurred in 1826:[15]

> During my visit to this monastery [Monastery Klisura] there was staying one old monk, named Gerasim, who was from the monastery of Dečani, but who had just been in Bosnia to seek alms. . . . And thus Father Visarion, abbot and host, gave us both dinner. And after we had dined, the following conversation occurred among the three of us.
>
> *Gerasim:* Dear brothers, can you imagine what happened two months ago in a village near Novi Pazar?
>
> *I:* And what happened, holy father? Come tell us.
>
> *Gerasim:* It happened that they dug up a vampire.

I: And what did they do with him?

Gerasim: What did they do? Why they ran him through with a hawthorn stake.

I: If that is what they did, it would have served them better to have gone to the tavern to drink raki, and to have left the dead body to sleep in peace.

Gerasim: And why leave the corpse in peace?

I: Because in this world there are no vampires.

Gerasim: There you are, just like our students nowadays. They don't believe in anything.

Visarion: Sir, I beg you not to speak in that way. How can you say there are no vampires in this world?

I: Because it is an impossible being. And I can't allow such a remark to pass with a clear conscience. But I beg you, Father Visarion, tell me, have you ever with your own eyes seen one?

Visarion: It is true that I have never seen one, but it is what people say.

Gerasim: But I have seen one with my own eyes; what do you say to that?

I: Then I beg you, Father Gerasim, tell me what this vampire that you saw with your own eyes looked like.

Gerasim: What it looked like! When they dug it up, it was not decomposed, its eyes were staring and its teeth were showing and clenched.

I: And what did this, your vampire, do?

Gerasim: And what did it do! At night he went about the village, scaring and strangling people; why he went into his own house and even slept with his wife.

I: Ha ha ha! He was a crude vampire, shame on him! To even have a woman on his mind. And what did his wife do, did she chase him out?

Gerasim: Of course not; she didn't dare, because he would have strangled her.

I: Tell me more, what else happened with your vampire?

Gerasim: What happened! When they dug him up, then Priest Stavro took a hawthorn stake, forced it between his teeth, and then took a piece of holy wood and put it between his teeth and along the holy wood poured into his mouth three drops of holy water and . . .

I: Now stop! I beg you, Father Gerasim, why didn't this vampire leap up and grab Priest Stavros by his beard?

Gerasim: You're again talking nonsense! How could he grab him by his beard, when during the day he is dead and has no strength; it is only at night that he gets power from the Unclean One, and comes to life, and then he goes about the village causing all sorts of chaos and misfortune.

I: Hmmm, so this vampire is dead in the day, but alive at night. I still just can't believe it. But tell me, what happened with your vampire in the end?

Gerasim: What happened! Why, after that, the elder Petko took that same hawthorn stake and stabbed him through the breast, and blood issued from his mouth and that was the end of him. Then they again buried him in the ground, and after that he never again left his grave, nor scared nor strangled people in the village. . . .

I, having listened to these words of the Monk Gerasim about the vampire, began to say to myself: God All-blessed! How can this people live in such error, ignorance, and superstition; and if a clergyman believes and talks such superstition, what will the common people think and say? And then casting my glance upward, said: All powerful God, give our lord Miloš a long and successful life that he may during his reign establish schools with talented teachers who can wipe out error and enlighten our people. And then I turned to the monk and in this way spoke to him.

I: Holy father, I from my side beg and advise you for God's sake not to believe that there are such monsters in this world as vampires, which could bring upon other men such injuries and misfortune, but the whole thing is only one simple and stupid superstition which does not serve any good purpose. And, tell me, Father Gerasim, what would you say if I said that even though you dug up your alleged vampire and found him not decomposed with staring eyes and clenched teeth, that still does not prove he was a vampire. And why not? That is because in some places is found earth which is salt-sulphur (salitro-sumporita), that is it is such that when you put a dead body, in which there is still considerable blood to be found, in such ground, then the blood will coagulate and the body will swell and the earth will not allow the body to decompose, but will keep it as firm as if it were magnetic iron. And such a dead body may for 77 or more years remain undecomposed in such ground. And if we want to decompose such a body we do not need a hawthorn stake nor a priest with holy wood and water, for there is no need to torture the corpse, but one need only dig it up, take it out of the ground into the air and let it lie there for only half an hour in the air and then put it back in the grave and cover it. Then after three days dig up the corpse again and you will see that it is already half disintegrated.

And now I will tell you briefly from where vampires and such superstitions originate: From nowhere else but the imagination and craftiness of men, as I will show by narrating the following case to you. Just listen to me.

In Hungary not far from my town of Baja, where I was born, there is still today a certain village in which there once appeared a vampire, as you would say. It frightened people and rode on them as it would a donkey, but it was mostly seen around the house of one young, pretty widow, whose husband two days before [its first appearance] had died and been buried; so always at night at 12 o'clock, with its white shroud, threaded with bells, and white cap and socks, it appeared, and when it arrived the whole household would panic, and everyone from fear would flee every which way, leaving only the pretty young widow in her bed. This alleged vampire would spend an hour or so in the house with the young person, after which, with loud cries, bangs, and the ringing of bells, it would leave. This went on for three months. During this time one sharp young man decided to follow the vampire, and if possible even to capture it. So he took with him two of his trusted friends, and they hid in the kitchen behind the door, each having in his hand a stout rope. The householder and his wife knew they were there, but the pretty young widow did not know a thing about it. When all was ready and it was approaching midnight, here came our pretty vampire with his white shroud, cap, and socks, according to his custom with bangs, noise, and bells ringing. All the household flew out of the house without their caps, and then he nicely approached the young daughter-in-law and lay down beside her. At that moment the sharp young hero in the kitchen crashed into the room and seized the handsome vampire by the arms. At this the vampire began to clang, moan, and to scratch. But it did not help him, because he was well held. Meanwhile the two comrades came running in with their stout ropes to help the first tie up the handsome vampire, and then to drag him to the village hall. And there there were five neighbors from her house. The next day they also took her to the courthouse, where she was put through a tough interrogation, and in the end they found, even proved, that she with her vampire had poisoned her husband whom she did not love; she had wanted to carry on a disgusting illicit love affair with the vampire and he also wanted to do it with her. But they were not able to do so with so many people living in the house, and no other place existed for them to go to. Afterwards both of them were taken to the county seat of Bač, where there took place a second intensive interrogation, and when it was clearly proved and both of them admitted their guilt, then the court announced its decision, namely that the vampire be hanged and the pretty vampirica have her head cut off below the gallows, and the sentence was carried out.

And that is your vampire, and under the name of vampires people not only carry out lustful doings, but also steal, burn houses, and commit other crimes. And as for bodies that do not decompose, and such are found naturally, there are also those that are embalmed.

[And Vujić then proceeded to explain embalming to the two monks, who had never heard of the process.]

Vujić's rational-scientific outlook should not be taken to represent a section of opinion in Serbia at the time. Vujić was a Serb from the Austro-Hungarian Empire, then on a grand tour of Serbia's churches and monasteries. He was soon, however, to settle in Serbia as director of the new theater Miloš was trying to establish in Kragujevac. The theater, which under Vujić's direction lasted only a few years, chiefly presented works of Vujić. Whether or not that explains its short life, I am in no position to judge. Vujić very well may have already been angling for such a post during his 1826 journey, which would explain the extreme flattery of Miloš—one example of which is seen in the cited passage—which runs through his whole book.

The documents cited in my text show that vampire beliefs were widespread in Serbia at this time. They were not limited to the ignorant peasantry but were also widespread among the clergy. Among Serbs the main issue was not whether or not there were vampires—for Miloš himself in not denying their existence may well not have been sure of this—but how was one to deal with them; should one use traditional village methods or should one take a more spiritual approach and call on the clergy to eliminate them through prayers? It would take many decades and the establishment of schools throughout Serbia—a task begun with vigor by Miloš—to embue people with Vujić's skeptical rejection. In fact, even today in modern Yugoslavia such beliefs have not been entirely eradicated.

What function did vampire beliefs serve? As an ancient belief passed on from generation to generation, vampires, of course, were simply a part of this world, as children learned without question from their elders. However, they did explain certain sudden and unusual events, and as blame was thrown on the dead they produced a far more harmless scapegoat than was seen when blame was thrown on the living, as also occurred in Serbia, when such ills were blamed on witches.

Notes

1. Vuk Karadžić, "Život i običaj naroda Srpskog," reprinted in V. Karadžić, *Prvi i Drugi Srpski Ustanaka* (Novi Sad and Belgrade, 1969), 330–331. The best general study of vampires in what was formerly Yugoslavia is T. Djordjević, "Vampir i druga bića u našem narodnom verovanju i predanju," published in the Serbian Academy of Sciences series, *Srpski Etnografski Zbornik*, knj. 66, second series, "Život i običaji narodni," knj. 30 (Belgrade, 1953), 149–219.

2. T. Djordjević, "Običaji narodna Srpskoga," knj. 2, published in *Srpski Etnografski Zbornik* (henceforth *SEZ*), 14 (1909): 431–432.

3. Djordjević, *SEZ*, 14 (1909): 432. This document is also contained in V. and N. Petrović, *Gradja za istoriju Kraljevine Srbije—vreme prve vlade Kneza Miloša Obrenovića*, vol. 1 (Belgrade, 1882), 393. Their text says "priest *and* vladika" (italics mine) instead of Djordjevic's reading of "or." The latter's reading seems more reasonable to me.

4. Djordjević, *SEZ*, 14 (1909): 432–433.

5. Ibid., 432.

6. Ibid., 433.

7. Ibid., 433.

8. T. Djordjević, "Nekoliko arhivskih podataka o našim narodnim običijima," *Glasnik Etnografskog Museja u Beogradu*, 13 (1938): 5.

9. Ibid., 5.

10. T. Djordjević, "Gradja za Srpske narodne običaje iz vremena prve vlade Kneza Miloša," *SEZ*, 19 (1914): 464.

11. Ibid., 465.

12. S. Maksimović, *Sudjenja u Požarevačkom Magistratu (1827–1844)*, ed. V. Živković (Požarevac, 1973), 216.

13. Ibid., 216–217.

14. Ibid., 219–220.

15. Joakim Vujić, *Putešestvije po Srbije* [1826], 2 (Belgrade, 1902), 2–11.

FRIEDRICH S. KRAUSS

South Slavic Countermeasures against Vampires

One of the pioneering figures in the history of folkloristics was Friedrich S. Krauss (1859–1938). A contemporary of Freud's in Vienna, Krauss is perhaps best known for two things: his numerous publications of Serbian folklore, and his courageous editing of Anthropophyteia *(1904–13), a periodical devoted to the publishing of erotic and "obscene" folklore that other folklorists of that time were unable to publish otherwise. It was essentially a German-language sequel to the earlier, comparable, French-language* Kryptadia *(1883–1911). Krauss was a true folklorist, and his more than 250 publications ranged from folk speech to legends and epics. However, his editing of* Anthropophyteia *got him into trouble with the local authorities, and he had to undergo numerous trials involving the violation of censorship laws.*

Krauss wrote two short discussions of vampires, the first of which was "Vampyre im südslawischen Volksglauben," Globus *61 (1892): 352–238. This essay, as its title suggests, is basically a presentation of various alleged reports of vampires in Yugoslavia. The second essay, translated for inclusion in this volume, is more specific. It concerns the protective measures employed to ward off vampires. From apotropaic techniques designed to fend off potential attacks from existing vampires to supposed sure-fire methods for preventing corpses from becoming vampires in the first place, Krauss provides a fascinating glimpse into a folk belief system, a system found wherever vampires were thought to frequent. For reasons which are not entirely clear, this second essay has apparently been overlooked by most students of the vampire.*

For more information about Krauss, see Raymond L. Burt, Friedrich Salomo Krauss (1859–1938) *(Vienna: Verlag der Österreichischen Akademie der Wissenschaften, 1990).*

About the method and manner of fully destroying a vampire, scholars have given unclear views, even though there is certainly no reason for such differences of opinion. The vampire is a dead person who comes to life during the night-time. So one destroys him just as one would annihilate any living be-

Reprinted from *Globus* 62 (1892): 203–204. It was translated from German into English by Johanna Jacobsen and Alan Dundes.

ing, namely by killing it, in this case usually either by driving a stake through its body or by burning the corpse. The disembodied spirit is freed or takes flight and is thus no longer able to cause harm to anyone.

If a widow confesses that her deceased husband has visited her as a vampire or other signs indicate that such an event has occurred—for example, nightly noises in the house, pots and pans flying about, a sudden death in the village, or even direct encounters with the vampire at a crossroads at night— then the most respected and senior men of the village will convene. The purpose of this assembly is to obtain permission from the living relatives of the vampire to dig up the grave to exhume the deceased, this to determine whether the suspect corpse has indeed become a vampire. The Muslims say that the body of such a vampire, even though it may have been lying in its grave for a long period of time, does not decompose. Only its eyes are big as those of oxen and are bloodshot as well. In such a case, one builds a fire in the grave, sharpens a hawthorn stake, and with it impales the body. Informants state that during the impalement, the vampire's body frequently writhes and twists, and that a large amount of blood spurts out of its body. While one group of people tends to the body of the vampire, the others present anxiously watch for the appearance of a moth (or butterfly) flying away from the grave. If one does fly out of the grave, everyone runs after it in order to capture it. If it is caught, it is thrown onto a bonfire so that it will die. Only then is the vampire completely destroyed. If the butterfly escapes, however, then, alas, woe to the village, because the vampire wreaks a frightful vengeance, which does not end until finally a period of seven years runs out.

In the upper Krajina, the Muslims and Christians believe that a vampire cannot be killed by any means other than by driving a hawthorn stake (*glogovi kolac*) through its body. Some informants have stated in my presence that one may also impale a vampire with a knife which has never yet cut bread. The Herzegovinians of the Orthodox Confession pierce the vampire through the dried hide of a young bull, because they believe (like the Serbians in the Morava and the Bulgarians in Rumelia) that anyone who is bespattered with the blood of the vampire will himself turn into a vampire, and that thereupon he must soon die. The Herzegovinian Orthodox do not burn the vampire. Nor do the Catholics of Slavonia. In the Drina region of upper Bosnia at the Serbian border, the Orthodox priest accompanies the farmers to the cemetery. They proceed to scrape open the grave of the deceased, stuff it full with a wagonload of straw, drive a hawthorn stake through both the straw and the corpse, and set fire to the straw. The fire continues to be fed until the body of the vampire has completely turned to ashes. Only then do they believe that any further return of the vampire has been prevented.

Farmer Lato Petrovic in Zabrgje reports:

About 150 years ago in the village of Cengic in the Zvornik district, there lived the wife of an Orthodox priest. After the death of this priest's wife (*popadija*), a raft of other deaths occurred in the village. At that time, all the members of the household of my mother's grandfather, Farmer Pero, died except for three young boys. So Pero decided to stand watch at night. In the kitchen of his own house, he lighted a large fire and waited. Suddenly, around midnight, the *popadija* appeared in the house. Pero, however, jumped up, seized a burning hawthorn branch from the fire, began to beat the *popadija* with it, and chased her out of the house. Still, she remained in front of the house and she shouted, "Come on out here, old man Pero, and beat me just a little and I will perish immediately." Pero answered, "I will not go outside and I will not let you into the house." Whereupon she retorted, "Just you wait, old man Pero, no son of yours will survive with whom you could plot." At the crack of dawn, Pero, along with the village magistrate and a farmer, went to the priest and informed him that the *popadija* had been resurrected and that she was snatching away people. The priest said, "It isn't true!" But Pero went to the courthouse in Zvornik and reported that the *popadija* had turned into a vampire and that just last night in the kitchen of his house, he had covered her shroud with soot when he struck her. The court granted him permission to dig up the grave. Together with the most respected men of the village, he exhumed the grave. There they found the *popadija* swollen up like a tub and they took a sharpened hawthorn stake, planted it on the *popadija's* stomach, and with a hammer drove it into her body. Then they built a huge fire and burned her to ashes and coals. But, sure enough, as they began to fill in the grave again, a snake crawled out of it. But Pero killed the snake on the spot. From that time on, they had peace and quiet in the village, and the sudden spate of deaths ceased.

Manda Superina in Pleternika told my mother: In the village of Mihaljevci, north of Pozega, a man fell off a wagon. His head got caught under the wheels and was crushed. And so he died. Eight days after the funeral, he returned, and began to sleep with his neighbor's wife. And sure enough, she became pregnant with his child. Thereupon, she informed the priest and told other women what had happened to her. One of the women advised her that she should take hemp and spin a large skein of thread, and that when the dead man next came to her, she should tie the thread to his big toe. Then she could discover where he came from. She was also told to make ready a large hawthorn stake. In the daytime, when the priest and the village folk opened the grave, they found the dead man lying on his stomach. They drove the hawthorn stake into his head and a large flame burst out of it. The skull exploded with a sound as loud as that of a cannon. The priest then at once gave the dead man his final benediction, and the dead man never returned again. The woman, however, gave birth to a child. The child died soon thereafter, but the woman is still alive. The narrator is a Catholic woman, and oddly enough, she had appealed to the Catholic priest of Velika. As a rule, Catholic priests do not play any role in the vampire hunts of Slavonia. In Dalmatia, where the Franciscan monk is very popular and believed, the people are more likely in such situations to turn to the priest for help. The monk is more sympathetic to the requests of the parish in which he is a priest.

Should a *kozlak* die, the old women in the village and also the remaining family members of the deceased take precautions with different measures against the anticipated imminent return of the *kozlak*. In some areas, it is the custom not to sweep out the room where death occurred for several days afterward. This, however, seldom seems to work. In spite of all this, the *vukodlak* or *kozlak* comes in at a certain hour of the night to disturb the tranquillity of the household and to torment the sleeping. The *kozlak* especially likes to rattle dishes, and he takes great pleasure, if there is a wagon around, in pulling it all around farmsteads. In such a crisis, the farmer will turn to his priest, that is, to the Franciscan who deals with written amulets. The priest must say prayers, and over and above that he must betake himself to the cemetery straight to the grave where the *kozlak* rests. He then has to summon him, await his appearance, and then run him through with a thorn. This thorn has to have grown in the high mountains in a place from which point the thornbush could not have seen the sea. Only in this case, or so it is believed, will the procedure work, and the *kozlak* will leave the people in peace.

It is no accident that it is the thorn that is used for impalement. The thorn is a natural—one could even say the original—human stabbing weapon. And it is easy to understand that its age-old utilization in ritual activities—in which category, in a limited sense, we can also consider vampire-slaying— has continued up to the present day. The thorn appears in the religious ceremonies of many peoples. Yet it seems to me that Liebrecht* is mistaken when he seeks to demonstrate that, just because the old Germans used the thorn in cremation, this leads to the following conclusion: "This explains finally, then, as a side observation, why in the Serbian legends the body of the vampire was impaled with a stake made out of hawthorn or a thornbush. It was a symbolic cremation." As evidence, Liebrecht cites the Bohemian "Lying Chronicler" Hajck (from the year 1337). A vampire would not stop

---

* Ed. note: This refers to the important mid-nineteenth-century folklorist Felix Liebrecht (1812–90). For the citation referred to by Krauss, see Liebrecht, *Zur Volkskunde: Alte und neue Aufsätze* (Heilbronn: Verlag von Gebr. Henninger, 1879), 65.

attacking the people "even when a stake had been driven through his body; only after his body was burned did he desist." For us there is no doubt that the Czechs at that time burned the corpse as a more powerful means of total annihilation in order to be fully certain of the desired result. Where do we find here even the shadow of symbolism? And where is the basis for a symbolic explanation of the custom?

In conclusion, we must consider one more belief, one which was a vital factor in the development of the custom of the blood feud. The soul of a murdered man, according to folk belief, could find no rest until revenge had been taken on the murderer. For this reason, the nearest blood-relative of the murder victim was obliged to seek blood revenge as a sacred duty. This is what is referred to in the old folk belief and legal proverb: Ko se ne osveti; taj se ne posveti (He who is not revenged, that person shall not find everlasting peace). However, blood feud is also based on principles of property law that cannot be explored here.

The Killing of a Vampire

Krauss's data regarding protection from Serbian vampires came from the late nineteenth century. But the belief in vampires in that part of the world did not suddenly disappear in the twentieth century, as the following essay attests. Classicist and ethnologist Veselin Čajkanović (1881–1946), stimulated by a newspaper article that appeared in 1923, wrote a response which discussed the traditional techniques utilized to neutralize or dispose of a vampire. The essay was translated from the original Serbian by Marilyn Sjoberg, whose valuable short introduction and notes have been retained.

As Sjoberg observes, Professor Čajkanović draws from the rich folklore collections of Vuk Karadžić, the founding figure in Serbian folkloristics. For more about this remarkable nineteenth-century folklorist, see Duncan Wilson, The Life and Times of Vuk Stefanović Karadžić (1787–1864) *and the references cited in the headnote to the reprinting of Karadžić's classic text of "The Building of Skadar," in* The Walled-Up Wife, *ed. Alan Dundes (Madison: University of Wisconsin Press, 1996), 3–4. For more details of Serbian vampires, see T. R. Djordjevic's essay (in Serbian) "Vampires in the Folk Beliefs of Our People,"* Recueil serbe d'ethnographie 6 (1953): 149–219.

Čajkanović was prolific but most of his many studies of religion and folklore were written in Serbian and hence remain unknown to scholars outside the former Yugoslavia, for example: Studije iz religije i folklora *(Belgrade: Srpska Kraljevska Akademija, 1924). The translator, Marilyn Sjoberg, is a specialist in Serbo-Croatian, writing her doctoral dissertation at Ohio State University in 1972 on the language used by poet Aleksa Santic (1868–1924): "Turkish Loanwords in the Language of Aleksa Santic."*

* * *

The following article is translated from Srpski knijizevni glasnik *(The Serbian Literary Herald) (Belgrade, 1923). Veselin Čajkanović, the author, was professor of classical languages and chairman of the classics department at Belgrade University as well as being a noted ethnologist.*

Professor Čajkanović's article on vampires and their despatch in the South Slavic areas is a very interesting one, especially so because a newspaper account of a Bosnian vampire that year triggered his article. Very little vampire lore has been made

Reprinted from *The Folklore Forum* 7 (1974): 260–271.

available to us; we find most bibliographies on vampires limited to English, German, and French sources. Therefore, Professor Čajkanović's contribution is very welcome, as it adds another dimension—which is not limited only to vampire lore among the Serbs, but also shows that such beliefs were still alive in the 1920s in some areas.

Professor Čajkanović makes use of classical analogy and of material from folk sources. Several references are made to the works of Vuk Karadžić (Vuk), the "father of the Serbian language," whose collections of folktales and folk poetry are classics. His Dictionary (Serbian-German-Latin) contains much valuable material concerning traditions and culture of the South Slavs; there is a complete description of "vampir" (cross-referenced to "vukodlak"—the root vuk means "wolf"), from which Professor Čajkanović has quoted with comments. It might be noted that, in some dictionaries, the word vampire is considered to be of Serbian origin.

The stake referred to throughout the text is glogovac (hawthorn stake), and glogovina is the hawthorn tree. It is interesting that glogovac has a second meaning, the aporia cratigi (a butterfly). As will be seen from the text, one possible form which may be assumed by a vampire is that of a butterfly!

I have sought to follow the author's article as closely as possible in all matters. I indicate his footnotes with asterisks (*), and I have added translator's notes where I felt them necessary in numbered notes. All references to Serbian journals are given in Serbo-Croatian; translations are in parentheses. Bold italic throughout the text indicates Professor Čajkanović's italics in the original text.

—Marilyn Sjoberg

A few days ago, in a patriarchal area of Bosnia, an unusual event occurred. In the village Tupanari (in the Vlasenicki jurisdiction), a vampire appeared. When it became intolerable, the peasants gathered, and, **more antique**, they dug it up from the grave, pierced it with a hawthorn stake, and then burned it.

Several Belgrade papers have written about this incident. According to the report in *Vreme* (Time) (number 511, May 23 of this year), we present below an excerpt. It ran thus:

> ... An old peasant Paja Tomic ... died ... the 9th of April this year. Shortly after his death, his wife Cvija began to complain that her dead husband had begun to return nights as a ghost and that he ran throughout the house scaring the inhabitants. There are some who believed Cvija and some who did not, though she has unceasingly asserted that her husband is a vampire and that he returns every night. Thus things went on for a whole month and then, it is said, her sons also became aware that there was a vampire in the house.

Stevo and Krsto Tomic, the sons of the deceased man, called the whole village to a discussion of what could be done about their father who had become a vampire. All of the peasants were in agreement that the vampire must be destroyed. They decided that they must dig up the corpse, burn it, and disperse the ashes. The decision was put into action. The peasants, armed with pickaxes and shovels, went to the cemetery. Some carried wood for the fire and one prepared a pointed hawthorn pole. The peasant crowd, led by the sons of the deceased Paja, arrived at the cemetery. The corpse was dug up, it was pierced by the hawthorn pole and thrown onto the stakes. After the body was burned, they dispersed its ashes, and those few charred bones which remained were thrown back into the grave. . . ."[1]

The people of the Vlasenicki jurisdiction preserve their ancient customs very carefully. Anyone who has, for example, subscribed to the Sarajevo *Glasnik zemaljskog muzeja* (Herald of the Local Museum) has surely been made aware of the fact that this area has given a great amount of material to researchers. Therefore, the above incident does not surprise us much. Moreover, the material we have from this area is usually of excellent quality. And this is true of the data which we can use from this most recent occurrence. The magical elements of the manner in which it was accomplished and the concepts and beliefs exhibited on this occasion—all are very ancient. The whole incident is valuable insofar as in some points it adds to and explains earlier data about a vampire and the killing of a vampire.

There is much that has been written about the belief in vampires in our area and among us. The classic source of such information is Vuk, *Rjecnik* (Dictionary), s.v. "vukodlak."[2] The theme is interesting, but it is substantial. Therefore, I shall speak here only concerning the article in *Vreme* (Time), and I shall limit myself to only those data in the article which show something new for the history of the Serbian religion.

The newspaper article reported that the vampire, Paja Tomic, appeared only to his wife; his sons became aware of him only after a whole month— only after his visits could no longer be hidden and when their mother had already called their attention to them. Obviously, the vampire had no intention of making himself known to his sons. What then was the vampire's exact purpose in his visits? Vuk Karadžić can give us the answer to this question. "A vukodlak [= vampire]—he says in his *Dictionary*, s.v. 'vukodlak'—sometimes returns to its wife . . . and sleeps with her; and they say that a child born of such a union does not have bones." And if the report of the Tupanari affair does not state this plainly, it is obvious that Cvija and the peasants of Tupanari make just the same assumption regarding the purpose of the vampire Paja. As can be seen among our people even today, such an ancient belief has been preserved: namely, a god or a demon *can have corporal union with a mortal woman*. We have evidence of this theme even in Serbian mythology and legends:

> Whenever there are Serbian heroes,
> Each one was nurtured by a vila,[3]
> And many were born of dragons.

occurs in the folk poem "Milos Obilic, the Dragon's Son." Compare also the myth of Trojan (in Vuk's *Dictionary*, s.v. "Trojan"), the poems about Empress Milica and the Snake from Jastrepac, the stories of the Medjedovic's, and so on.[4]

However, all of these examples (even if they are collectively strong enough to confirm the fact) are not individually, sufficiently concrete. However, it is quite a different matter when we consider the vampire. He is a demon who concretely, *in persona*, approaches a woman. It can be seen, moreover, from the Tupanari affair that this very ancient belief, known also among other peoples, remains unshaken among our people well into the twentieth century!

It is interesting that even among our people there were incidents—so-called *Nektan's deception*—that is, even here there were people who, in the name of a vampire, "succeeded in gaining entrance into discreet women's chambers"; Joakim Vujik tells one such example in his *Travels;* other examples are mentioned in the journal *Karadzic* and others. It seems that Vuk assumed such situations when he, not without some discernment, said, "The vampire sometimes comes to visit his wife, *especially when his wife is young and beautiful*, and he sleeps with her." The people of Tupanari, reports the newspaper article, pierced the vampire with a hawthorn pole, and then they threw it on the stakes and set it afire. Their aim was, it can be understood, to make the vampire ineffectual and to destroy it.

Piercing with a hawthorn stake and burning are very ancient measures for killing a vampire.

Evil spirits and all unclean demons fear the hawthorn and, generally, all thorns. When the ancient Germanic tribes sentenced to death "cowards and outlaws," they threw thorns onto their graves: it is obvious thus that the soul of the executed person could not return to avenge itself.* The Carthaginians

---

* In primitive societies, capital punishment is always accomplished in such a way as to protect the ones perpetrating it from the wrath of the man killed: e.g., he will be buried alive, so that his soul cannot leave again; or his grave will be piled high with rocks (the aim being to keep the soul inside); or the punishment will be carried out by a group, so that the soul of the

and Romans also threw thorns and rocks onto the graves of the deceased. A witch (which is, in fact, an underground demon, the female counterpart of a vampire) is also afraid of thorns. During "Walpurgis Night" in central Europe, hawthorns are placed on the doors of a household as a deterrent to witches. When a witch wishes to fly from a house, it is necessary to recite the poem: "not with a thorn, not with lightning. . . ." One understands that the thorn of the hawthorn is especially strong in magical effect, as is the hawthorn tree generally. In eastern Serbia, many drive a small hawthorn peg into the grave beside the cross, and thus the corpse cannot turn into a vampire. The women in Bosnia, when going into a house where there is a corpse, carry a hawthorn thorn with them, which they throw away upon leaving the house. The hawthorn is a charm and an antidote and, moreover, it is used against snakes; they believe in Bosnia that one can catch the devil himself with it. When one mentions a vampire, or in some way calls forth some kind of a demon, our people have this phrase which they add: "and in his way, put madder and hawthorns!"

Because the hawthorn stake is a sure means against a vampire, the vampire is pierced by it. To what purpose? Along with the proverb "Without a hawthorn stake, nothing can happen to it," Vuk observes: ". . . will not die easily, unless he is *killed*, like a vampire." Thus, Vuk obviously follows along with the popular belief and thinks that a vampire is killed with a hawthorn stake. This belief, generally (as can be seen in nearly all accounts of vampirism), is very widespread among our people; the best proof that our people actually desire to *kill* a vampire with a hawthorn is that sometimes, instead of a stake, a sword is used and the vampire is stabbed *many* times, whether with a yataghan or with a stake. Sometimes, indeed, he is even "killed" with a gun. But has our people always believed that a vampire can be killed? We know that religious concepts can change; in the same way, it can happen that one and another contradictory concepts can exist at the same time. The idea that a vampire can be killed by a hawthorn stake appears relatively later. Previously, our people, it seems, believed that a vampire *could not* be killed, at least not by a single means such as staking, even though the stake be of hawthorn. Staking a vampire is not enough, because the soul, the *vegative* soul, tied to blood, to the heart, to muscles, and to the intestines, continues to exist until the last part of all this exists, and the vampire will exist up until

---

deceased will not know exactly who is guilty of his death, e.g., each person present would throw a stone or (as in Montenegro) there would be a volley of rifle fire, etc. Among these customs can be mentioned the prescription that, during a burial, *everyone* had to throw dirt onto the grave.

the least bit of his body exists. Only when all that remains of his body are the bones—when his soul has departed elsewhere, generally for the kingdom of the dead—will he then annoy us no further. Thus, it seems our people, by staking the vampire with a hawthorn pole, had originally not the intention of killing him (since they must have been cognizant of the fact that this was impossible), but rather they sought to *magically intervene and to bind him to his grave*, to prevent his exit from the grave and his dangerous wanderings in their environs. In oriental tales, the genie or spirit, locked in some kind of a container, can lift every lid but that one on which is Solomon's word; crazy Jovan, in the poem "Jovan and the Gigantic Chieftain," can break every rope, but the string on a musical instrument; and thus the vampire can remove every stake, but not that of hawthorn wood: he in imprisoned, *riveted to his grave* by this stake. There are analogies to the use of a hawthorn stake among ancient Germanic tribes. Those corpses whose return was feared were *secured in the grave* by piercing them with a hawthorn stake. In eastern Frisia, a female corpse which had been impaled and covered with thorns was found in an ancient grave. We also have direct proof that our people intended, originally, not to kill the vampire but to rivet it to its grave. In southern Dalmatia and in Bosnia, when a vampire appears, "the people will dig up its grave, place the vampire on its stomach and *secure a hawthorn stake at the grave, so that the vampire may not raise itself from the grave any longer*"—says Vid Vuletic from Vukasvic (Karadžić 3, 1901, 213).

While this manner of employing a hawthorn stake had as a goal only to limit the freedom of movement of a vampire, *burning* had as a goal the complete destruction of the vampire. Burning is a very well-known custom. Even today corpses are burned in huge crematoria, but these instances are exceptional and rare; earlier, however, among classical and oriental peoples, and even in prehistoric Europe, this custom was practiced much more frequently and in many areas it was general.

The difference between modern and ancient burning is that, today, usually nothing remains of the cremated corpse, while earlier its bones remained; there is a further difference insofar as today this custom is practiced for purely practical, hygienic, and sometimes, perhaps, sentimental reasons, while in the distant past, the reason for burning was quite a different one. According to the explanations which the history of religions gives to this custom (because there are also other rational explanations), the true purpose of burning was to destroy the corpse or, more exactly, to destroy those parts of it in which the soul might remain, and those are, as we have just seen, the blood, the muscles, the heart, the eyes, the intestines, etc. When these parts were destroyed, there remained only the bones, and we are thus secure from the eventual return of the departed, because the soul cannot be bound to the bones.* Thus, it is in *our* interest that we burn the departed. But it is also in *their* interest. In that period when, in the Mediterranean countries, they began to burn the dead, a new religious concept appeared, which, for later mythology and poetry, proved very fertile. This was the idea of a general, communal, organized kingdom of the dead. The popular imagination found that kingdom at times under the ground, at times in the far west, or at the other side of the sea, or in the skies, etc. When a person died, his soul was bound to the grave for a certain time (usually some symbolic number of years, for example, seven) but its ultimate aim was to attain that kingdom and there to find its peace. What are the conditions that will enable it to go there? There is *one* condition: the body must as a preliminary *decompose*. Until that happens, the soul will be bound to it, and therefore, it will be unsatisfied and unhappy. How unhappy and unsatisfied such a deceased person can be can best be seen from the fact that the word for such an undecayed corpse began, with time, to mean a deeply unhappy, disconsolate person in general: the word *ocajnik*, which today means only "unhappy, disconsolate person," in Vuk's *Dictionary* has the single meaning "an undecayed body in the grave, a human body which cannot decompose." A dire curse in Montenegro is: "May you not decay for a thousand years!" The folk poem "The Repentance and Confession of Kraljevic Marko" reads: His mother implored Marko, that Marko's human blood would pass: "because you will never decompose"; and a little later the old prior says to Marko, "Sorrowful son, Kraljevic Marko, . . . your human blood must pass or you will never die, nor will your body decay." Our blessing "God pardon *him*" and "God pardon his *soul*" does not mean "God pardon him of his sins"[5] but rather: "God allow him, or just his soul, to be free of his body." In the poem which we have just mentioned, Kraljevic Marko finally receives the prior's blessing: ". . . This morning, I shall, by God, give you communion . . . *that you are pardoned from this world. . . .*"

Thus by burning the body we can accomplish two things: we can free the soul of the departed from his body, which hinders it in its journey, and we can personally protect ourselves against the possibility of its returning to attack us. *That* was the reason for the penetration of the belief, in the distant

---

* According to the beliefs of our people, the soul can be in the bones only while a person is alive; see, e.g., Vuk, *Srpske narodne poslovice*, 1597: "His soul burned in his bones. Whenever someone wishes to say that someone is very old, and at the same time does not wish him to die"; cf. also Vuk, *Pesme* (Poems) 2, 74, 79, etc.: ". . . Are you, brother, in life?" "Yes, I am, brother, it is bad: . . . I can just barely carry my soul in my bones."

past, that it was necessary to burn the dead; that is the reason that even today our people burn vampires.*

In many Serbian areas, for example, in Montenegro, only a hawthorn stake is used on the vampire; in Dusan's *Legal Code*, 6 in Article 20 (which is, of course, concerned with the killing of a vampire), only burning is spoken of. Meanwhile, in Tupanari the vampire was first pierced with a hawthorn stake and only then burned, and such a process was considered normal by Vuk Karadžić; it means that, in the areas which he had in mind, the vampire was regularly **both** staked **and** burned. But this seems, if not contradictory, surely excessive. Why is a vampire both staked and burned? When a vampire is already riveted to his grave, why then burn him? And, conversely, if he is to be burned, why then stake him? Isn't only one of these measures really sufficient? The answer is extremely simple: here **two customs remain, an older custom and a more recent one**. These people, who are unusually conservative in questions of cult, have retained the older custom even when it became illogical and unnecessary. This amassing of customs, superimposing the new upon the old, the compromise between the old and the new beliefs, is a very frequent phenomenon in the history of religion. A few days ago, a prophetess from Slavonia came to Belgrade to the national Parliament.

---

* Neither our people nor primitive peoples, in general, are consistent in the concept of the soul. The soul can be: (1) a vegetative soul, one which is tied to the blood (cf. especially the classic source in the Third Book of Moses 17:14: "Because the soul of each body is its blood, that is the soul" [trans. note: cf. Leviticus 17:14, King James Version: "For it [blood] is the life of all flesh; the blood of it is for the life thereof"]), the heart, the muscles, and others; (2) breath, more exactly the last breath which escapes from one's lips (etymologically the word *duša* 'soul' is cognate with the word *duvati* 'to breath'); (3) man's (spiritual) double (among the Germanic people). It leaves man when he sleeps and when he dies. Dreams are reality: when we sleep, our soul, "our double," leaves from our mouth (e.g., in the form of a fly or a bird), and later returns to the body; whatever the soul sees or experiences on that occasion is what we have *dreamed*. That is why it is considered bad to wake someone suddenly, because the soul might not have time to return to the body. For this kind of a soul or spirit, compare also Vuk, *Dictionary*, s.v. "vjestica" 'witch': "A woman is called a witch who . . . has within her some kind of *demonic spirit/soul*, which leaves her when she is sleeping and transforms itself into a butterfly, a hen, or a turkey, and flies about the house and eats people. . . . A woman who is a witch, once this spirit has left her, lies as though she is dead and if a person places her head where her feet had been, she will not awake again." Our people sometimes believe that a vampire has a vegetative soul (thus he can annoy us only until his body has decomposed); sometimes, however, they believe that the vampire's soul or spirit is a *fylgja* (a doublet): see, for example, the Glisic story *After Ninety Years*, in which the vampire's soul leaves from his lips in the guise of a butterfly; and Vuk, *Dictionary*, s.v. "vukodlak": "A person is called a vukodlak who . . . after death . . . is entered by some kind of demonic spirit (as is a witch also), which revives him," etc. The first belief is the older.

Through the conviction with which she spoke, because she had not "sold her gifts for money," in general because of her whole appearance, she was a real prophetess in the ancient (not in the modern) sense of the word—the last representative of those divine women, her predecessors who feel in themselves *sanctum aliquid et providum.* What she said is, for us, at this moment, secondary; but her appearance is interesting because, once, she went to the **cemetery to beg God for rain.** Turning to **God** for rain is an observance of the new faith; but why did she go to the cemetery? Because according to the beliefs of the old faith, the souls of our ancestors give us rain. Instead of bringing other proofs to confirm this (I shall put them forward in a separate article), I would suggest only the belief that if one dreams of the dead there will be rain. In the efforts of the prophetess to produce rain, we have obviously two things: the new ritual (appealing to the Christian God), along with that which has remained the *old* (the magic of the cemetery.) In the poem "Jovan and the Gigantic Chieftain," crazy Jovan's eyes are put out. A vila arrives to aid him: "When she looked at crazy Jovan, his eyes were put out, she washed him with Haladzijnski water, and the vila *prayed to God*, and Jovan's eyes were restored." Here also we have an example of a compromise between the old and the new beliefs. The vila, as we know very well, *is herself* very *capable* of both taking and restoring sight—why then the intervention of the Christian God? In the poem "Ivo Senjanin the Begler-Beg" we have another similar disagreement—a conflict between the new and the old beliefs: "And there the vila both looks and listens, and from the mountain she flies down to the hero, with her right hand she guards Ivo, and with her left *she takes out a dagger, and then she puts out the eyes of the Turks.*" The removal of the eyes with a dagger is a *new* element, because we know that a vila, in the same way as the Greek Artemis, by her very glance or even just her presence, could remove one's sight. When it thunders and lightnings, it is not good to cross oneself. Why? When it is known that the cross is a sure and universal protection against every demon and against every evil in general, this prohibition seems strange. According to folk explanation, "God drives the devils away by means of thunder and the devil, fleeing from thunder and lightning, can approach a person to hide under the cross and protect himself from these blows, thus it can easily happen that the person holding the cross will also suffer from the thunder and lightning" (Milicevic). This explanation is not exact, because it cannot be imagined that it would ever occur to the devil, who is very frightened of the cross ("He flees like the devil from a cross"),[7] to hide behind a cross. The explanation is not difficult to find when one assumes that this prohibition existed in a religious environment which still had not reconciled itself with the new conditions. The cross, which is the symbol of the new god, is a charm, surely, against evil spirits, but—it must not be forgotten—mainly against the demons of a *lower* order. So, against one such mighty god as was the old god of thunder—a god who through centuries was important as *summus deus* and was respected above all others—we are not absolutely sure that the cross can be effective. On the contrary, it might only evoke the anger of that god, and therefore, we do not use it. And so forth. We have many customs in which the old and the new concepts, the old and new rituals, stand one beside the other. We have one such situation in the custom of both staking and burning a vampire.

Now, which of these two customs is the older? Obviously, the older is the custom of piercing with a hawthorn stake. For if we were to assume that burning is the older custom, it becomes very difficult to imagine that people would then, at one such radical a means as burning, feel the necessity to seek still another means which is less obvious and sure. Thus it follows that the custom of burning a vampire can be ascertained as a custom of a relatively more recent date.

The custom of burning, as we have already said, was well-known to many people among whom were some who lived in our neighborhood (for example, Germans and Thracians), or who were in close connection with us (for example, the Czechs and Russians). Was it then, as we might expect, well-known to our forebears also? Mr. Sima Trojanovic, *Srpski knijizevni glasnik* (The Serbian Literary Herald) (3: [1901]: 55ff., 125ff.), has attempted to give an affirmative answer. Mr. Milojie Vasic, (*Brankovo kolo* [Branko's Circle], 1901) in his paper on this subject did not accept Mr. Trojanovic's results.

The question is not easy, and it is subject to revision. We cannot foresee what the results will be, but one thing is obvious: that we must take the burning of a vampire as a departure point in these investigations (as Mr. Trojanovic has already done). This is the only sure cremation which our Serbian religion knows. But because of the fact that a vampire is burned, it is clear that our people were aware that through burning a corpse it could be completely safe. And from this partial burning to a more general burning, only one step was necessary.

Did our ancestors take that step and generalize burning to all situations?

I shall, in only a few words, touch upon both one and the other possibility.

In my opinion, there are two facts which rather weaken the assumption that burning was practiced among the ancient Serbs. First of all, burning was not necessary. Our ancestors had other means of protecting themselves from the dead of whom they were suspicious. That was, in the first place, as we have seen, the hawthorn stake. The other possibility was Maschalismos, decapitation and dismemberment, which were known generally among all primitive peoples. From a report to Prince Milos in the year 1829, it is seen that some people from Ubljan "with a stake . . . crushed, severed the head and placed it at the feet" of a suspicious corpse, and in Krusivacka Tesica in the year 1836, the peasants "dug a certain corpse from its grave and beat it . . . , shot it with guns and finally cut off its head." The third means is *supplemental burial.* That custom is known among the southern Serbs. The corpse is dug up after three years and its bones are ritually cleaned (with wine, etc.), the decay around the bones is carefully cleaned off and thrown away—obviously the purpose is that the soul be completely "pardoned" from the body. All these means were sufficient to remove a dangerous corpse from one's door. The hawthorn stake, decapitation and dismembership, and supplemental burial—all of these have been preserved even down to the present day; this means that they have existed, without interruption, from ancient times. What with all these other means, was burning also necessary?

For another thing, today there is no trace of the custom of burning—if it at anytime existed—either in the traditions or in the customs. And this surprises us most. The people in all of their customs in general and in their funeral customs in particular are very conservative; if a new idea or a new custom arrives, the people will preserve the old custom along with the new or in totality (as is the situation with the hawthorn stake and cremation, or in *substitutions* and *symbols*). Live people were sometimes thrown as sacrifices into the Nile or the Tiber—later dolls were thrown instead of people; the ancient Jews, when some one of them died, would tear their clothes—today's Jews only cut them imperceptibly with a knife; a living person was supposed to be entombed in a foundation (see "Zidanje Skadra" [The Building of Skadar])—today it is sufficient that, instead of the person, only his shadow or his measurements are walled in. And so forth. The Romans first buried their dead, later they cremated them; but the custom did not completely disappear because, even in the era of cremation, one part of the deceased's body, for example, a finger, was ritualistically buried in the earth. Some Slavic tribes, while they were still living on the sea coast, buried their dead by placing them in a boat, which was then pushed out to sea; when these tribes later settled to the south in the interior, they continued to bury their dead in a box, shaped like a boat, and when they acquired the custom of cremation, they also burned their dead in a boat. All of the ancient forms of burial are preserved among us Serbs in substitutions; for the substitution of decapitation, of dismembership, and of complete destruction, one need only consider the custom of "cutting" the corpse, and that most often in the *head* or the *forehead* or the neck. As a substitution of the custom of staking a corpse with a hawthorn pole, consider the observance of pricking a suspicious corpse in the hand with a hawthorn; or the practice of putting a hawthorn under every corpse; or, generally, all usages of the hawthorn with respect to these bodies. The custom of burying the dead in the house under the threshold existed among our people in the very distant past; and this custom is preserved symbolically even down to today: in an area of Bosnia, the deceased's nails are cut and these are buried under the threshold, and in the Krusevac area, the measurements of the corpse are taken with a thread and that thread is then buried under the threshold. Every form of earlier burial is preserved, even if it be in substitutions, but for burning we have no sure example of substitution, nor allusion.* Is this accidental?

On the other hand, it is worth mentioning that in Bosnia, prehistoric necropoli with the remains of burnt bones have been found. The necropoli are not dated, but they obviously belong to a period earlier than the Serbian population of Bosnia. It is interesting that the custom of the burning of a vampire is best preserved exactly here in Bosnia, as we have been shown by the incident in Tupanari and the information in Vuk (which in any case rests on the data from western Serbia and Bosnia). Dare we tie these facts together? An analogy from the far eastern part of the Balkan Peninsula would speak for the possibility that burning existed: Jirecek says that, on the coasts of the Black Sea up until recent times, *all corpses* were burned out of the fear that they would become vampires.[8]

As can be seen, the question is not solved; it will be possible to say more about the burning of vampires when more data have been collected.

Notes

1. As is known and as can be seen from information in South Slavic sources, e.g., in Vuk Karadžić's *Rječnik* (Dictionary), 3d ed. (Belgrade, 1898), this is the prescribed technique for the destruction of a vampire.

2. *Vukodlak* and the word *vampir* are both South Slavic words for *vampire*.

3. The vila is a South Slavic wood or water nymph, a fairy, an undine, a dryad; she lures sailors to their doom, and she is the cause for a hunter's or fisherman's nonreturn.

4. These are all from South Slavic folk literature.

5. Here Professor Čajkanović gives the Serbo-Croatian "Bog da ga prosti" and "Bog da mu *dušu* prosti" = God pardon him and God pardon his soul; were this to

* The examples which Mr. Trojanovic gives, in my opinion, are not sufficiently clear and would more likely be of a cathartic character.

83

mean "God pardon him his sin," it would be in the dative case and not in the accusative, e.g., "Bog da mu oprosti" or "Bog da mu *duši* orprosti."

6. The Zakonik, a famous legal code, one of the most important documents extant of the fourteenth-century Serbian social conditions and culture, was published during the reign of the Serbian king Stephen Dusan (1331–55).

7. A proverb.

8. Konstantin Jirecek, *Das Fürstentum Bulgarien* (Vienna, 1891), 110.

Not applicable to Dracula examination

JULIETTE DU BOULAY

The Greek Vampire: A Study of Cyclic Symbolism in Marriage and Death

Having sampled the vampire traditions of Romania and Serbia, we now turn to the vampire in modern Greece. The reader will surely observe many similarities between the Greek vampire and the Romanian and Serbian vampires. Indeed, there is unavoidable overlap in all the essays contained in this volume, inasmuch as they were written in different time periods from diverse disciplinary perspectives and addressed to quite variegated audiences. In this case, we have a British social anthropologist, Professor Juliette du Boulay of the University of Aberdeen, who, on the basis of her own fieldwork carried out in Greece, seeks to find an explanatory model to illuminate some of the curious facets of vampire beliefs. Anthropologists are famous for their efforts to find patterns in culture, and Professor du Boulay's proposed structural model that she believes may underlie the Greek vampire belief system is nothing if not provocative. It is certainly a welcome change from the endless purely anecdotal reports of vampire sightings found throughout the vampire literature.

The vampire belief system in Greece is evidently pretty deep-seated. We know this because vampire legends continue to be recounted by Greek-Americans. Generally, the creatures of legend are closely tied to landscape, so much so that they remain behind when emigrants leave their native land. Accordingly leprechauns stay in Ireland, trolls do likewise in Scandinavia, and so do other legendary supernatural creatures associated with American immigrants abide topographically trapped in the original homeland. In the case of Greek-Americans, it is not that the vampires appear in the United States, but rather that some of the first-generation Greek-Americans tell of encounters with vampires they remember from the "old country." See D. Demetracopoulou Lee, "Greek Accounts of the Vrykolakas," Journal of American Folklore 55 (1942): 126–132; and Robert A. Georges, Greek-American Folk Beliefs and Narratives (New York: Arno Press, 1980), 96–99.

The phenomenon of the vampire in Greece, with its unexpected horror and savagery, has been noted by Hellenic scholars from many disciplines, including that of anthropology, but as yet no attempt has been made to form an

Reprinted from *Man* 17 (1982): 219–238, with permission from the Royal Anthropological Institute of Great Britain and Ireland.

interpretation of it. In this article I offer an explanation which draws on fieldwork conducted in 1971–73 in Ambéli, a mountain village of North Euboea. My interest had been aroused by the prevalence there of a particular cyclic pattern "like the dance" (*sán horós*) to which villagers gave great significance, and which, I argue, is fundamental to their beliefs relating to the vampire.

Anthropology has dealt with cyclic patterns in two principal contexts. On the one hand, circular patterns of marital alliance, ritual movement, or neighborly exchange appear as an indigenous concept in such societies as occur, for example, in Highland Burma,[1] Indonesia,[2] and the Basque country.[3] On the other hand, cyclic imagery is used as an analytical concept of the anthropologist, amongst which notable examples are the studies of Lévi-Strauss and Needham on marriage alliance.[4]

In this article an indigenous concept forms the central theme, for the "dance" to which the villagers refer is the traditional ring dance of rural Greece, which takes the form of an open-ended circle and is led always in the auspicious anticlockwise direction defined by villagers as "to the right" (*dhexiá*).[5] A pattern "like the dance," then, consists of a spiralling motion which proceeds anticlockwise and is conceptually right-handed, and is a category which is in many contexts of village life consciously invoked. Thus the cyclic symbolism presented here is rooted solidly in the understanding of Greek villagers, and analysis is carried out strictly within their terms of reference.

Cyclic imagery—whether indigenous or anthropological—has in turn been interpreted within two alternative frameworks. First, the cyclic pattern may be seen as constituting an asymmetric exchange of people or goods—an approach developed by Mauss, Sahlins, and, in the European context, by Hammel; and it is to this literature that Ott looks to interpret indigenous Basque symbolism.[6] The interest of this understanding lies in what it reveals of social organization and of the principles which order it: exchange is seen primarily as a mechanism which orders relationships, and thus as an important contributor to solidarity. A second type of interpretation, however, by no means exclusive of the first but differing in emphasis, has incorporated an attempt to understand the symbolic aspect of cyclic imagery. The thrust of this form of analysis, while it has detailed certain features of social organization, has been primarily towards elucidating fundamental categories of thought,[7] which again are often associated with such concepts as left and right.[8] Emphasis has been on bringing together symbolic correspondences observed in widely divergent contexts, thus making possible an interpretation of specific institutions by revealing in them the operation of a unified system of meaning. Thereafter the coherence of these meanings may give rise to a variety of consequences of which solidarity may or may not be one, and it is the meanings themselves which hold the clue to understanding the part they play within the social order.

It is this second approach which I have thought most suitable for an analysis of the Greek vampire, for the customs which cluster around the vampire show that what is on one level a principle of alliance can become on another level a principle of great destructiveness, in which society appears as much threatened by the phenomenon as consolidated. These consequences flow from an underlying structure of ideas: an understanding of a life-giving right-handed movement, which, prevalent throughout the culture, is here linked to a particular understanding of blood and the organization of marriage rules. The vampire is consequently explicable as the manifestation, at a crucial point of transition between the living and the dead, of the symbolism which also governs incest prohibitions, and which represents in general the onward and irreversible flow of life.

The Puzzle of the Greek Vampire

While revenants in general may be known as vampires (*vrykólakoi*), there is a special type of case in which a person is thought to have been, between death and burial, taken over by the devil in such a way as to become a true "vampire." This event involves not only the body but also the soul—the soul becoming in some way so crucially involved with this demonic influence that it "becomes a demon" (*yínetai dhaímonas*), and, thus impelled, reanimates its own body. It is this reanimated body which, resisting the normal course of decay, returns to the living and, appearing in any chosen form—human or animal—drinks the blood of its own kin. The living, in the face of such an emergency, are forced to protect themselves in the only way available. With the use of certain ritual means to destroy the power of the devil, they at the same time destroy the soul.

completely different from European Slavic folklore

This belief is common throughout Greek culture,[9] and the causes thought to engender such a transformation of the soul have been noted in some detail.

Lawson,[10] summarizing evidence from modern Greek folklore as well as from his own observations, lists nine types of vampire or revenant: (1) those who do not receive the full and due rites of burial; (2) those who meet with any sudden or violent death (including suicides), or, in Maina, where the *vendetta* is still in vogue, those murdered who remain unavenged; (3) children conceived or born on one of the great Church festivals, and children stillborn; (4) those who die under a curse, especially the curse of a parent or one self-invoked, as in the case of a man who, in perjuring himself, calls down on his own head all manner of damnation if what he says be false; (5) those who die under the ban of the Church, that is to say, the excommunicated; (6) those who die unbaptized or apostate; (7) men of evil and immoral life in general, more particularly if they have dealt in the blacker kinds of sorcery; (8) those who have eaten the flesh of a sheep which was killed by a wolf; (9) those over whose dead bodies a cat or other animal has passed. Campbell[11] says that, among the Sarakatsani, people who are believed to turn into *vrykólakoi* are "persons whose lives were corrupted in sin, committed suicide, drowned or were unbaptized; or persons whose bodies were not guarded by their kinsmen in the period between death and burial, or whose bodies, although guarded, were leaped over by a cat." Blum and Blum[12] quote a number of random stories in which a huge variety of cases are cited, which include the cat crossing over the body, as well as lying, drunkenness, stealing from a school or a church, and so on.

The major part of these typical cases, with the exception of the unavenged dead (which is locally specific), thus appears to be related to two main classifications corresponding more or less to cases of (a) unabsolved sin or (b) ritual neglect by the living. Lawson's work reflects this classification, for he discerns two corresponding concepts of the dead, which often had their own terminology and which create a distinction between revenants and vampires. Thus the depraved or sinful dead remained uncorrupt and, being unable to find rest in decay, might wander as revenants, exciting pity but certainly not terror. They would usually be discovered to be undecayed at the exhumation, which customarily takes place several years after death,[13] and they were sometimes known as the "drumlike" (*tympanaíoi*) or "undissolved" (*álytoi*) dead. These characteristics contrasted sharply with those of the "vampire" proper, which showed itself immediately after death in violent attacks on its own kindred, and inspired a terror and revulsion which could reach the heights of panic.

Lawson then engages on the task of showing that the uncorrupt revenant was a traditional Greek conception, a "reasonable and usually harmless" creature,[14] and that this was superseded by the vampire which, bloodsucking and life-destroying, derived from the Slavs. Each of these phenomena had separate causes, the essentially Slavonic causes for the creation of the vampire being, in Lawson's view, the last two of the nine he cites[15]— eating the flesh of a sheep killed by a wolf (which, however, he notes as a rare belief in Greece), and allowing a cat or other animal to cross the body (which we have seen to be common to this day). This distinction too is important, although the historical argument plainly owes much to Victorian Hellenism; its chief drawback is simply that to provide a historical derivation is not to provide the meaning of the belief or to give any reason as to why it is adopted.

My own evidence in fact corroborates the distinction observed by Lawson, for the villagers of Ambéli distinguish clearly between the generalized category of the uncorrupt dead and specific instances of vampires (which alone are termed there *vrykólakoi*). In this village and the surrounding area there is no indication at all that lack of corruption in a body at the time of the exhumation is a sign of a vampire, for it is universally believed that a vampire reveals itself within forty days or not at all, and that an uncorrupt body at exhumation is not a vampire, but a soul with "sins" (*hamartíes*). And thus while it is said that the service which may be read for a corpse found uncorrupt at exhumation is designed to release the soul from sin and free it into the future life, actions performed at the grave of a vampire are conducted explicitly to achieve the vampire's sudden and permanent destruction; and it is stated clearly that this involves, necessarily, the total and permanent loss of the soul. Moreover, while the villagers of Ambéli believe that the soul of a suicide is "taken" by the devil (*tín paírnei ó dhaímonas*), and that the soul of an unbaptized child is "lost" (*hánetai*) (a word used also for the fate of the soul after exorcism), the ideas both of a suicide and of an unbaptized child are quite distinct from that of the vampire, for this is a soul which has not merely been taken by the devil, but has itself actually become a demon.

While it may be, therefore, that the experience of villagers in other parts of Greece has been genuinely different from that reported here, it is possible also that the two categories of the uncorrupt dead have become confused in the ethnography, so that the dead who remain whole within the period of forty days and are discovered as vampires become conceptually merged with those dead who because of "sins" are found to be uncorrupt at exhumation. This would be particularly explicable in view of the overlap in various cases, for even in Ambéli, where the distinction between the two main categories of the dead is incontrovertible, there is still a sense in which the uncorrupt dead with "sins," and therefore "in hell," parallel the uncorrupt vampire who is possessed, and destroyed, by the devil. It is, however, also made clear that the action which turns the dead into a vampire is precise, time-limited, and has an immediate and tangible result, whereas the idea of "sins" provides a general category involving both the known world of obvious evil-doing and the unknown world of spiritual consequences: although there is an implicit understanding that the sinful dead are in some way related negatively to the living, this is in no sense comparable to the terrible return of the vampire to its kin in its active search for blood.

It is the specific phenomenon of the vampire, then, which I examine here, and I consider it in relation to its characteristic cause—the ritual infringe-ment which results from cats (and, as will be shown, other objects) crossing over the body; for this is the only cause particularly connected with the true vampire which persistently recurs in all the sources quoted. It is also the only one which governs the still-living fear of the vampire in the village of Ambéli.

It is apparent that belief in vampires, especially that aspect which relates to the fatal nature of a cat's action in "crossing over" the dead body, is one which, as Lawson documents, was embarrassing and irrational to the Church, and seemed to a European—and especially a Hellenist—shocking and unjust. The effects of this belief did not stop at ritual, however, for fear of vampires in many Greek villages plainly inspired the inhabitants to a degree of terror which was by any reckoning destructive of the social fabric. Such destruction is testified to by relatively skeptical clerical sources: a seventeenth-century source quoted by Lawson[16] refers more than once to numbers of people dead "of fright or of injuries," amounting in one case to more than fifteen, and a nineteenth-century source, which he also quotes, speaks similarly of the possibility of whole villages being devastated in an epidemic of panic deaths. Although one may question whether some of these writings were not relying on reports exaggerated by the same panic, this is itself a document to the terror induced by the vampire, and this terror has naturally lent itself to dramatic use. Byron, in *the Giaour*, uses the idea of the vampire (invalidly, according to the present argument) to sanction a curse on the killer of Hassan:

> But first, on earth as Vampire sent,
> Thy corse shall from its tomb be rent:
> Then ghastly haunt thy native place,
> And suck the blood of all thy race;
> There from thy daughter, sister, wife,
> At midnight drain the stream of life;
> Yet loathe the banquet which perforce
> Must feed thy livid living corse;
> Thy victims ere they yet expire
> Shall know the demon for their sire,
> As cursing thee, thou cursing them,
> Thy flowers are withered on the stem.

Novels also capitalize on vampire beliefs to create convincing and frighten-ing effects; for example, Karkavitsa[17] includes an episode about a man, con-fused with a person recently dead, who creates such terror among the villagers that they pelt him with stones and eventually set fire to his house in an effort to dispose of him. Aside from fiction, relatively recent instances of terror are documented in two cases quoted by the Blums.[18] In one the parents of a girl in a coma, unable to believe the doctor's diagnosis and terrified of her return as a vampire, besought him to leave her as she was, and in the end buried her alive; while in the other, a man, stirring in his coffin just before his burial, was stoned to death by panic-stricken villagers.

Even without these instances, however, there is irony enough in the thought of a human soul being taken over, through no evil-doing of its own, by the devil, and ultimately destroyed forever. In the following pages I do not attempt fully to resolve the evident paradox revealed at this level of understanding; but in explaining the deep structures of thought from which it springs, I hope to provide some understanding of the counterbalancing intuitions which are entrenched in the culture, and which, it must be assumed, act to sustain the villagers in their acceptance of this belief, even while they at the same time provide the motive force for it.

Some Aspects of Death and Burial in North Euboea

The theme of blood is paramount at many of the rituals connected with death in Ambéli, for it is believed that at the moment of death Cháros, or the Angel, sent by God to bring the soul to judgment, with his drawn sword cuts the victim's throat, and drenches with blood not only the dead person but also the house and everyone in it.[19] The word for this act is *slaughter* (*spházo*)—a word used, except for this one context, specifically in connection with the killing of animals. It means precisely "to cut the throat of," an association made still more pointed by the custom on St. Michael's Day which forbids the killing of any animal, because on that day, the villagers say, "only one slaughters (*móno énas spházei*), that is to say, the Angel of Death himself. There is indeed another word commonly used for the act of dying, which means "to un-soul" (*xepsycháo*), and images the process by which the soul is thought to come out of the mouth with the last breath, "like a baby" (*sán moró*); and it is this word, and never that meaning simply "to die" (*pethaíno*), which is used about this last moment. But the action of Death as an act of slaughter occurs not only in generalized accounts, but also in graphic conversations about the recently dead. I remember a family who, even when recalling the death of their father after a long illness, described the moment of death in words which drew upon the traditional imagery: at one moment he had been alive, and the next—"Cháros slaughtered him" (*tón ésphaxe ó Cháros*). It seems, then, that while the crucial action of the dying person is to deliver up his soul, the action which brings this about is the sudden and violent spilling of his blood.

As a consequence of this, after the moment of death, one of the first acts— by the women of the house and any close female relatives and neighbors—is to wash the body with water and soap, and then a little wine. And as a consequence of this, also, it is considered essential that everyone present in the house at the moment of death, members of the family and visitors alike, should immediately change all their clothes. These clothes must be left in an outbuilding and on no account be taken into any of the houses of their owners until washed on the third or fifth day (*moná*, in uneven numbers) after the death. In earlier times it was also the custom to sponge over the floor of the room in which the death had occurred, and later to whitewash the walls and ceiling, and to do the same to the room in which the body had been laid out if this were a different one. After this there was for a year a prohibition on white-washing the rooms again. These last-mentioned customs have now lapsed, but that regarding the washing of the clothes is strictly kept, and the reason given is always in the terms of the same idea: "It seems as if there is blood everywhere."

While washing the body is the immediate means of transforming the savagery of the event, the fresh clothes then placed on the body, and in particular the shroud (*sávano*) which covers them, carry an added symbolism. The shroud is an unsewn length of white material, approximately thirteen feet long and one foot wide, cut in such a way as to fit over the head of the dead person and stretch down to the feet at both the front and the back. It is worn under the jacket or cardigan, but over the trousers or skirt, and is the most important of all the clothes worn, for it is in this garment that the soul is said to appear in the other world.

The interpretation of the shroud given in the village is that it represents the stole (*trachilió*, or dial. *trachomándilo*) worn by Orthodox priests when they are fully vested. The stole is worn in representation of the high priesthood of Christ and in revelation of the priest's sacramental function in his name; the shroud as a lay representation of the stole reveals, therefore, an understanding by the villagers of a sacramental function in every man.

The body thus passes through a vital transition from the moment of death until the moment when it is prepared for the visiting of the community: the pollution of death, seen categorically as one of blood, is washed away by water and wine, after which clean clothes and the shroud are put on, and finally candles are lit and the body censed. By this time the change from pollution to holiness has become so extreme that the body is, as it awaits burial, conceived in the same terms as that used for the relics of the saints—"the holy relics" (*tá ághia leípsana*). The achievement of this state of holiness, however, is until burial essentially unstable, and must be kept in equilibrium by continual care against a sudden catastrophic revival of the original blood pollution, and the transformation of the soul into a vampire.

As already indicated, in Ambéli only one type of action is believed to create a vampire, and this is often initially framed in terms of the prohibition against cats. This statement is, however, if questioned, always enlarged either to a phrase such as: "a cat . . . a mouse," or to the categorical assertion that while cats are especially dangerous, in fact nothing at all should be allowed to pass over the unburied dead. The proscription of cats is thus not itself the focus of belief, but rather a short-hand expression of a danger which is much more general, and which is represented by any action which crosses over the body, whether "stepping across" (*draskyló*) or "passing over" (*pernáei apáno ápo*) it. And it is this action—whether it is performed by stepping across the body, or by handing anything across it to someone on the other side, or by leaning over the body to place something on the ground opposite—which creates the conditions for a demonic possession so absolute that, whatever the virtue of the person during life, the soul loses forever its own nature, and becomes immediately an urgent and terrible danger to those it leaves behind. I once heard it said that vampires go "wherever they are sent" (*ópou tón ríxane*), but, as is normally affirmed and as a proverb quoted later also indicates, the predominant belief is that vampires always return to their own kin. Coming in any guise, human or animal, they return to attack either their own family or their own flocks, damaging and eventually killing them—an action often described as "suffocating" (*ná pníxei*)—by going up the nose and drinking their blood.

Once a vampire has been suspected, proof of its existence is sought at the graveyard, in the presence of a hole in the grave about the size of two cupped hands held together, around the region of the corpse's head and chest. Those who can bear to, I was told, look in and see the gleaming eyes of the vampire in its depths. The remedies which then have to be practiced, between the hours of Vespers on Saturday and the end of the liturgy on the Sunday morning (since between those hours the vampire is compelled to remain in the grave), consist of "boiling" (*zimatáo*) the vampire by pouring a mixture of about four kilos of boiling oil and vinegar into the hole in the grave, and "reading" (*dhiávasma*), that is to say exorcism, by the priest. The effect of these actions is dramatic, for they cause the soul, with its demonic power, immediately to "burst" (*skázei*) or "be lost" (*hánetai*); it is extinguished in a moment, and neither heaven nor hell knows it thereafter. Nothing avails, therefore, to undo the harm that has been done, and henceforward no candles are lit for the soul, no remembrance food is made, the long sequence of memorial customs lapses utterly.

There is plainly a contradiction here between the belief that on death the soul leaves the body through the mouth and is taken by the Angel, and the belief that through some subsequent fortuitous action it can be taken over totally by the devil, thus fatally reanimating the body. This contradiction presents a difficulty, not only because the same word *psychí*, denoting the soul, is used in both contexts, but also because villagers do not differentiate in any conscious sense between the two uses of the word. Nevertheless, there are hints in certain accompanying beliefs relating not only to the dead but also to the blood, which may suggest that at a relatively inexplicit level the soul is understood in what are virtually two distinct senses.

The blood theme will be developed in detail elsewhere, but with reference to the theme of the dead it may be said here that there exists in rural Greek thought, running alongside those beliefs which relate to the destiny of the soul separated from the body and taken by the Angel, a parallel belief that the rupture between the body and the person who inhabited it is not made absolute on death, but is only finally completed when the flesh, as villagers say, "has dissolved" (*échei liósei*) from the bones—a process indicating also the dissolution of sins—and when the bones are exhumed and brought up "into the air" (*stón aéra*). According to this latter series of ideas, then, possession by the devil of the *body*, of the flesh and blood, would necessarily involve in some way the possession of a psychic element of the person also—of that psychic element whose dissolution is equivalent to the dissolution of sins; and this is said to occur despite the fact that another psychic element has already left the body with the Angel. The distinction between these two elements of the "soul" (*psychí*) cannot be pressed too far, for, as has been said, the villagers do not explicitly mark a difference of sense, and they speak merely of the "soul" in both contexts. Yet at the same time they are untroubled by the contradiction between the two uses, and the nascent distinction thus suggested would account for the fact that they are much less concerned about the fate of the vampire's soul than they are about the reanimation of the corpse, and for the corresponding fact that they are much less fearful of actually becoming a vampire than they are of making or meeting with one.

Whatever the explanation of this contradiction, however, the necessity of preventing, or alternatively destroying, the vampire, carries in Ambéli urgent and total assent, and the consequences of this belief govern the actions of everyone to come near a body during the period of the wake. The wake itself is often referred to as a process of "guarding" (*filáne*) the body (a word which implies guarding it from being "crossed over"), although this is not its only purpose; and indeed for the twenty-four hours which elapse between death and burial, the body is never for one minute left alone. However, the wake itself holds its own dangers: in a small room crammed with people it is easy for someone to make a mistake—and in fact the last case of a vampire in the village, an event remembered by all the older villagers, occurred through a child inadvertently crossing over the body as it lay on the floor. The child was immediately handed back again in an attempt to undo the evil, but to no avail, and for several nights after the burial the dead woman returned as a great heavy woolly apparition, terrifying her husband and children, until the hole in the grave was discovered and the vampire exorcised. For three Saturdays the villagers poured boiling oil and vinegar into the hole in the grave and the priest read the service, and all was quiet thereafter.

The danger, then, is extreme, and at the wake there is persistent avoidance of any action which could be construed as passing over the body. This precaution is continually reinforced by the injunction that, as chairs, cushions, cups of coffee, and so on are needed and passed around, and as people come and go, those concerned should "take care" (*ná proséxeis*) and "not cross over" (*mín tó draskylás*) the body of the dead.

In this passing of things round the body there is a suggestion of the cyclic movement that I shall argue is central to the understanding of the vampire; but in the meantime I draw attention to other patterns of circular movement which occur alongside these events in the course of the wake.

When the body is laid out, it is placed "facing the sun" (*prós tón ílio*), that is to say with the feet, and thus the face, towards the east, lying "on the ground" (*katageí*) on a white sheet, which in turn is sometimes placed on a goat weave rug. The eyes are closed and the hands crossed right over left on the breast, and usually a cloth is laid over the face which reaches down to, but does not cover, the hands. Candles are placed around the body—always in an uneven number—and the candle known as the *ísou* is placed over the navel. *Isou* derives from *ísos*, meaning "equal" or "equivalent," and this candle is made soon after the moment of death by someone who rubs wax around a collection of threads cut to the same length as the height of the dead person. This long candle is then coiled round and round, anticlockwise, spiralling outwards from the center, in a flat circular mat—and when this is done the center of this coil is pulled up and lit, so that in its burning the candle consumes itself in the direction according to which it was made. During the night of the wake it must be allowed to burn itself down to one-third of its original length only, before it is extinguished and an ordinary candle lit in its place. The second night it is lit and burns down through the second third of its length, and on the third night it is lit again and entirely consumed.

The placing of the *ísou* on the navel reinforces the symbolism of the spiral with which the *ísou* is itself informed, since the navel is conceived by the villagers as being the center of the body and itself formed in a spiral. This spiral can at times become unwound, giving rise to pains in the area, and sickness—an ailment known as the "unwinding of the navel" (*xéstrima toú aphaloú*), or sometimes merely the "unwinding." If not attended to it passes eventually, but can be cured quite pragmatically, without the use of spells, by winding it up again. There are various ways in which this is done, but all (except for cupping) work according to the same principle, which is to re-form the true spiral of the navel by twisting it back "like the dance" in an anticlockwise direction. The vital significance of the maintenance of this direction will be made clear, but it is already implied in the startled response to my inadvertently miming in this context a spiral going clockwise, "towards the left" (*aristerá*); "You don't dance like that! Don't do it that way or the person will die!"

Finally just as the shroud is, of the clothes, the one indispensable article, so the *ísou* is, among the candles, the most essential; for it is the *ísou* which is supposed to give the soul of the dead person light for the forty days during which it is said that it remains in touch with the earth, and it is with the *ísou* before it that the soul finally, at the end of this period, appears before God.

The right-handed, or anticlockwise, spiralling movement according to which the *ísou* burns recurs throughout village life in a great variety of contexts, and it is seen again in the censing of the body carried out at intervals throughout the wake. In this context it is performed in the same way as in everyday life—that is to say with the customary and anticlockwise movement of the hand, which villagers say is "right-handed" (*dhexiá*) and "like the dance" (*sán horós*)—to spread the incense. A complete right-handed circle is also described round the body (as in normal circumstances it is described round the room) before the incense is set down again beside the head. And it is particularly significant that this same pattern used to be reiterated in the singing of the laments at a wake, which were also, I was told, passed around the body "like the dance."

This assimilation of the lament to the dance, as in all instances when the dance pattern is being invoked, is of great importance, and may illuminate the description of the same ritual from other parts of Greece quoted by Alexiou.[20] Describing antiphonal lamentation at wakes throughout Greece she writes, with a reference to Pasayannis:[21]

> Although the arrangement of the mourners varies in different parts, it is not random. The procedure is strict and formal; one of the kinswomen usually leads off, helped by the rest who wail in chorus, and then, when the chief

96

mourner from the other side wishes to "take up" the dirge, she stretches her hand over the body and grasps the hand of the mourner on the left. By this silent stretching of the hand, the dirge is passed over from one group to the other all day long.

In the light of the pattern observed in North Euboea, and in the light also of the general fear in Greece of cats (and by inference anything else) crossing the body, it seems legitimate to interpret this passage as describing not a movement crossing over the body, but one which is circular and goes around it. Thus if one takes the chief mourner who stretches her hand "over the body" and grasps the hand of the mourner "on the left" to be stretching out her left hand to the right hand of the mourner opposite to her at the body's head or foot, this is consistent with a movement not in fact across the body but around it, and in a right-handed direction. And it is striking that the action of stretching out the left hand to take the leader's right is the way in which people used to enter the dance, for traditionally those who wished to join the dance always entered at the head of the line. Thus in the district of Ambéli the dance pattern, invariably associated with a right-handed (anticlockwise) auspicious movement, used to be repeated in the singing of laments, so that the lament, taken from the left and given to the right, and similarly, received by one person and given by another, was, although sung antiphonally by two groups, not exchanged to and fro but passed symbolically on and on in a continuous right-handed circle.

An Analogue in Kinship—Katameriá

Lack of space compels me to summarize an argument which will be set out at length elsewhere, and which concerns ideas about the flow of the blood and its relationship to conceptions of kinship and the incest prohibition. The rule to which I draw attention here is known as *katameriá*.[22]

Katameriá (pl. *katameriés*) is a word for which only a clumsy translation can be found, but it is likely to be derived from *katá méros*, "according to its place," and best rendered as "a process for putting things according to their category."[23] It is thus an abstract concept which is given meaning only by context, since the precise categories are peculiar to each situation.

Because kinship reckoning in Ambéli is cognatic, covering four generations from ego to his great grandparents, the marriage rule which results prohibits marriage between all descendants of a common great grandparent. Thus up to the degree of second cousin, collaterals are "kin" (*sói*), but after this they have "unkinned" (*xesóïsane*) and can marry. Some ambiguity is experienced concerning marriages between those in categories immediately outside the relationship of second cousin, because, as it was explained to me once, "kinship has passed, but a vein of blood endures" (*pérase tó sói, allá vastáei fléva*). However, this idea does not, and apparently even in the 1930s did not, act as a customary prohibition, but simply as involving a degree of disquiet. There was, nevertheless, one sequence of marriages, in addition to those within the canonical kindred, which used to be forbidden by a clear rule—a rule which was still in the late 1950s enforced against one proposed marriage in the village, and which continued to be of concern to some older people up to at least the early 1970s. This rule, known as *katameriá*, prescribed, to put it briefly, that after a couple had married, any future marriages between the collateral kin of the wife and the collateral kin of the husband should follow the initial movement of the sexes. Thus once a woman had married, her male collateral kin could not after that point take a woman back from her husband's collateral kin; and any man from her kin, if he did so, was said to have "turned back" (*gýrise*) to take his wife, and to be courting disaster. This expression, "to turn back," always, when it is used symbolically, indicates an inauspicious action; and in this case the agent by which misfortune occurred is revealed unequivocally as the blood, for, as the villagers say, in such a case "the blood returned" (*gýrise tó aíma*), bringing with it misfortune or death.

My evidence refers only to a single generation, and does not establish whether or not any descending generations used to be taken into account in calculating the applicability of the rule of *katameriá*, although it is possible that such a calculation might at one time have been made. However, the inclusion in the calculation, by some people, of lateral kinship as far as second cousin, indicates that the principle was one which could operate over a wide field of kin, and was thus a significant influence towards the distribution of marriages through the community.

The meaning of *katameriá* is one which is not immediately apparent from the way in which the rule is normally presented, for at first sight it appears as if it expresses a prescription for the unidirectional exchange of men and women between their respective kindreds in such a way as to represent men going one way and women another. However, as I have argued elsewhere,[24] all the attitudes to the marriage of men and women, together with a significant element of the vocabulary used, imply an essential understanding of men as "in the house" (*mésa stó spíti*) with women "destined for a strange hearth" (*xenogoniá*), and thus represent men as the static, women as the moving, principles. In the light of this it therefore becomes apparent that what *katameriá* is stating is not two opposite transitive movements of women and men between the kindreds, but a principle which, accepting men to be identified with the natal kindred in a way in which women are not, dictates the movement of their women out, and prohibits their return. Thus for a particular category of kinsmen to give women back—before due time has passed—to a category from which it has previously taken them, is to turn backwards and to "return" the blood to its original source. *Katameriá* is thus a rule which incorporates two important statements about Greek kinship; it states the auspicious nature of the asymmetric progression of the women through the kindreds,[25] and it states also that this progression of women is an analogue of the progression of blood.

The reason given for the *katameriá* proscription—fear of the "return" of the "blood"—reveals clearly that the marriage relationship is conceived in *some way* as extending from the bride or groom to a category of the kin into which he or she has married, although the sense in which this could be so plainly cannot rely on the facts of blood relationship as they are seen to operate in the physiological kindred. A complex symbolism of the blood is hinted at here, which may be illustrated in two additional instances. One concerns a concept of the relationship believed to exist between a god-parent and the child which he or she baptizes, for this relationship, created primarily with the oil with which the god-parents anoint the child, is said to involve the child "taking a vein [of blood]" (*paírnei fléva*) from the god-parents. And it is consistent with this that the children of the god-parent and the god-children are, it is said, "as of one blood" (*sán aíma*), and may not marry. This case indicates the possibility, in village thinking, of a type of blood link created by sacrament rather than by procreation, and one way in which such a link may be understood is illustrated in my second instance, which highlights the point already made in *katameriá* and deals with the link thought to be created between affines. This occurred during a conversation concerning marriage and certain of the quasi-blood relationships created thereby, in answer to my questioning of the rationale behind them. My interlocutor suddenly picked up a glass and, making as if she were drinking a glass of water, said: "If you drink water it becomes part of you. So it is with blood."

The course followed by this blood as it flows through the community is not directly expressed by the villagers, but it is revealed by following through the implications of *katameriá*. The movement of women between the kindreds is equated with the movement of blood, and expresses the prin-ciple that this movement should be unidirectional and should not be re-versed. It is thus a movement which is characterized by a cyclic progress, since the blood not only circulates through the community, but may also, after the prescribed generational delay, return to the descendants of the original kindred. It is for this reason that the idea of a spiral constantly recurs in the imagery of the blood. This is most commonly manifest in the expression "the blood endures to the seventh *zinári*"—a *zinári* being the long belt which was traditionally wound spirally round and round the waist; but it also occurred in the words *mia vólta* ("one cycle" or "one revolution"), which I once heard used in description of the progress of kinship outwards to third cousin. *Zinári* is a relative term, the analytic interpretation of which depends on context, but it here means approximately "generation." One *vólta*, or "cycle," on the other hand, was, in the case quoted above, being used to describe the cycle of time and of marriages which must pass before the women may again return—as is ultimately necessary in a small and residentially stable population—to the descendants of the kindred which sent them out. Too hasty a return, as in the marriage of second cousins or of those who run counter to the movement of *katameriá*, is to cause the blood to turn back and to court disaster.

Neither the imagery of *zinári* nor that of *vólta* defines the direction conceptually followed by this spiral. However, the interpretation of the principle of *katameriá* provides an implied definition, for in *katameriá* the movement of the blood is seen to be analogous to the movement of women through the community in marriage; and in marriage, as the persistently recurring symbolism in all the processional movements show, this progression is envisaged as right-handed. Thus the movement of the blood—the correct procession of *zinária*—runs symbolically in a right-handed spiral which must always maintain its momentum and be perpetually guarded against a return on itself.

The "return" of the blood to the kindred, the ominous reversing of this right-handed spiral movement of the blood, has close parallels in the fatal return of the vampire to its own kin, although I only once heard such a connection between these two ideas being consciously made by villagers. Its occasion was, however, significant; for it arose in a discussion by two women of a marriage between second cousins which had taken place in the village some years before. The women were agreeing that for a marriage to be propitious the participants had to go to "strange blood" (*xéno aíma*)—a statement which is frequently heard and which is the mirror image of the doctrine already noted, that, in cases of the union of similar blood, "the blood returns," bringing catastrophe. In this context the comment then uttered takes on a startling significance, for, said as an aside and half under the breath, it took the form of a well-known proverb: "The vampire hunts its own kindred" (*vrykólakas tó sóï kynigáei*). The image of the vampire returning from the grave to hunt its own kin sprang intuitively to mind in the context of the blood which in second cousin marriage returns to destroy its originators.

The Intolerable Reversal—An Interpretation of the Vampire

As was stated earlier, the village understanding is that death is caused by Cháros cutting the throat and letting the blood pour out of the body, and that at this moment also the soul comes out of the mouth like a baby. The immediate concern of the living, then, is to deal with both the negative and the positive aspects of death—to purge the blood pollution and to assist the soul in its journey to the other world.

The immediate fate of the soul is enshrined in a tradition which, broadly speaking, teaches that for forty days after death the soul is taken by its angel around the scene of its earthly life, where it learns about the merits and defects of all the actions it performed when in the body; and at the fortieth day, it is taken up to God for the judgment, and there sent to its "allotted place" (*thésis*).[26] In connection with this journey of the soul, the theme of the *ísou* must be recapitulated.

It will be remembered that the *ísou* is the candle which gives light to the soul during its journey; it is made immediately after the death, its length being calculated according to the height of the dead person, after which it is twisted into a flat right-handed spiral and placed on the navel of the body to burn to two-thirds of its length. During the two subsequent nights the remaining two-thirds are burned, until it is finished. Set over the navel and burning in the life-giving right-handed spiral, the *ísou* is plainly an image of life, and the correspondence of its length with the height of the body—not to mention the name *ísou* or "of the same (length)"—is clear indication of its symbolic correspondence with the person who has just died. Again the three days of the burning of the *ísou* on earth are thought to correspond with the forty days of the soul's journey over its past life; and thus it seems that the *ísou*, representing the interim period during which the soul is neither of this world nor of the next, relates the one to the other through the judgment finally passed on the soul's accumulated lifetime of deeds. The burning of the *ísou* appears to represent, from birth to death, a replay of the life which has just ended, together with the soul's progressive enlightenment as, taught by the Angel, it comes to understand the significance of all it did during life. Thus it is all the gathered deeds both good and bad recollected and comprehended by the soul as the past years and places are revisited, that the flame of the *ísou* symbolizes, as the soul appears before God.

While, however, the forty days spent revisiting the past, and the ultimate appearance of the soul before God, reveal a belief in a just judgment awaiting the soul, which has left the body at the end of its life on earth, the belief in the annihilation of that other aspect of the soul, which, apparently fortuitously, becomes a vampire, appears to relate to an antithetical structure of thought. Yet the meaning of this belief as well, although capricious and impersonal in expression, has its origin in the same understanding of life—and of the life after death—which informs the idea both of the *ísou* and of the judgment.

As has been shown already, the chief contrast between life and death is that between blood and not-blood which emerges at the moment of death, when the life blood of the living is shed to its last drop by the brutal act of Cháros. The soul leaves the body for the "other world" (*állos kósmos*) at that precise moment when the last of the blood of this world pours symbolically out into the house; and the soul is the opposite of fleshly life and blood—a "shadow" (*ískio*), a "breath" (*anása*), "air" (*aéras*). In a dominant folk description of the "other world" the insubstantial souls everlastingly flit about like shadows, in a world where "there is no sitting down" (*dhén káthondai*), "there is no drinking or merrymaking" (*dhén pínoun dhén glendáne*); a world where the dead only half recognize each other, never able to grasp even their memories for certain. This last idea is given a powerful rendering in the demonstration by villagers of how the dead meet each other—passing by each other and stretching out their right hands behind them, infinitely quietly, to grasp the hand of the other, while still looking ahead and in the very act of separation, saying, "Somewhere I've seen you before" (*kápou sé eídha*). In this enactment the impression is of continual drifting motion, of perpetual non-encounter, of everlasting existence in a bloodless world lacking in all reality. And when it is remembered that the villagers, in life, are involved habitually in the most vivid and vital face-to-face relationships, it becomes apparent that the opposition between the world of the living and that of the dead is seen as fundamental and absolute.

The moment of death, then, is the polar opposite of life, and this opposition is expressed predominantly in terms of blood. It is thus entirely consistent with this symbolism that the greatest fear that the living have of the dead, and for the dead, is lest this metamorphosis from the world of the living to that of the dead should in any way fail to be maintained, and it is consistent too that the failure of this metamorphosis should be seen in terms of the physical reanimation of the dead. Thus the period of the wake is shown to be a transitional time during which the proper state of the dead is liable to reversal, and vampires—those dead whose transition into the other world has somehow been arrested before completion—return not as ineffective revenants, but as living demons, illegitimately demanding blood.

While the presence of a phenomenon like the vampire may thus fit coherently into the rural Greek tradition relating to the afterlife, the means by which a soul is transformed into such a vampire may appear less logical. In fact, however, its logic is equally clear, for the prohibition on cats crossing over a dead body involves a particular ritual action of great significance. It has been said that in Ambéli the prohibition is not confined to cats only, but extends to all objects, animate and inanimate, and that on this level no distinction is actually made between, for instance, a cat or a candle. Cats are singled out to embody the proscription not because they possess an intrinsic power of evil, but because, being domesticated and yet at the same time unsocialized, the danger in their case is particularly acute that they might cross over a dead body. Other animals would be kept away by the mere presence of people, and dogs in any event are never allowed inside the house; but a cat could well perform the fatal action, even in a crowded room. In such a situation therefore cats are, indeed, dangerous.

The prohibition on crossing over the body is subject to interpretation on various different levels. A phrase in the village describes the situation of a person living alone and likely to die alone: "The cats will eat him" (*thá tón fáne oí gáttes*). It could therefore be argued on a sociological level that this fear of vampires finds its origin in the need for the young to look after the old, and that the custom thus guards against anyone being left alone "to be eaten by the cats." Although, however, this may well have been one consequence of this belief, the realities of the culture make it necessary to look further and to understand the meaning of vampires in terms more akin to those in which the villagers themselves see them.

Initially, it becomes evident that if a body lies on the floor in the middle of the community, and if there is a prohibition against stepping over or passing anything across it, there is being voiced an imperative on preserving the space above the dead—who has by now been transformed into "holy relics"—which no one and nothing must enter. The earth, on which the body is traditionally laid, is thus linked to the upperworld and to the underworld by means of the dead person, who provides the central point at which the two worlds meet.

There is here a clear suggestion of an axis leading from one world to the other, though it is no more than a suggestion. However this sense of a sacred space above and below the dead is emphasized by the second consequence of the prohibition, for the corollary of having a space into which nothing earthly must enter, but which nevertheless is the focus for the tasks of the living community, is that the community and its possessions must circulate around it. In Ambéli in the present day things are passed impartially to and fro, round either the head or the feet. But on my asking an old woman which way they used to be passed in the old days, the answer came immediately: "Like the dance." "Not to the left?" I inquired. "No," emphatically, "the devil comes from there." It appears, then, that persistent symbolism of the right-handed spiral movement "like the dance," evident throughout village culture but recurring with particular frequency in the rituals of death, is repeated yet again in the symbolism which protects both the community and the dead from the phenomenon of the vampire. The present-day custom is faithful to the insistence on a circular movement round the body, but has failed to perpetuate the true right-handed direction; the older custom, it appears, created a continual reassertion of traditional realities as people, cushions, chairs, babies, cups of coffee and all the paraphernalia of the wake, processed in an unending dance around the dead person in the center. The world—to use an exact translation of the Greek for "people," "community" (*kósmos*)—revolves, literally, around the dead person, at whose own center, on the navel, the right-handed spiral of the *ísou* burns.

The precise meaning of this dance of life around the dead is closely related to the context of blood in which it is found. It has been shown that this blood is thought to run in a unidirectional, right-handed spiral, and that its direction must be perpetuated through the flow of marriages *katameriá*—"according to category" or "to strange blood"—through the community. Contravention of this—the contraction of a marriage against the direction created by the necessity of *katameriá*—cause the blood to "return" as a catastrophic force, bringing misfortune or death to those from whom it originated. The parallels between this belief and that concerning the creation of a vampire are striking.

On the death of a person, as has been said, Charos slits the victim's throat and spills his blood, slaughtering the body and at the same time releasing the soul to its review of its past life and its passage to God. The body and blood of physical life are thus separated from the soul of the spiritual existence, and the customs thereafter are designed to maintain this separation until, with the consignment of the body to the earth, it is assured. The blood, that is to say, must flow one way, out of the body, and the body itself be laid to rest in the earth. One thing only can interrupt this process, and this is an action symbolized by the "stepping over" of the body, for this causes the blood to flow back into it, reanimating it as a demon and sending it back to the living in a hunt for the blood of its own kin. This action plainly parallels that carried out for those marriages which are not *katameriá;* for just as the cutting across of the proper categories of blood causes the blood "to return" to the kindred and results in misfortune and death, so the breaking of the dance around the dead symbolizes the return of the blood on itself, pouring back into the dead, reviving it with demonic life, and sending it in a horrific search for its own kind. And this relationship between the two images becomes even clearer when it is remembered that the fusion of two kindreds on marriage was described by one woman as the action of "drinking blood"—an action which, if enacted between the correct categories of people, ensures the on-flowing of the life blood of the generations, but if enacted between kin or in defiance of the rule of *katameriá*, turns the blood 'back' and results in stagnation or death. Thus it is plain that the movement of the blood from kindred to kindred according to the correct categories of relationship, as well as the pouring out of the blood in death, are seen as aspects of the same life-giving spiral, and that the interruption of the flow in either case causes the blood to reverse its true life-giving character and to return home down the spiral of relationship as a deadly force. It was, then, for this reason that the subconscious connection was made by the woman who recalled, in the context of second cousin marriage, the vampire returning to its kin; for the image of the vampire is a parallel to the image of marriage within the kindred.

[handwritten marginal note: This encapsulates the crux of the author's argument]

Conclusion

The district of Ambéli is only a small part of Greece, and it would be unwise to suppose that the detailed expression of the themes of blood, marriage, and death found there would be discovered in exactly the same forms throughout Greece. Particular refinements of dress, ritual, and behavior often show a creative variety from region to region; and it is appropriate, in conclusion, to draw out what appear to be the essential and invariate principles of the interpretation put forward. In brief, the explanation given here identifies the spiral pattern of the dance first with the inflow of blood through the generations by means of marriage, and second with the outflow of blood in a death auspiciously accomplished—both these flows being in a vital sense irreversible.

Because of the great number of contexts in Greek village life in which this image of the spiral is found, it seems that in spite of the close similarities between the incest prohibition and the custom relating to vampires, it is inappropriate to explain one in terms of the other. What seems more likely is that the custom relating to vampires reveals, not a literal equivalence at a death with the incest taboos which operate during life, but a continuity of understanding which informs the processes both of life and death. Thus the symbolic equivalence of blood with life is carried to its logical conclusion in the insistent theme of the bloodlessness of death; while at the same time the auspicious spiral which, during life, must be perpetuated by the correct flow of blood in marriage, is at death perpetuated by the symbolic outpouring of blood from the dead, and the vital prohibition against its return. In this way the image of continual movement that protects the life in the blood as it circles through the generations, protects also, at the moment of death, the soul from being trapped in a physical form which is neither alive nor dead. According to the understanding implicit in both contexts, it is motionlessness which is the true death, for motionlessness here involves retrogression. Blood going to "strange" blood pours in a life-giving spiral through the community; while blood going to blood that "resembles itself"—that is to say, stays where it is—halts and doubles back. Similarly, the life in which the outpouring of the blood in death has not been frustrated moves on without check into the new and auspicious categories of the other world, while a life in which this outpouring is, by some inauspicious action, checked and turned back on itself, returns to devour the succeeding generations, and imperils the destiny of its own soul. Thus the women moving outwards from kindred to kindred, and the soul moving freely from this life to the next, are parallel images derived from the same understanding of life.

There is then, on one level, a chasm between life and death in Greek rural thinking which is unbridgeable, insofar as if bridged it gives rise to the primary horror that Greeks experience, the extinguishing of which takes precedence over all personal justice and all affection of the living for the dead. On another level, however, it appears that the principle of ongoing right-handed movement, which establishes the bloodlessness of the body, preventing the return of the vampire and consolidating the "otherness" of the dead, ensures not only the health of the living community, but also the safe passage of the soul into the other world. Thus the spiral dance of life, while it divides irrevocably blood from nonblood and the living from the dead, at the same time permeates the opposed worlds of life and death, and transcends, though it does not reconcile, their opposition.

Notes

I acknowledge with thanks a generous grant from the Social Science Research Council, which supported my fieldwork.

1. E. R. Leach, *Political Systems of Highland Burma* (London: Athlone Press, 1954).

2. R. H. Barnes, *Kédang* (Oxford: Clarendon Press, 1974).

3. S. Ott, *The Circle of Mountains* (Oxford: Clarendon Press, 1981.)

4. C. Lévi-Strauss, *Les Structures élémentaires de la parenté* (Paris: Plon, 1949); and R. Needham, *Structure and Sentiment* (Chicago: University of Chicago Press, 1962).

5. It should perhaps be mentioned that the concept of the "right" and the "left" hand is primarily a symbolic rather than a physical category, and that because of this

the physical direction implied by either category, in any particular culture, can vary. In Greece, and among the *Kédang* (Barnes, *Kédang*), right-handedness is conceived to involve motion in an anticlockwise direction, while among the Basques (Ott, *The Circle of Mountains*), the motion conceived as right-handed is one which proceeds clockwise. What is as important, then, is not the literal direction conveyed by either classification, but only whether the rule which orders this classification remains constant. In Greece the rule is unambiguous—that the dance pattern, anticlockwise motion, right-handedness, and an auspicious connotation, are all invariably associated with one another.

6. M. Mauss, *The Gift* (London: Cohen and West, 1954; originally published in 1925); M. Sahlins, *Stone Age Economics* (Chicago: Aldine-Atherton, 1972); E. A. Hammel, *Alternative Social Structures and Ritual Relations in the Balkans* (Englewood Cliffs, N.J.: Prentice-Hall, 1968).

7. Leach, *Political Systems;* Needham, *Structure and Sentiment;* Barnes, *Kédang.*

8. R. Hertz, *Death and the Right Hand,* trans. R. and C. Needham (Aberdeen: Aberdeen University Press, 1960); V. Turner, "Ndembu Circumcision Ritual," in *Essays on the Ritual of Social Relations,* ed. M. Gluckman (Manchester: Manchester University Press, 1962); R. Needham, ed., *Right and Left* (Chicago: University of Chicago Press, 1973).

9. M. Alexiou, *The Ritual Lament in Greek Tradition* (Cambridge: Cambridge University Press, 1974), 48.

10. J. C. Lawson, *Modern Greek Folklore and Ancient Greek Religion* (Cambridge: Cambridge University Press, 1910), 375–376.

11. J. K. Campbell, *Honour, Family and Patronage* (Oxford: Clarendon Press, 1964), 337.

12. R. Blum and E. Blum, *The Dangerous Hour* (London: Chatto and Windus, 1970), 75–77.

13. This exhumation of the bones is a ritual common throughout Greece, and is in Ambéli normally carried out either three or five years after a death. The bones are washed with water and wine, placed in a box, and finally put into the ossuary.

14. Lawson, *Modern Greek Folklore,* 390.

15. Ibid., 410.

16. Ibid., 367–373.

17. A Karkavitza, *O Zitiános* (Athens: "Angkyra," 1977).

18. Blum and Blum, *The Dangerous Hour,* 71–72.

19. Cháros cutting his victim's throat is not, of course, the only image of death in rural Greece, although it is certainly the dominant one in Ambéli. Amongst others, there is for instance the image of the dying person wrestling with Cháros on the marble threshing floor—well-known in Greek folksong. Such images as this, however, incorporating as they do the idea of violence, do not run counter to the image of Death as one who slaughters, and the generality of this latter idea is depicted either with a sword (*spathí*) or with a "double bladed knife" (*dhíkopo machaíri*). Thus I would claim that the understanding of Death as the spiller of blood which is presented here, on which much of the argument depends, is not confined to Ambéli and

its environs, but is found in many parts of Greece, and is coherent with other rural Greek images of death.

20. Alexiou, *The Ritual Lament*, 40.

21. K. A. Pasayanis, *Maniátika moirológia kaí tragoúdhia* (Athens, 1928).

22. J. du Boulay, *Portrait of a Greek Mountain Village* (Oxford: Clarendon Press, 1974), 146, 165.

23. This differs slightly from a derivation which I give in du Boulay, *Portrait*, 146, where I propose a root in *katamerízo*, meaning "to divide up in proportion." I now think this derivation, although relevant, is not sufficiently basic.

24. This is argued more fully in "The Meaning of Dowry: Changing Values in Rural Greece," *Journal of Modern Greek Studies* 1 (1983): 243–270.

25. It should be made clear at this point that there is no question here of a descent group of any sort being involved, as in the instances of prescriptive alliance cited by Lévi-Strauss, *Les Structures élémentaires*, and Needham, *Structure and Sentiment*. The "kindred" (*tó sóï*) in Ambéli is a group of blood relations which, never more than four generations in depth, is centered always on one particular group of siblings, and is thus, as a group, constantly being redefined. Nevertheless it is still the case that the kindred is, *for each individual*, a finite entity with fixed limits, and it is in relation to these individually defined groups that both the marriage rule and the rule of *katameriá* are invoked.

26. There is reason for supposing that this understanding is a compressed version of a more differentiated teaching which derives from the vision of St. Makários. The story runs that St. Makários asked to see the fate of the soul after death, and accordingly he was shown that for three days the soul circles around the earth reviewing its past deeds, and is then taken before God. For the next six days it is taken to paradise to see the joys of the saints, after which it is again taken before God. Finally, until the fortieth day, it goes down into hell, after which it appears before God for the judgment on its own life. While, however, there are some vestiges of this understanding still evident in the village, the simpler version given in my text is by far the most common.

Repeat from his book?

PAUL BARBER

Forensic Pathology and the
European Vampire

The vast majority of books and articles devoted to the vampire offer little that is new on the subject. Instead they are rather vampirelike themselves, feeding on the flesh of previously published books and articles. The same cases of vampire attacks are repeated again and again with little or no insight to reward the reader. It is for this reason that the following essay, by historian Paul Barber, deserves plaudits and praise. Barber, research associate at the Fowler Museum of Cultural History at the University of California at Los Angeles, offers a new and exciting interpretation of the vampire. In an attempt to demystify the supernatural, Barber provides a down-to-earth natural explanation of the vampire phenomenon. His theory has the advantage of being able to account for a good many of the characteristics of the vampire in terms of that creature's alleged physical attributes. The erudite essay included here in this volume was expanded into a book-length exposition entitled Vampires, Burial, and Death: Folklore and Reality *(New Haven: Yale University Press, 1988), which readers intrigued with his argument should definitely consult.*

If there is in this world a well-attested account, it is that of the vampires. Nothing is lacking: official reports, affidavits of well-known people, of surgeons, of priests, of magistrates; the judicial proof is most complete. And with all that, who is there who believes in vampires?

—Rousseau, *Lettre à l'Archevêque de Paris*[1]

I

The modern reader might assume that the vampires of the eighteenth century were much like the ghosts of today, which exist in a rather murky underworld, far from the haunts of Scientific Method. In actuality, however, as one might gather from Rousseau's remarks, nothing could be further from the truth: a number of "vampires" were actually dissected by surgeons, who

Reprinted from the *Journal of Folklore Research* 24 (1987): 1–32.

compiled a report in which they came to the conclusion that there was in fact something very spooky going on.

Moreover, whatever was happening, it was not only spooky, it was catching: the vampire infected his victims, causing them to become vampires as well, so that the phenomenon tended to occur as an epidemic. In the late seventeenth century, such an epidemic of vampirism occurred in Poland and Russia, and the French *Mercure galant* carried the following account of it:

> They appear from midday to midnight and come to suck the blood of living people and animals in such great abundance that sometimes it comes out of their mouths, their noses, and especially, their ears, and that sometimes the body swims in its blood which has spilled out into its coffin. They say the vampire has a kind of hunger that causes him to eat the cloth he finds around him. This revenant or vampire, or a demon in his form, comes out of his tomb and goes about at night violently embracing and seizing his friends and relatives and sucking their blood until they are weakened and exhausted, and finally causes their death. This persecution does not stop at one person but extends to the last person of the family, at least as long as one does not interrupt its course by cutting off the head or opening the body of the vampire. Then one finds his body, in its coffin, limp, pliable, bloated, and ruddy, even though he may have been dead for a long time. A great quantity of blood pours from his body.[2]

Such accounts became common in the eighteenth century, and the best-attested of them, the *locus classicus* of vampire stories, told of events that occurred in the 1720s, near Belgrade, when a man named Arnold Paole died an accidental death, after which several people died suddenly of what had been traditionally viewed as "vampirism." Forty days after his burial, Paole was exhumed:

> [It was found] that he was complete and incorrupt, also that completely fresh blood had flowed from his eyes, ears, and nose, and the shirt and graveclothes were also bloody. The old nails on his hands and feet, along with the skin, had fallen off, and new ones had grown. Since they could see from this that he was a true vampire, they drove a stake through his heart, according to their customs, whereupon he let out a noticeable groan and bled copiously.[3]

A few years later there was another such outbreak of "vampirism." Among others, the authorities found:

> A woman by the name of Stana, twenty years old, who had died in childbirth three months before, after a three-day sickness, and who had said before her

death that she had painted herself with the blood of a vampire in order to be free of him, wherefore she herself, like her child—which had died right after birth and because of a careless burial had been half-eaten by dogs—must also become vampires. She was whole and undecayed. After the opening of the body a quantity of fresh, extravascular blood was found *in cavitate pectoris.* The *vasa* of the *arteriae* and *venae,* like the *ventriculis cordis,* were not, as is usual, filled with coagulated blood, and the whole *viscera,* that is, the *pulmo, hepar, stomachus, lien et intestina,* were quite fresh as they would be in a completely healthy person.[4]

Clearly these accounts, however well attested—and the people present at Stana's disinterment included "two officers, military representatives from Belgrade, two army surgeons, a drummer boy who carried their cases of instruments, the authorities of the village, the old sexton and his assistants"[5]—contain details that cannot possibly be true and so must be dismissed. It is quite obvious, for example, that a dead body cannot groan, that blood coagulates after death, that a corpse is pale, not flushed, and is subject to rigor mortis, and that decomposition takes place shortly after death, certainly in less time than forty days.

Or do we know these to be "facts"? As we shall see, they do not stand up at all well under scrutiny. In fact, it will be shown here that the closer we look at the descriptions of "vampires" in their graves, the more accurate—as descriptions—these prove to be. Far from being merely fanciful horror stories, the vampire stories prove to be an ingenious and elaborate folk hypothesis that seeks to explain otherwise puzzling phenomena associated with death and decomposition—phenomena that are now well understood. Viewed as a theory, the vampire lore may be—as we now know—quite wrong, but like the Ptolemaic astronomy, it is capable of describing events accurately and has predictive value. In its history, however, it differs from such theories as Ptolemy's in that it was not the creation of a single person and no single Copernicus ever came forth to refute it—that was done piecemeal, over centuries—so that in modern times we no longer even understand how and why it came about.

To complicate the matter further, while modern forensic analysis has brought about an understanding of the phenomena of death and decomposition, this understanding simply has not reached most of us yet. We do not choose to spend a great deal of time thinking about how our bodies will decay after death. Thus it is that we remain convinced that—to give just one particularly dramatic example—a dead body cannot groan, as Arnold Paole's is said to have done; but however persuaded you are of this, you would be well advised not to make any sizable bets on the matter

111

without consulting your local coroner, for he will most certainly tell you otherwise.

In order to understand the vampire lore, then, we will have to unravel two sets of misconceptions: theirs and ours. In attempting to do so we will ask an obvious but neglected question: if bodies do not, in fact, turn into vampires, then what does happen to them? And do the actual events have any relation to those of the folklore?

From time to time scholars have attempted to explain the vampire lore by suggesting that perhaps the bodies were not dead at all, but were those of people buried alive, by accident. That would account for their bleeding, groaning, etc. No one, as far as I can tell, has published a serious study of this view, probably because it flies in the face of all our best evidence: the "vampires" we have the best information on were dug up (like Paole) long after their interment. Consequently, to prove that they were merely in a coma, one would have to prove that human beings can survive deprivation of air, food, and water for weeks and months at a time.

In looking for a simpler explanation, we will proceed as follows:

1. We will summarize the stories about vampires and revenants, using as our data those details that occur again and again in such stories. In the course of our discussion it should become apparent that our informants are themselves all looking at the same data—dead bodies perform pretty much the same worldwide—but with a wealth of information at their disposal the informants make different choices in identifying the characteristics of their particular native monster. As we shall see, the vampire and the revenant are identical in their origin: both start out as dead bodies. It is just in the telling that they diverge, and the principal source of their divergence is based on an ingenious interpretation of a striking but quite normal phenomenon associated with death and decomposition (see below, number 4). This is not the reason, however, why I will not concern myself with the much-debated typological distinctions between the vampire, the revenant, and their other relatives: it proves unexpectedly difficult to talk about the genus "revenant" without doing violence, from time to time, to the technical terms for the various species. Consequently, rather than either qualify my terms endlessly or make up a new, all-encompassing term, I shall ask the reader to accept for now the following working definition of a vampire/revenant: "any dead human being who, in folklore, is believed to return to life in corporeal form." I shall use the term *revenant* where possible, as it seems to me the more general term, but where the process of transformation is at issue, I shall use *vampirism* rather than *revenantism*, for reasons that probably need no elaboration.

In the interests of economy, I shall limit the discussion to European vampires and revenants. Actually, however, such creatures occur in folklore throughout the world, as one would expect, and scholars have remarked on the similarity of "vampires" in China to those in Europe.[6]

2. Second, in attempting to understand the folklore of death, we will study what actually happens to a body after death.

3. And finally we will put the two sets of data together—what people knew about vampires and what we now know about dead bodies—and see if they do not in fact correspond remarkably well.

II

The following, then, is a summary of information that has been reported about vampires and revenants:

1. Murder victims,[7] suicides,[8] and victims of plague[9] tend to become revenants. Indeed, revenants cause plague.[10] They were often unpopular people even before their deaths.[11]
2. The earth is disturbed at the revenant's grave, or there are holes in the earth.[12]
3. The body has not decomposed, is bloated, and is flushed and ruddy. "If, after a period of time, it remains incorrupt, exactly as it was buried, or if it appears to be swollen and black in color, having undergone some dreadful change in appearance, suspicions of vampirism are confirmed."[13] (Note that what is being said here is that, if the body has not changed, then it is that of a vampire, whereas if it has changed—then it is that of a vampire.)
4. He may suck blood from his victims, evidence of which is the bloating and the blood at the lips of his body when he is found in his grave.[14]
5. The friends and neighbors of the revenant die after his death.[15]
6. He can be heard in the grave, chewing on his extremities or on the shroud, especially in times of plague.[16]
7. He is most likely to be about in the winter.[17]
8. His body is warm to the touch.[18]
9. He has an evil smell.[19]
10. His body shows no signs of rigor mortis.[20]
11. His hair and nails have continued to grow after death.[21]
12. His principal natural enemies are wolves and dogs.[22]

13. The revenant cannot cross water[23] and must return to his grave by sunrise.[24]

14. Potential revenants may be disposed of in swamps.[25]

15. It takes some time for a person to become a revenant after death. Most accounts mention either nine days[26] or forty days.[27]

16. A revenant can be killed by the following means:
    a. Pierce him with a stake (in different areas, different types of wood are specified).[28] Sometimes a needle is specified.[29]
    b. Cut off his head.[30]
    c. Cut out his heart.[31]
    d. Burn him.[32]
    e. All of the above.[33]

17. A revenant may be kept in his grave by pinning him to his coffin or to the ground in his grave,[34] or by securing the grave with bolts or weighing down the body.[35]

18. Revenants may be controlled by the harnessing of their compulsions, as by scattering poppy or millet or mustard seeds in their graves (they must then gather them up one by one), or by putting a fishing net or a sock into the grave with them (they must unravel these, usually at the rate of one knot per year).[36]

19. Flames shoot out of the mouths of some Slavic vampires.[37]

20. When a revenant is killed in his grave, he is apt to scream or groan and to move suddenly, and fresh blood flows from his wounds.[38]

21. You may protect yourself from a revenant by means of garlic.[39]

22. Vampires and other revenants are frequently described sitting up after death, sometimes in the grave or coffin.[40]

23. Vampirism is a phenomenon of the villages, not of the cities; of the lower classes, not the upper.[41]

One misconception about the folklore of vampires might be noted here. Contrary to popular belief, the species "vampire" is not a native of Hungary, although, as we shall see, Hungary has representatives of the genus. The Western idea that vampires are Hungarian is, however, a rather old tradition itself, dating back to the eighteenth century, when some of the incidents of "vampirism" took place in what was then part of Hungary.[42] This idea was given added force when the makers of the movie version of Bram Stoker's novel chose a Hungarian (Bela Lugosi) to play the part of Count Dracula, a figure derived from Vlad the Impaler, a prince (not a count) of Wallachia (not Transylvania), who has in common with the Hungarians the fact that no tradition of vampirism at all—in folklore at least—attaches to him.[43]

III

As noted, any attempt to make sense out of the folklore of death must begin with considering the facts of death. We shall discuss these under the following categories:

1. Decomposition: characteristics
2. Coagulation and decoagulation of blood
3. Decomposition: duration

Our primary sources will be two standard texts: Glaister and Rentoul's *Medical Jurisprudence and Toxicology*, hereafter to be referred to as "Glaister," and Albert Ponsold's *Lehrbuch der gerichtlichen Medizin*. In addition, I shall cite the views of Dr. Terrence Allen, deputy medical examiner of the Los Angeles Chief Medical Examiner's Office, who answered several questions for which I could not easily get adequate answers from the literature.

1. *Decomposition: characteristics.* Glaister and Ponsold give an exhaustive account of the stages of decomposition, but only a few details are important to our discussion:

—The face of the body undergoes swelling and discoloration.
—The abdomen distends because of the gases given off by the microorganisms that cause decomposition.
—A blood-stained fluid escapes from the mouth and nostrils.
—The nails are shed and the hair is loosened, while the beard appears to grow (but does not) because the facial skin sinks back.
—The abdominal and thoracic cavities burst open.[44]

2. *Coagulation and decoagulation of blood.* The blood does in fact clot after death, but when the source of oxygen has been cut off very quickly, as when death is sudden, the blood soon liquefies again and remains in that condition.[45]

3. *Decomposition: duration.* In the popular imagination, decomposition is viewed as both a quicker and a more complete process than it necessarily is. In the movies, for example, the decay of a body is typically shown to be complete, with nothing left but bones that remain in anatomically correct relation to one another.

The reality is very different indeed. According to Glaister, "Putrefaction begins at about 50°F, and is most favored by temperatures ranging from 70° to 100°.[46] The temperature of the ground, a few feet below the surface, is normally well below this ideal temperature. European oenologists, in fact, expect the temperature of a wine *cave* to be around 54° Fahrenheit. It will be seen from this that a body will not, in fact, decompose quickly in a grave at all. "It may be accepted as a general principle," says Glaister, "that a body decomposes in air twice as quickly as in water, and eight times as rapidly as in earth."[47]

Moreover, under certain conditions bodies may not decompose at all. Where there are hot, desiccating sands or currents of dry air, mummification may take place.[48] Where there is a superabundance of moisture, little air, and few microorganisms, a process called saponification may take place, which preserves the body indefinitely.[49] The bodies of those who are poisoned tend to resist decay simply because the poison kills the microorganisms that cause decay.[50]

And finally, bodies can be preserved by immersion in acid peat bogs, as is the case with the so-called Bog People, many of whom date from the early Iron Age. According to Christian Fischer:

> The reason for the preservation of the bog bodies (and of other organisms also) lies in the special physical and biochemical makeup of the bog, above all the absence of oxygen and the high antibiotic concentration. The manner in which the body was deposited is also of great importance—for example, placed in the bog in such a way that air was rapidly excluded. It is important not only that the bog water contained a high concentration of antibiotics but also that the weather was cold enough (less than 4°C) to prevent rapid decomposition of the body). If the body had been deposited in warm weather, one can assume that the presence of anaerobic bacteria in the intestinal system would have had a destructive effect on the interior of the corpse before the liquid of the bog could penetrate the body.[51]

In numerous cases such bodies were preserved so well that, in modern times, on their discovery by peat-cutters, their discoverers have gone to the police rather than to an archaeologist, as it was apparent to them that a murder had taken place, and they believed it to have been a recent event, rather than one from two thousand years in the past.

IV

It remains for us to look once again at our information about vampires, this time with an eye to asking ourselves if we cannot now make sense of it, in light of what we know about what actually happens to bodies after death.

1. *Murder victims, suicides, and victims of plague tend to become vampires.* Note that these three categories of the dead have in common that they are inadequately buried, the first two for obvious reasons—murderers tend to give only limited attention to the niceties of funerary procedures, while

suicides ignore them completely—the last because, during epidemics, so many people died that burial was often very hasty. The Blums, in fact, quote one informant who actually defines the Greek *vrykolakas* as an unattended dead body: "These were dead people who had died alone and had no one there to take care of them."[52] And the people of Oldenburg, getting right to the heart of the matter, came to the conclusion that vampirism could occur simply because a body was not buried deeply enough.[53]

This is because what is really happening is not that bodies are turning into revenants, but that they are coming to the attention of a populace that has only a very inadequate understanding of how a body decays. The bodies that are buried well do not draw attention to themselves later, as did, for example, that of the child in the account quoted earlier, which was dug up by dogs "because of a careless burial." Moreover, as Glaister points out, people who die suddenly, in apparent good health, do not decompose as rapidly as those who die after a long illness.[54] It will be seen that murder victims and suicides are especially likely candidates for "vampirism": not only are they not buried properly, but, because of their sudden death, they do not decay quickly.

To these considerations must be added the fact that even normal burials are often not very deep, for reasons that will be immediately clear to anyone who has ever tried to dig a deep hole without the aid of a backhoe. Creighton cites a nineteenth-century account of Bedouin burials that illustrates this problem: "The deceased is buried the same day or on the morrow. They scrape out painfully with a stick and their hands in the hard-burned soil a shallow grave. I have seen their graves in the desert ruined by foul hyenas, and their winding-sheets lay half above ground."[55] Where the soil is rocky, shallow burial—or another form of disposal of the corpse—becomes inevitable.[56] And Edmund Schneeweis observes that the Serbo-Croatians generally dig their graves to a depth of one to one-and-a-fifth meters.[57] In view of this, it is no surprise that they have always had more than their share of "vampires."

2. *The earth is disturbed at the grave of the vampire.* If a body is given a shallow burial, then undergoes bloating, the surface of the earth will, in fact, be disturbed. It was once believed that one could detect the presence of a vampire in a grave by attempting to lead a horse across the grave. If the horse balked, the grave contained a vampire.[58] If there is anything at all to this story, it could be that the horse was balking simply because of the looseness of the dirt over the grave, occasioned by the swelling of the corpse, or because it could smell the corpse. The action of predators (see number 13 below) and the settling of the earth would also presumably disturb the surface of the grave.

3. *The body is intact and is bloated, and the face is flushed and ruddy.* If the

body is buried, there is nothing surprising about its preservation, since it has been protected from air, moisture, maggots, and warmth, the principal agents of decomposition. But even if it is lying in the open a body will sometimes remain intact for a long time, especially in cold weather.

The bloating occurs because the internal organs, which decompose first, produce gases that then have no escape route. Krauss remarks that the Slavs believed that "ein Vampyr wäre von dem Blute der Menschen, die er ausgesogen, ganz rot und aufgebläht"[59] ("a vampire was all red and swollen from the blood of the people whom he had sucked out"). Here we see that the description (if not the explanation) is accurate enough: a corpse does in fact bloat and change color, and the color may vary considerably, ranging from pale through red to livid and even black. I have in my files, in fact—courtesy of the Los Angeles Medical Examiner's Office—a slide of a decomposing Caucasian corpse that I originally thought to be that of a black man, so darkened was the skin.

Probably one of the things we are seeing in regard to a flushed and ruddy face is what is referred to as postmortem lividity or livor mortis.[60] When death occurs, the oxygen in the blood is used up, whereupon the blood turns dark in color, and because circulation has come to an end, the corpuscles—now dark—are caused by gravity to sink toward whatever is the low side of the body. Since the plasma and corpuscles separate (when the blood liquefies), and since the plasma is lighter than the corpuscles, both in weight and in color, it will be seen that the face of a body may be pale if it is supine, dark if it is prone. If Hans Naumann is right, then, and the "weisse Frau" is to be derived from the characteristic pallor of a (supine) dead body, then it would seem as if his "schwarzer Mann" might have a corresponding origin, except that the figure is a reflex of the appearance of a *prone* body.[61]

That this is possible is suggested by the fact that potential revenants were normally buried face down, so that they would not find their way to the surface.[62] It will be seen that such a burial practice would cause the face of the corpse to discolor—note Krauss's observation above—thereby proving to those who buried it, then dug it up again, that their original presumption was correct, and the corpse really was that of a vampire.[63]

While it is entertaining to speculate on the matter, however, it does not seem to me as if one can hope to prove or disprove Naumann's thesis: the "weisse Frau" and "schwarzer Mann" are strictly in the domain of legend. Unlike the vampires and revenants, they are not exhumed in the form of actual bodies from actual graves. Moreover, the coloration of a dead body is a more complicated matter than is suggested by this very brief analysis, because decomposition also changes the color of the skin.

4. *There is blood at the lips and nose.* Again, this is normal in a decomposing

body. It occurs because the lungs, which are rich in blood, deteriorate after death and are under pressure from the bloating of the internal organs. A blood-stained fluid is forced out through the mouth and nose.

It will be seen now why it was believed that the vampire drank blood: here you have a body that is clearly full of something that was not there when you buried it—it is bloated—and there are obvious traces of blood at the lips. Furthermore, the gravesite is disturbed (by the swelling of the body). The villagers, instead of remarking to one another that here is an obvious case of bloating, resulting from the production of gases by microorganisms and accompanied by traces of blood-stained fluid induced by pulmonary edema, conclude that the body has been climbing out of the grave to suck blood, and that that is why, when you drive a stake through it to kill it, it proves to be full of blood. (See number 20 below: liquid blood.)

Worldwide, there are some common means of dealing with his phenomenon of bloody fluid escaping from the mouth of the corpse. Frequently the mouth is tied shut, as is done with the elder Bolkonski in *War and Peace*, and in much of Europe this is considered important, since, if it were not done, the body would become a revenant.[64] I have seen Peruvian mummies (in the Ethnographic Museum in Vienna) with wool stuffed into their mouths, and it seems likely that this is done to soak up the liquid. In Australia soft plant fibers are said to be used similarly.[65]

5. *The friends and neighbors of the vampire die after his death.* I suspect that what is important here is not relationship but propinquity. We would say that they all died of the same contagious disease, which the people close to the "vampire" are more likely to catch than those distant from him. Their view is that the vampire must have climbed out of his grave—the earth above the gravesite is disturbed, after all—and attacked his friends and neighbors at night, sucking their blood. It must have happened at night because no one saw him.

6. *He can be heard in the grave, chewing on his extremities or on the shroud.* It will be seen how startled people would be to find that a sound was issuing from a grave, as we all know that the dead are unusually quiet by nature. Nevertheless, dead bodies can make a certain limited number of sounds, and there is considerable reason to believe that the sound described here is that of the body rupturing as the result of the bloating caused by decomposition. This bursting of the body, which can be quite audible, is not necessarily sudden, like that of a balloon being popped; it can be a prolonged event, like the sound of the air escaping from a tire. Some years ago, on a hike in Monterey County, I came upon the body of a Hereford calf that was undergoing this dreadful experience. The pressure of the gases was forcing what is called purge fluid to escape from the body. This was very audible, even from

some distance away—indeed, I heard the body before I saw it. The emission of purge fluid, incidentally, would seem to account for stories of bodies that are heard making noises in the grave, are dug up, and are found to be "lacerated and swimming in blood."[66] It could be, incidentally, that this belief—that the dead can be heard chewing in their graves—reinforced the age-old custom of providing the dead with food and drink.

If the swollen body is punctured, of course, the rupturing is apt to be sudden and dramatic, and this process has been unforgettably chronicled (the body in this case being that of an elephant) by John Taylor in his *African Rifles and Cartridges.*[67] Taylor describes an "immense out-rush of stinking gas and muck." That our vampires perform similarly is suggested by the practice (attested both for Poland and Yugoslavia) of covering them with a hide or cloth or dirt to prevent the blood of the vampire from spurting onto his killers, as this would kill them or cause them to go mad.[68]

The observation that the vampire chewed on his extremities seems to result from the tendency, in wet climates, of the limbs of corpses to lose their flesh while the trunk, perhaps because it is covered with clothing or a shroud, does not appear to have done so. One can observe this in pictures of Tollund Man. Also, Evans remarks that saponification is more likely to take place where the body is covered.[69] I suspect, but cannot think how I can prove it, that the eating of the shroud is simply an interpretation of the effect of capillary attraction on the shroud, as the mouth is emitting fluids. That this is plausible is suggested by the common belief that such eating can be prevented by the simple expedient of keeping the shroud away from the mouth of the revenant.[70]

There are fairly numerous accounts, incidentally, of the bursting of the body of the vampire. Trigg gives one such account:

> Among some gypsies it is believed that a simple curse is sufficient to destroy a troublesome vampire. In one Rumanian gypsy folktale, for example, a vampire is quickly destroyed simply by saying to him, "God send you burst." On hearing this the vampire was so enraged that he literally burst, leaving nothing but a large pool of blood where he had stood.[71]

Here we have two common motifs, the swelling (and subsequent bursting) of the corpse and the suspiciously liquid blood. Murgoci gives another account of a vampire that burst with anger, and Vakarelski observes that Bulgarian vampires, when killed, leave only liquid blood behind.[71]

Finally, the reader may protest that the bursting of the body, being an event of limited duration and taking place under the ground, would presumably not be easily noticed. This is of course true, which is why it is that such things tend to happen during epidemics—that is, when hundreds of people are being buried, and not very deeply at that. It could be that at such times it would be hard *not* to notice such sounds, especially since people would be frequenting the graveyard more than usual. In any case, folklore is rich in accounts of sounds being emitted from graves.[73]

7. *He is most likely to be about in the winter.* Here we must recall that a vampire is characterized, among other things, by his disinclination to decay properly. The decay of the body is of course retarded by low temperatures: note Fischer's remark (in section III above) about how only those bog bodies would have remained intact that were deposited in the bogs in cold weather.[73] In the eighteenth century, when Flückinger's famous *Visum et Repertum* was published, no one seems to have noticed that the vampires of Medvegia (see above: Stana, on p. 110) were dug up in January! That the bodies had not decayed, which was such a source of astonishment to the doctors who investigated them, can scarcely come as a surprise.

8. *His body is warm to the touch.* This could be because the process of decomposition generates heat. According to Ponsold it is actually possible for the temperature of the body to *increase* after death, as a result of decomposition.[74] In the eighteenth century the botanist Pitton de Tournefort observed first-hand the dissection of a Greek *vrykolakas* and wrote an account of it in which he describes trying, without success, to explain this phenomenon to the people of Mykonos. De Tournefort's description of the stench from the body—and he maintains that it was in fact merely a dead body—was sufficiently graphic that his account was thoroughly bowdlerized, both in English and (later) French publications. An accurate version of it can be found in Jan Perkowski's *Vampires of the Slavs.*[75]

According to Dr. Allen, such a rise in temperature would be uncommon: normally the body would be in equilibrium with the ambient temperature. He points out, however, that a body will frequently seem warm because one's hands are cold, which is why modern books on forensic investigation insist that one determine temperature with a thermometer, not by touch.

9. *He has an evil smell.* Surely no comment is necessary by now.

10. *His body shows no signs of rigor mortis.* In fact, rigor mortis is a temporary condition. Glaister discusses in detail the factors that determine its time of onset, length, etc.[76] Incidentally, Aidan Cockburn tells of a Chinese mummy, two thousand years old, of which "the tissues were still elastic and the joints could be bent."[77]

11. *His hair and nails have continued to grow after death.* Sometimes the teeth grow as well, although this is more commonly noted in fictional vampires than in those of folklore. The hair, nails, and teeth do not in fact grow after death: they merely appear to do so as the skin shrinks back. Eventually

two other events take place: the nails fall off and a phenomenon known as skin slippage occurs (both these events may be seen in the account of Arnold Paole in section I above).

A recent article in *National Geographic* shows and discusses this phenomenon of the apparent lengthening of the fingernails.[78]

12. *His principal natural enemies are wolves and dogs.* This belief clearly arises out of a misinterpretation of a common phenomenon: the tendency of wolves and dogs to dig up and eat corpses that are not either buried deeply or protected in some way, as by a casket. We have seen how, in the account quoted in section I, the child's body had been half-eaten by dogs, because of a careless burial, and Dr. Allen tells me that it is quite common for animals to dig up bodies that have been buried superficially. They may even carry off parts of the body. Many burial practices can be shown to be attempts to deal with this problem. The Bedouins, for example, have been said to have preferred to bury their dead in rocky areas to that they could cover the graves with stones to protect them from wolves. If the burial was in sand, then brush was used for this purpose.[79]

Some years ago I inadvertently conducted an informal experiment on this issue when I buried the body of a pet chicken in my yard only to discover that (to state the matter within the context of Russian mythology) Mother Earth repeatedly rejected the unclean corpse, until finally I dug a deeper hole, covered the corpse with rocks, filled the hole, and issued a stern warning to my dog. Years later I realized that I had encountered a typical problem of burial and had responded with a typical solution.

Incidentally, one of the lesser-known ecological niches is filled by white wolves that, in certain areas, occupy graveyards and keep down the vampire population.[80] This suggests that when the wolf is found digging up a corpse, and the corpse is found to be undecayed—hence a vampire—then the wolf is seen as an ally of the villagers. This could explain the extremely close relationship between werewolves and vampires: in eastern Europe, the werewolf, after his death, becomes a vampire.[81] The clustering of the three ideas—death, werewolf, and vampire—may occur simply because death produces a corpse which attracts a wolf.

And finally, when wolves or dogs dig up a body, it will be seen that they are far more likely to bring a limb to the surface than the trunk of the body, simply because it is easier to do so. This may account for the fact that the *lugat*, a type of Albanian revenant, which is otherwise invulnerable, is no match for a wolf: "he [the wolf] bites his leg off, whereupon the lugat retreats into his grave and decides to remain quiet from now on."[82] It may also account for the origin of stories in European folklore of how a hand reaches out of the grave. Sometimes the hand is that of a child that struck its mother,[83] or it is that of someone who has brought down a curse upon himself, such as a patricide, a thief, or a perjurer—a group not unlike that of our standard revenants.[84] Here too the curse may be less significant than the inadequate burial. Such stories, however, occur in various degrees of elaboration, and I do not mean to suggest that each of them had its origin in an actual event—only that the event is not as improbable as it must seem at first sight.

13. *The vampire cannot cross water and must return to his grave by sunrise.* Here we must remember three things: (a) the body is not buried very deeply; (b) it has bloated spectacularly (up to nearly twice its original size), filling up with lightweight gases, thereby increasing in buoyancy; and (c) it may well be buried in ground that has a high water table, such as a swamp. It is extremely common for bodies of murder victims to be disposed of in water with enough weight to submerge the body, but not enough to keep it submerged when putrefaction causes it to bloat. According to Dr. Allen, in fact, it is almost impossible to keep a body submerged. He provided me with a photograph of a body that had floated to the surface even though it was weighed down with a piece of cast iron that weighed 145 pounds! The body itself weighed five pounds *less* than the weight that it had carried up to the surface of the water, and we must note that we have no way of knowing what was the upper limit of the lift provided by the bloated body. We know only that it would lift at least 145 pounds (125 when one takes into account the buoyancy of the iron in water).

Here we see yet another reason why it is that the vampire emerges from his grave: his body may simply be more buoyant than its surroundings. It should also be pointed out that, according to Glaister, waterlogged soils tend to retard decomposition.[85] Thus we may imagine the following scenario: if the earth is waterlogged and the body bloats, rising to the surface, the local inhabitants, coming out in the daytime and finding the "vampire," quite intact, at the surface, might conclude that

(a) the vampire did not make it back to his grave by dawn, or

(b) a vampire cannot cross water.

Still another interpretation of the same phenomenon seems to be implied in Murgoci's report that "vampires never drown, they always float on top."[86]

That bodies of suspected revenants frequently ended up in water, incidentally, is well attested. In Russia, for example, where the revenant was believed to be responsible for droughts, the practice arose of digging up the body and throwing it into a lake or stream, apparently on the assumption that, with a sufficiency of water at its disposal, it would leave the clouds alone.[87]

14. *Potential revenants may be disposed of in swamps.* Some light may be

thrown on this practice merely by asking about alternatives. Even leaving aside the hydrotropic character of the soul, which is presented as the rationale for numerous funerary procedures,[88] the possibilities are limited by the nature of the problem. If you wish to dispose of a dangerous corpse, you will naturally choose a site that is away from human habitation. You could go into the hills, if there are hills, but it must be remembered that you are obliged to transport a corpse. Such corpses have proved to be preternaturally heavy,[89] unless of course it is merely the fear and trembling of their bearers that makes them seem so.

In any case, it seems likely that you would choose low uninhabitable ground over high uninhabitable ground, unless the death occurred on high ground. When this is the case, as it is with the revenant Glam in *Grettir's Saga*, the body is likely to be covered with rocks or brush to keep it in place.[90] For one thing, there may not be a deep enough soil for burial; for another, it is apt to be rocky soil, which is difficult to dig in.

When a body is disposed of in a swamp, on the other hand, the problems are different. While the depth of soil is likely to be adequate, the high water table might make it impossible to dig a deep hole. And once you know that the body is apt to become a revenant (i.e., bloat and come to the surface), you will be forced to come up with means of preventing this from happening. Some of the more obvious means would be puncturing the corpse (to release the gases), weighing it down with rocks, and holding it down with a latticework of branches.

Fortunately, we are not reduced to mere speculation on this point, for close to two thousand bodies—quite well preserved in many cases—have been dug out of bogs in Europe, many of them held down in just the ways I have described.[91] Some of these were clearly the "bad dead" of their age, people who had died "before their time" and so refused to decompose properly.

15. *Length of time for the transformation to take place.* Both numbers—nine and forty—are simply examples of mythic time, which occurs in standard quantities. One of the German terms for a revenant is *Neuntöter* (nine-killer),[92] and in Swabia it was said that a drowning victim remains underwater for nine days.[93] In the Bible, such things as days in the wilderness and the duration of floods occur in units of forty, and the number has made its way into vampire lore because in the Eastern Orthodox church it was believed that, after death, the soul remains on earth for that length of time. As for the *actual* time required for a body to "become a vampire" (which is to say, become swollen and discolored), that is simply incalculable: there are too many variables.

16. *To kill a vampire, you must pierce him with a stake.* The staking of a

vampire makes a certain kind of sense when you consider that what is being "killed" is a bloated corpse. The most direct way of reducing it to what it was is to puncture it.

This puncturing of the body is common even before burial, as a prophylactic measure: "should the devil inflate [the skin of the body], then the air would escape."[94] Other examples of such puncturing are common in the literature.[95]

Frequently sharp objects have been buried with the body in order to puncture it if it should bloat. Richard Beitl, for example, describes sickles being buried with bodies in Transylvania "allegedly in order to prevent the swelling of the body,"[96] and Norbert Reiter says that the Slavs buried bodies with a sickle around the neck of the corpse, "so that the vampire would cut his throat if he left the grave."[97] Perkowski quotes a Romanian informant who says that the sickle must be driven into the corpse's heart,[98] and according to Csiszár, the Hungarians attempted to prevent the bloating of the body by putting iron objects on it: "There are also evil souls of a sort that spoil the corpse. When they creep in, then the stomach bloats and the dead person acquires a smell. [To deal with this] one puts iron implements on the stomach of the dead person."[99] (Note that the stench and bloating are regarded here as something unnatural.) Balassa and Ortutay give a similar report for Hungary, saying that a sickle "is laid on the body to prevent bloating" and adding that such sickles have been found in graves dating back to the ninth century.[100] Tekla Dömötör also remarks that—in Hungary—people laid either a sickle or some other metal object on the dead person "so that the corpse would not bloat," and says that "in reality this occurred so that the dead person would not come back as a revenant."[101] It will be seen that both interpretations are correct, since it is the bloating—and consequent disturbance of the burial site—that is interpreted as the dead person trying to get out of his grave. The sickle is expected to prevent this by puncturing the body. This function of the sickle, incidentally, might cause one to puzzle over a possible relationship to the traditional conception of death as a skeleton carrying a scythe or sickle.[102] Sickles are in fact often found in the presence of skeletons because of the above-mentioned burial practice, and both Burkhart and Schneeweis suggest that one of the Slavic words for vampire (*prikosac*) may be derived from a word for scythe.[103]

In addition to sickles, Schneeweis mentions various iron implements—knives and swords and axes—being used thus. In his opinion, such implements may have been intended "to prevent the return of the soul into the body."[104] Frequently the deterrent effect of these objects has been attributed to the magical quality of iron,[105] and while it is beyond the scope of this article to deal with the subject adequately, I cannot help wondering if the weight and sharpness of iron were not originally the significant characteristics (weight for holding the body down, sharpness for puncturing it), especially since there are common reports of other, nonferrous implements being used in this way. Often, for example, we are told of sharpened stakes that have been driven into graves, so that the body might be punctured if it tries to come to the surface,[106] and Krauss describes both knives and hawthorn stakes being used in this way in Serbia.[107]

Also, in addition to those cases where the sharp object is clearly meant to puncture the body, there are others where its function has apparently been reanalyzed, as when Strackerjan reports that, in Oldenburg, the needle with which the shroud was sewn had to be laid into the coffin—not just any needle would do.[108]

And finally it must be noted that such puncturing of the dead body is as common now as in the past, and for some of the same reasons. In Guyana, for example, after the Jonestown massacre, a doctor was sent in to puncture the bloating corpses so they would not burst.[109] And the practice of embalming, which in the United States dates from the time of the Civil War (because bodies were being brought home by train), may be viewed as a kind of preemptive strike against "vampirism," in that it is intended to prevent all those messy events that are brought about by decomposition.

Embalming, incidentally, might seem to imply a radically different conception of the afterlife than does cremation, since the one method preserves the body while the other destroys it. Looked at another way, however, the two methods have the same function: both render the body inert—unable to develop into something ugly and threatening. Puncturing the body, on the other hand, while it would have an immediate and dramatic effect on the condition of the body, would not end the process of change, which may explain why, so often in the history of vampirism, we find that bodies were dug up repeatedly and each time "killed" in some new way, until eventually—as with de Tournefort's *vrykolakas*—they were cremated.

As for cremation, it proves to be a rather complicated subject, an understanding of which requires some consideration of the physics of combustion. I discuss it in detail in *Vampires, Burial, and Death*.

17. *Keeping the revenant in his grave by pinning the body or weighing it down.* Here again we are seeing methods of dealing with a purely mechanical problem: the tendency of the corpse, having bloated, to disturb the surface of the earth, or even to pop up to the surface if the ground is waterlogged. I have before me a photograph (from the second page of the *Los Angeles Times*, dated 11/1/1985) that shows a coffin floating in a flooded graveyard, in Louisiana. According to the caption, several coffins floated up out of the ground in the floodwaters left by Hurricane Juan. This particular one was

tied to a tree by someone who believed, apparently, that a dead body could not only leave the grave under the right conditions, but could not even be counted on to remain in its vicinity. Sealed coffins, like bloated bodies, are remarkably buoyant.

It must come as no surprise to find that we have large quantities of archaeological evidence demonstrating that bodies were in fact frequently pinned or weighed down. Ludwig Pauli describes such burials in detail in his book on Celtic beliefs, and Edmund Schneeweis observes that the gravestone originally was intended to keep the dead person in his grave.[110] Burkhart, incidentally, argues that, of all the methods of laying the dead, the oldest is probably that of *mechanically* holding the body in place.[111] Clearly the reason why this is so is that bodies tend not to stay put, both because of their buoyancy and because they are attacked by animals.

18. *Controlling revenants by means of their compulsions.* The accounts of revenants being obliged to unravel nets appears to be a reinterpretation of a common practice of keeping bodies in their graves by means of nets. Erhard Eylmann, in his *Die Eingeborenen der Kolonie Südaustralien,* gives an account of aborigines wrapping the body in a net "so that the dead person would not leave the grave and do harm to the living."[112] It may be, then, that the original purpose of this practice was forgotten—the net was intended as a mechanical restraint—and a reinterpretation came into being, according to which the net was there to give the revenant something to do. The use of the various grains may have been an extension of the idea of occupying the revenant.

Even in modern times, incidentally, the net is sometimes mentioned merely as a means of keeping a body from becoming a revenant, with no reference to his practice of unravelling the net.[113]

19. *Flames come out of the mouth of the vampire.* As implausible as this seems at first sight, it is actually likely that something of this sort would, in fact, happen when a "vampire" is cremated. This is because the body of the supposed vampire is swollen to bursting with the gases of decomposition, and these gases (mostly methane) are highly flammable. Since the gases are forming interstitially within the tissues as well as within the thoracic and abdominal body cavities, the staking of the body, while it will release some of the gas, will not release all of it by any means—especially when you consider that, throughout much of Slavic territory, the stake had to be driven in at one blow. A second blow revived the vampire.[114] This is perhaps one of the reasons why the last-resort method of disposing of a vampire is always that of burning him.

While I had no doubt that flames would shoot from the body of a burning "vampire," I thought it best to get the opinion of an authority and asked Dr.

Allen about this theory. He offered me a more striking confirmation than I could have hoped for, saying that he had a colleague who had acquired the habit of dramatizing the presence of gases in a dead body by touching them off with a match when he made his first incision. The resulting flame, according to Dr. Allen, shot between one and two feet in the air.

20. *When a vampire is killed in his grave, he is apt to scream or groan and to move suddenly, and fresh blood flows from his wounds.* It must be remembered that what is being "killed" is a bloated corpse. An attempt to drive a stake into it will force air past the glottis, which is still intact, thereby creating a very lifelike groan. Such sounds (Pensold refers to this as the *"Totenlaut"*) are common even when a body is moved, let alone when the thoracic cavity is being violently compressed, as would happen in the staking of a vampire. Among medical personnel the reaction to such sounds is likely to be one of humor, as when an attendant, on hearing a body groan, said to Dr. Allen, "Don't *hurt* him!" I have also heard an account—and here we may have entered the domain of legend—of a bystander who was asked to help carry a body and, when it emitted a sound, dropped his end, saying, "If he can talk, he can walk."

It takes little imagination to conceive of how such sounds would affect the people engaged in attempting to kill a vampire. Incidentally, we have other, more pedestrian accounts in which the sounds are not interpreted as a human scream or groan at all. Wuttke, for example, cites an account in which the sound is compared to the squeal of a pig.[115] And Aribert Schroeder quotes the following account from eighteenth-century Serbia:

> The investigation of the doctors determined that the four questionable corpses, which had lain in the earth for twenty days, had remained incorrupt. Out of fear that vampires or snakes might take them over, the inhabitants of the village beheaded the corpses, drove a stake into the man's heart, whereupon they heard a loud cracking sound, and burned all the corpses.[116]

Several things about this account are particularly interesting. First of all, note that, as in many accounts of revenants, we are told that authorities have been brought in, people who might be expected to know about dead bodies. Second, note how little these authorities actually did know, as is suggested by their astonishment at finding that the bodies had not decayed, underground, in a period of twenty days. Man's final decay had long since been a literary motif, but not, it seems, a scientific study.

Finally, note the "overkill." The body is beheaded, a stake is driven into the heart, and the corpse is then burned. The account itself is very straightforward, but the rather extreme efforts to kill the revenant hint at the climate of fear in which the events took place. The hysteria over vampirism can be seen in Köhler's accounts of conflicts, in the eighteenth century, between citizens and the authorities over whether a suicide (i.e., a potential revenant) was to be buried in the churchyard—conflicts that were often resolved by military force.[117]

As for the movement of the body, clearly this occurs because the attempts to drive a stake through it causes a redistribution of the gases of decomposition—much like what happens when you push down on a balloon. I have conducted no experiments here, for all the obvious reasons.

The blood, of course, is not really fresh at all (as de Tournefort points out, by the way): it is the fact that it is *liquid* that shocks the vampire-killers. We have seen that this is a normal circumstance under certain conditions.[118] Here again one needs little imagination to conceive of the effect a bleeding corpse would have on people who already suspect that it is still alive.

21. *Garlic will protect one from a revenant.* I find myself wondering if garlic was originally a specific against the stench from the dead body, on the principle that one strong smell may be opposed with another. De Tournefort, as we have seen, describes the Greeks using frankincense to mask the odor, and de Groot, in *The Religious System of China*, makes the following remarks:

> It is a general conviction that any one who calls at a mortuary house incurs a kind of pollution, especially so if death has been untimely or caused by disease. Some condolers therefore wisely hide a few garlic roots under their garments, convinced that the strong smell will prevent the influences of death from clutching to their bodies; on leaving the house they throw the roots away in the street.[119]

Note that in China, as in Europe, the garlic is held to be useful when one is in the presence of a dead body, but in de Groot's account, it is specifically the strong smell that is held to be the active agent. This passage, by the way, clearly implies an awareness of contagion. One sees this also in accounts of how everything associated with the dead person—the utensils he ate with, the water used to wash him, the straw he lay on—must be thrown out, burned, or buried with him. As de Groot's text suggests, such "pollution" (i.e., contagion) is most to be feared when death is "untimely or caused by disease." The "vampires" illustrate this principle well: the fear of them was simply the fear of death, brought about by agents that were known to be contagious, while the actual mechanism of contagion was not understood. (Since we do understand the mechanism, we are not afraid to "catch our death" from a victim of stroke; but our recent experience with the AIDS epidemic has had some similarities to the vampire scares of the past.)

22. *Vampires and other revenants are frequently described sitting up after death, sometimes in the grave or coffin.* Such stories are so persistent, and they occur over such a wide area,[120] that I finally began to wonder if there was something to them, although I could not think of a satisfactory explanation. The evidence remains contradictory: Dr. Allen, for examples, while himself doubting that such is possible, nonetheless tells me that a colleague of his claims to have seen a movie of this very phenomenon.

The Blums quote a classic instance of such real or supposed movement of the body:

> On my mother's island a man was very ill and became unconscious. The people thought that he had died, and so they prepared the funeral. After the ceremony there was a movement in the coffin and slowly the man began to rise. Well, the people there believed he was becoming a vrikolax; in their fright they threw everything they could find at him—sticks, rocks, anything. In that way they did kill him when before he had only been in a coma.[121]

The incident may have happened this way. But if we suppose that the body can in fact "sit up like a Turk" after death, as it is frequently described doing,[122] then we would have a plausible explanation for why it is that such bodies—as in the above account—always seem to end up being dead after all.

The Greeks make distinctions between different types of revenants, and the distinctions seem always to be related to demonstrable physical characteristics of dead bodies. This can be seen most easily in the etymologies of the terms for the revenant (except for *vrykolakas*, which is clearly borrowed from the Slavic):[123]

1. τυμπανιαῖος: "drumlike," because of the taut, distended skin, resulting from the bloating of the body.
2. ἄλυτος: "unloosed," which is to say, incorrupt. The body has not decayed.
3. σαρκωμένος: "one who has put on flesh," that is, bloated.
4. ἀναικαθούμενος: "one who sits up" in his grave.
5. καταχανᾶς: Lawson derives this last from the Greek word for *gape*. I may be more persuaded of this etymology than Lawson was, as I can attest, by grace of the L.A. Medical Examiner's Office, that the gape of a decomposing body (brought about by the swelling) is a particularly striking and unforgettable sight. This is one of the reasons why, even now in Greece, the mouth is tied shut.[124]

In addition, he gives three terms—ἀνάρραχο, λάμπασμα, λάμπαστρο—that he finds unintelligible. The second two would seem to be derived from the root λαμπ-, from which our *lamp* is derived and should mean, respectively, "that which is lit up" (abstract noun) and "that which lights up" (agent form). Lawson would seem to be ignoring the obvious etymologies because they do not appear to make sense—unless, that is, one notices that such terms all seem to be related to the condition of a dead body. Then one need only look for a mechanism whereby a dead body can give off light, and W. E. D. Evans, in *The Chemistry of Death*, describes such a mechanism:

> It was observed in antiquity that dead fish and meat could appear to glow with a pale light, and the wonder and fear that this must have brought to primitive man observing the phenomenon in the darkness of night or the gloom of a cave can well be imagined. Old stories, often re-told, linger on in oral tradition telling of the glowing of exhumed human remains. . . .
>
> These fearful concomitants to the exposure of entombed or buried bodies seem to have become unfashionable in recent years; perhaps modern times have made mankind too familiar with death, and by scientific pathways have come sophistication and disenchantment. At all events, the luminescence of remains is now to be explained by natural, rather than supernatural history.
>
> Luminescence of dead animal remains is most commonly due to contamination by luminous bacteria such as Photobacterium fischeri, the light emanating from the organisms and not from reactions in the decomposing tissues. The organisms swarm over the remains and give light, particularly while the temperature is in the range of 15° to 30°C.[125]

The first word, ἀνάρραχο, would seem to be derived from ἀνά plus ῥαχίς ("up" plus "spine"), which becomes plausible when you consider that revenants are commonly reported sitting up after death and that Lawson has already given one derivation that suggests this habit (number 4 in the list of Greek terms above).

If this is so, then we are confronted with the following conclusion: most native Greek words for the revenant refer to demonstrable physical characteristics of a dead body. It seems most reasonable to conclude that the two concerned with sitting up do so too.

The matter is not easily resolved, but there is certainly no doubt that some movement is possible after death. Rigor mortis causes all the muscles to stiffen, and because the flexor muscles of the arms are stronger than the extensors, the arms may move slightly across the chest. Moreover, when rigor mortis ends, as it must, gravity may again cause some movement, which could account in part for the extremely common stories of bodies being found in a changed position.[126] (The bloating and bursting of the body would also change its position, and such changes presumably contribute to the idea that the body has left the grave.)[127] Cremation causes considerable movement of the corpse.[128] And movement would certainly occur—seemingly at the volition of the corpse—if one were to try to adjust the limbs of the body while it is in rigor mortis: they would spring back to their original position.

Finally, though, I must acknowledge that I have not found sufficiently clear evidence here to persuade me that I have located the source of this tradition. It may be that the phenomena are brought about by funerary or burial practices that I am not taking into account.

23. *Vampirism and class.* It is only in fiction that a vampire is likely to be from the upper classes—Count Dracula, for example. Actually, rich and important people tend to be buried properly, and their families have sufficient influence to prevent them from being dug up again. Consequently, the classic vampire—in folklore, at least—far from being the urbane count that the movies have introduced us to, tends to be a peasant with a drinking problem.[129]

V

It has been remarked that vampire stories occur only in areas where the dead are buried, not where they are cremated,[130] and the reasons for this will now be obvious. It will also be clear why it is that such stories are by no means an isolated phenomenon but occur worldwide. They tend to correlate with the practice of exhumation, as in Greece, Bulgaria, and Serbo-Croatia, and the local variations are based on such things as whether the blood at the lips, combined with the bloating, is taken to be evidence of blood-sucking. Since the phenomena being observed are quite diverse, one would also expect to encounter in folklore creatures that are seemingly quite different from the revenant but are related by their origin: carrion-eating ghouls, for example, like those of India,[131] which serve to account for the process of decomposition, except that here the body in the grave is viewed as the victim rather than the monster. It should be an easy matter, in fact, to predict reflexes of the phenomena of decomposition; we might look for creatures that swell up, change color, drip blood, refuse to die, burst (as do trolls, for example), and give off a noisome stench.

It should also be profitable to consider the possibility that certain changes in funerary customs—the cremations of the Urnfield Culture, for example—came about not because of changes in religious beliefs, but because there was an "epidemic of vampirism." Such epidemics would tend to occur when people were forced to look closely at the decomposition of corpses, as in times of plague. Because of this, a reconsideration of the history of funerary practices would seem to be in order, approaching the question from the point of view that it is in fact very difficult to dispose of a body in such a way as to keep it disposed of, and that our funerary practices probably reflect ever-renewed attempts to deal with this problem.

And finally, after having gone to such lengths to argue that the lore of the vampire arose out of misconceptions concerning the nature of decomposition, I must concede that there are well-attested accounts of actual dead bodies being involved in the drinking of human blood. It is not as people believed, however, for by a peculiarly gruesome and chilling irony, the blood of the supposed vampire was regarded as a specific against vampirism and was baked in bread,[132] painted on the potential victim,[133] or even drunk.[134] Blood was actually consumed, in other words, but by the "victims," and it was the blood of the supposed vampire.

The vampires themselves, it would appear, were and are dead.

Notes

I would like to thank Professor Felix Oinas for his valuable comments on two versions of the manuscript of this article. The refereeing process was most helpful.

1. Jean-Jacques Rousseau, *Lettre à l'Archevèque de Paris*, quoted in Voyslav M. Yovanovitch, *"La Guzla" de Prosper Mérimée* (Paris, 1911), 316. All translations are my own unless otherwise indicated.

2. From the *Mercure galant*, 1693–4, quoted in Stefan Hock, *Die Vampyrsagen und ihre Verwertung in der deutschen Litteratur* (Berlin, 1900), 33–34.

3. Johannes Flückinger's account quoted in Georg Conrad Horst, *Zauberbibliothek*, (Mainz, 1821), vol. 1, 256.

4. Ibid., 257–258.

5. Basil Copper, *The Vampire in Legend, Fact, and Art* (Secaucus, N.J.: Citadel Press, 1974), 44.

6. See, for example, G. Willoughby-Meade, *Chinese Ghouls and Goblins* (New York, 1928), 224.

7. L. Strackerjan, *Aberglaube und Sagen aus dem Herzogthum Oldenburg* (Oldenburg, 1867), vol. 1, 154. See also Christo Vakarelski, *Bulgarische Volkskunde* (Berlin: Walter de Gruyter and Co., 1968), 30.

8. W. R. S. Ralston, *The Songs of the Russian People* (London, 1872), 409. See also J. C. Lawson, *Modern Greek Folklore and Ancient Greek Religion* (Cambridge, England, 1910), 408; Vakarelski, *Bulgarische Volkskunde*, 30.

9. Adolf Wuttke, *Der deutsche Volksaberglaube der Gegenwart* (Hamburg, 1860), 222.

10. Ibid.

11. Rossell Hope Robbins, *The Encyclopedia of Witchcraft and Demonology* (New York: Crown Publishers, 1959), p. 523. See also, Friedrich Krauss, *Slavische Volksforschungen* (Leipzig, 1908), p. 125; Lauri Honko "Finnish Mythology," in *Wörterbuch der Mythologie* (Stuttgart, 1973), vol. 2, 352.

Vampirism can also come about by a variety of other means, as when an animal jumps over the corpse. Space does not permit a complete accounting here, but I discuss these in detail in *Vampires, Burial, and Death: Folklore and Reality* (New Haven: Yale University Press, 1988).

12. Raymond McNally and Radu Florescu, *In Search of Dracula* (New York: Galahad Books, 1972), 148. See also Elwood B. Trigg, *Gypsy Demons and Divinities: The Magic and Religion of the Gypsies* (Secaucus, N.J.: Citadel Press, 1973), 155; W. Mannhardt, "Über Vampyrismus," *Zeitschrift für deutsche Mythologie und Sittenkunde* 4 (1859): 259–282; R. P. Vukanovic, "The Vampire," *Journal of the Gypsy Lore Society* 37 (1958): 30; Krauss, *Slavische Volksforschungen*, p. 130; Vakarelski, *Bulgarische Volkskunde*, p. 239. Vukanovic's article was published in installments; I shall cite it by the year.

13. Trigg, *Gypsy Demons*, p. 157. See also D. Demetracopoulou Lee, "Greek Accounts of the Vrykolakas," *Journal of American Folklore* 55 (1942): 131; Joseph Klapper, *Schlesische Volkskunde auf kulturgeschichtlicher Grundlage* (Breslau, 1925), 213; Fr. von Hellwald, *Die Welt der Slawen* (Berlin, 1890), p. 369; Mannhardt, "Über Vampyrismus," 271; Vukanovic, "The Vampire" (1958), 22, 25; Hock, *Die Vampyrsagen*, 29.

14. Hock, *Die Vampyrsagen*, p. 3. See also Ernst Bargheer, *Eingeweide, Lebens- und Seelenkräfte des Leibesinneren im deutschen Glauben und Brauch* (Leipzig, 1931), 82; Mannhardt, "Über Vampyrismus," 264.

15. Montague Summers, *The Vampire, His Kith and Kin* (New York: University Books, 1960), 161. See also Bernhardt Schmidt, *Das Volksleben der Neugriechen und das hellenische Alterthum* (Leipzig, 1871), vol. 1, 164; Juljan Jaworskij, "Südrussische Vampyre," *Zeitschrift des Vereins für Volkskunde* 8 (1898): 331; Lawson, *Modern Greek Folklore*, 387.

16. Hock, *Die Vampyrsagen*, 31–32, 43–44. See also Johann Heinrich Zedler, *Grosses vollständiges Universal-Lexikon* (Graz: Akademische Druck- und Verlagsanstalt, 1962), vol. 44, 664. This is a reprint of an edition published in 1745. See also Mannhardt, "Über Vampyrismus," 269, 274; Bargheer, *Eingeweide*, 78–79, 85.

17. Dagmar Burkhart, "Vampirglaube und Vampirsage auf dem Balkan," in *Beiträge zur Südosteuropa-Forschung* (Munich, 1966), 219. See also Krauss, *Slavische Volksforschungen*, 125.

18. Summers, *The Vampire*, 179. See also Mannhardt, "Über Vampyrismus," 275.

19. Ibid. See also Edmund Schneeweis, *Serbokroatische Volkskunde* (Berlin: de Gruyter and Co., 1961), p. 9; Vukanovic, "The Vampire," (1960), 47; Lawson, *Modern Greek Folklore*, p. 367.

20. Pitton de Tournefort, *Relation d'un voyage du Levant* (Paris, 1717), vol. 1, 133. See also Hanns Bächtold-Stäubli, *Handwörterbuch des deutschen Aberglaubens* (Berlin: de Gruyter, 1934–1935), vol. 6, 818; Richard Beitl, *Deutsches Volkstum der Gegenwart* (Berlin, 1933), 32; Bargheer, *Eingeweide*, 84.

21. Johann Heinrich Zopf, *Dissertatio de vampyris serviensibus* (Duisburg, 1733), 7. See also Maximilian Lambertz in *Wörterbuch der Mythologie*, 490; Schneeweis, *Serbokroatische Volkskunde*, 9.

22. Rade Uhlik, "Serbo-Bosnian Gypsy Folktales, N. 4," *Journal of the Gypsy Lore Society* 19 (1940): 49. See also Vakarelski, *Bulgarische Volkskunde*, 239; Schneeweis, *Serbokroatische Volkskunde*, 10; Lee, "Greek Accounts," 128; Vukanovic, "The Vampire" (1960), 49; Trigg, *Gypsy Demons*, 154–155.

23. Schneeweis, *Serbokroatische Volkskunde*, 9; Vukanovic, "The Vampire" (1958), 23; Schmidt, *Das Volksleben*, 168; Trigg, *Gypsy Demons*, 154; Hock, *Die Vampyrsagen*, 27; Lawson, *Modern Greek Folklore*, 368.

24. Burkhart, "Vampirglaube," 219; McNally and Florescu, *In Search of Dracula*, 150.

25. Julius von Negelein, *Weltgeschichte des Aberglaubens*, vol. 2: *Haupttypen des Aberglaubens* (Berlin and Leipzig: de Gruyter, 1935), 124. See also Jan Machal, *Slavic Mythology* (Boston, 1918), 231; Dmitrij Zelenin, *Russische (ostslavische) Volkskunde* (Berlin and Leipzig: de Gruyter, 1927), 328; Paul Geiger, "Die Behandlung der Selbstmörder im deutschen Brauch," *Archiv für Volkskunde* 26 (1926): 158.

26. Hock, *Die Vampyrsagen*, 24, 36; Hellwald, *Die Welt der Slawen*, 368.

27. Friedrich Krauss, "Vampyre im südslawischen Volksglauben," *Globus, Illustrierte Zeitschrift für Länder und Volkskunde* 61 (1892): 326. See also Hellwald, *Die Welt der Slawen*, 368.

28. Agnes Murgoci, "The Vampire in Roumania," *Folkore* 37 (1926): 328 [ed. note: see also herein, pp. 12–34]. Also Veselin Čajkanović, "The Killing of a Vampire," *Folklore Forum* 7, 4 (1974): 261; trans. Marilyn Sjoberg, originally published in Belgrade in 1923 [ed. note: see also herein, pp. 72–84]. See Adelbert Kuhn, *Sagen, Gebräuche und Märchen aus Westfalen* (Leipzig, 1859), 175, for early accounts of staking in Saxo Grammaticus and Burchard of Worms.

29. Trigg, *Gypsy Demons*, 152. See also G. F. Abbott, *Macedonian Folklore* (Cambridge, 1903), 219.

30. Wuttke, *Der deutsche Volksaberglaube*, 221. See also J. D. H. Temme, *Die Volkssagen von Pommern und Rügen* (Hildesheim: Georg Olms Verlag, 1976), 308; originally published in Berlin in 1840. And Paul Drechsler, *Sitte, Brauch und Volksglaube in Schlesien* (Leipzig, 1903), 317; Klapper, *Schlesische Volkskunde*, 212; Franz Tetzner, *Die Slawen in Deutschland* (Braunschweig, 1902), 462. Archaeologically, such beheading is well attested. See, for example, Ludwig Pauli, *Keltischer Volksglaube* (Munich: C. H. Beck'sche Verlagsbuchhandlung, 1975), 145–146.

31. Augustine Calmet, *The Phantom World*, ed. Henry Christmas (London, 1850), vol. 2, 38; This is a translation of his *Dissertations sur les apparitions des anges, des démons et des esprits, et sur les revenants et les vampires* (Paris, 1746). See also Hock, *Die*

Vampyrsagen, 42; Bargheer, *Eigenweide*, 37; Burkhart, "Vampirglaube," 222; Lawson, *Modern Greek Folkore*, 412.

32. August Löwenstimm, *Aberglaube und Strafrecht* (Berlin, 1897), 103. See also Christopher Frayling, *The Vampyre, A Bedside Companion* (New York: Scribner, 1978), 30; Robert Pashley, *Travels in Crete* (London, 1837), vol. 2, 201; Krauss, *Slavische Volksforschungen*, 133, 135; Trigg, *Gypsy Demons*, 157; Čajkanović, "The Killing of a Vampire," 261.

33. See Aribert Schroeder's account following. See also Arthur and Albert Schott, *Walachische Maerchen* (Stuttgart and Tübingen, 1845), 297; Edm. Veckenstedt, *Wendische Sagen, Märchen und abergläubische Geschichten* (Graz, 1880), 354–355; and Harry A. Senn, *Were-Wolf and Vampire in Romania*, East European Monographs (Boulder, 1982), 67, for a summary of methods of killing the vampire.

34. Summers, *The Vampire*, 202; Schmidt, *Das Volksleben*, 167; Bächtold-Stäubli, *Handwörterbuch*, 819; Jaworskij, "Südrussische Vampyre," 331; Iván Balassa and Gyula Ortutay, *Ungarische Volkskunde* (Budapest: Corvina Kiadó, and Munich: C. H. Beck, 1982), 726.

35. Hock, *Die Vampyrsagen*, 28.

36. Dieter Sturm and Klaus Völker, *Von denen Vampiren oder Menschensaugern* (Carl Hanser Verlag, 1968), 524; Arthur Jellinek, "Zur Vampyrsage," *Zeitschrift des Vereins für Volkskunde* 14 (1904): 324; Bargheer, *Eigenweide*, 86; Mannhardt, "Über Vampyrismus," 260, 262, 265–265; Bächtold-Stäubli, *Handwörterbuch*, 819; Hellwald, *Die Welt der Slawen*, 367, 370; Abbott, *Macedonian Folklore*, 219–220; Beitl, *Deutsches Volkstum*, 187; Wuttke, *Der deutsche Volksaberglaube*, 222; Trigg, *Gypsy Demons*, 153; Hock, *Die Vampyrsagen*, 28; Murgoci, "The Vampire in Roumania," 341.

37. Schneeweis, *Serbokroatische Volkskunde*, 9. See also Norbert Reiter (Slavic) in *Wörterbuch der Mythologie*, 201; Vukanovic "The Vampire" (1958), 23.

38. Mannhardt, "Über Vampyrismus," 264, 268; Zedler, *Universal-Lexikon*, vol. 46, 478; Vukanovic "The Vampire" (1960), 47; Drechsler, *Sitte, Brauch*, 318; Bächtold-Stäubli, *Handwörterbuch*, 818–819; Hock, *Die Vampyrsagen*, 31–33; Trigg, *Gypsy Demons*, 157; Edward Tylor, *Primitive Culture* (London, 1871), vol. 2, 176; Joseph von Görres, *Die Christliche Mystik* (Regensburg, 1840), 282.

39. Murgoci, "The Vampire in Roumania," 334; Vakarelski, *Bulgarische Volkskunde*, 305.

40. Hellwald, *Die Welt der Slawen*, 371–372; Abbott, *Macedonian Folklore*, 219; Trigg, *Gypsy Demons*, 142, 149; Bächtold-Stäubli, *Handwörterbuch*, 818.

41. Voltaire made a remark to the effect that vampires are not to be found in London or Paris (quoted in Sturm and Völker, *Von denen Vampiren* 484).

42. Tekla Dömötör, *Volkslaube und Aberglaube der Ungarn* (Corvina Kiadó, 1981), 122. Krauss points out that Medvegia, which Arnold Paole made famous, was actually in Serbia under Hungarian rule (Krauss, *Slavische Volksforschungen*, 131). See also Bargheer, *Eigenweide*, 81 and Mannhardt, "Über Vampyrismus," 273.

43. Grigore Nandris, "The Historical Dracula: The Theme of His Legend in the Western and in the Eastern Literatures of Europe," *Comparative Literature Studies* 3,

4 (1966): 369. See also Senn, *Were-Wolf*, 41ff. I am indebted to Dr. Senn for his helpful clarification (in conversation) of some details relating to the history and folklore of Romania, especially in the matter of Dracula. Incidentally, there is some question as to which of several Vlads in Romanian history was Stoker's model.

44. John Glaister and Edgar Rentoul, *Medical Jurisprudence and Toxicology* (Edinburgh and London: E. and S. Livingstone, 1966), 117. See also Albert Ponsold, *Lehrbuch der gerichtlichen Medizin* (Stuttgart: Georg Thieme Verlag, 1957), 290–296.

45. Glaister and Rentoul, *Medical Jurisprudence*, 115–116; Ponsold, *Lehrbuch*, 292–293.

46. Glaister and Rentoul, *Medical Jurisprudence*, 120.

47. Ibid.

48. Aidan and Eve Cockburn, *Mummies, Disease and Ancient Cultures* (Cambridge University Press, 1982), 1 (abridged paperback edition).

49. Glaister and Rentoul, *Medical Jurisprudence*, 124.

50. Ibid., 121.

51. Christian Fischer, "Bog Bodies of Denmark," trans. Kirstine Thomsen, in Cockburn, *Mummies*, 177. See also P. V. Glob, *The Bog People*, trans. from the Danish by Rupert Bruce-Mitford (New York: Ballantine, 1973); and Alfred Dieck, *Die europäischen Moorleichenfunde: Göttinger Schriften zur Vor- und Frühgeschichte*, ed. Herbert Jankuhn (Neumünster: Karl Wacholtz Verlag, 1965).

52. Richard and Eva Blum, *The Dangerous Hour: The Lore of Crisis and Mystery in Rural Greece* (New York: Charles Scribner's 1970), 71. Hock (*Die Vampyrsagen*, 23) also remarks that people who are not buried at all tend to become vampires. See also E. H. Meyer, *Mythologie der Germanen* (Strassburg, 1903), 94.

53. Strackerjan, *Aberglaube*, 154.

54. Glaister, and Rentoul, *Medical Jurisprudence*, 121.

55. Charles Creighton, *A History of Epidemics in Britain* (Cambridge, 1891), vol. 2, 165.

56. Creighton, *History*, vol. 2, 167.

57. Schneeweis, *Serbokroatische Volkskunde*, 90. One would expect to find a correlation between "vampirism" and the custom of exhumation. This seems to be present in the Balkans. The duration of the first burial may be from three to eighteen years, after which the body is dug up again: "If the body has still not disintegrated, then it is believed that a curse weighs on it" (Schneeweis, *Serbokroatische Volkskunde*, 103). Note that this custom implies that bodies may not disintegrate even after years in the grave, let alone days or months.

For a discussion of the practice of exhumation in Greece, see Loring M. Danforth, *The Death Rituals of Rural Greece* (Princeton, N.J.: Princeton University Press, 1982). Danforth describes inhumations taking place after five years, in the area where he did his research. Lawson (*Modern Greek Folklore*, 372) and the Blums (*The Dangerous Hour*, 75) mention a time span of three years. See Vakarelski (*Bulgarische Volkskunde*, 309) for an account of exhumations in Bulgaria.

58. Murgoci, "The Vampire in Roumania," 327.

59. Krauss, "Vampyre," 327.

60. Glaister and Rentoul, *Medical Jurisprudence*, 111–112.

61. Hans Naumann, *Primitive Gemeinschaftskultur: Beiträge zur Volkskunde und Mythologie* (Jena, 1921), 49. Also Vukanovic "The Vampire" (1958), 23: "... it is believed that the body which is to become a vampire turns black before burial."

62. Pauli, *Keltischer Volksglaube*, 175. See also Geiger, "Die Behandlung," 159; Reiter, *Wörterbuch*, 201; Zelenin, *Russische (ostslavische) Volkskunde*, 393; Mannhardt, "Über Vampyrismus," 260, 270; Čajkanović, "The Killing of a Vampire," 264; and Věroboj Vildomec, *Polnische Sagen*, introduction and notes by Will-Erich Peuckert (Erich Schmidt Verlag, 1979), 78.

63. See note 57: exhumation correlating with vampirism.

64. Edmund Schneeweis, *Feste und Volksbräuche der Lausitzer Wenden* (Nendeln, Liechtenstein: Kraus Reprint, 1968), 81; originally published in Leipzig, 1931. There are at least two other reasons, by the way, for blood to appear at the mouth of a corpse: a traumatic injury may cause this (as in a murder victim), as will pneumonic plague, which causes vomiting of blood. See Creighton, *History*, vol. 1, 122.

65. Ronald and Catherine Berndt, *The World of the First Australians* (Chicago: University of Chicago Press, 1965), 410. Lawson (*Modern Greek Folklore*, 405) says that, on the Greek island of Chios, "the woman who prepares the corpse for burial places on its lips a cross of wax or cotton-stuff . . . ."

66. Wuttke, *Der Deutsche Volksaberglaube*, 222. See also Klapper, *Schlesische Volkskunde*, 213, and the account from the *Mercure galant* (Section I).

67. John Taylor, *African Rifles and Cartridges* (Highland Park, N.J.: Gun Room Press, 1977), facing p. 342; reprint of 1948 edition.

68. Burkhart, "Vampirglaube," 222; Trigg, *Gypsy Demons*, 156; Vukanovic, "The Vampire" (1960), 45, and (1959), 117; Otto Knoop, *Sagen und Erzählungen aus der Provinz Posen* (Posen, 1893), 139.

69. W. E. D. Evans, *The Chemistry of Death* (Springfield, Ill.: Charles C. Thomas, 1963), 49.

70. Bächtold-Stäubli, *Handwörterbuch*, 814. This interpretation is also suggested in a curious nineteenth-century Hungarian novel that analyzes the vampire lore. I found a German translation of the novel. Ferenz Köröshazy, *Die Vampyrbraut* (Weimar, 1849), 268. (On the title page, the author's name is given in reverse order, in the Hungarian manner.) See also Karl Bartsch, *Sagen, Märchen und Gebräuche aus Meklenburg* (Vienna, 1879), 93.

71. Trigg, *Gypsy Demons*, 154.

72. Murgoci, "The Vampire in Roumania," 349; Vakarelski, *Bulgarische Volkskunde*, 239.

73. See, for example, Sturm and Völker, *Von denen Vampiren*, 511, 526, 441, 442, 444; Edward Westermarck, *Ritual and Belief in Morocco* (London, 1926), vol. 2, 548; and Bargheer, *Eigenweide*, 79.

74. Ponsold, *Lehrbuch*, 290.

75. Jan Perkowski, *Vampires of the Slavs* (Cambridge, Mass., 1976), 109ff.

76. Glaister and Rentoul, *Medical Jurisprudence*, 52.

77. Cockburn, *Mummies*, 1.

78. Jens P. Hart Hansen, Jørgen Meldgaard, and Jørgen Nordqvist, "The Mummies of Qilakitsoq," *National Geographic* 167, 2 (February 1985): 190–207; see p. 201. See Trigg, *Gypsy Demons*, 146, for long teeth of vampire; also, Otto Knoop, "Sagen aus Kujawien," *Zeitschrift des Vereins für Volkskunde* 16 (1906): 96.

79. J. J. Hess, *Von den Beduinen des innern Arabiens* (Zürich and Leipzig: Max Niehans Verlag, 1938), 164. Note, in this connection, the practice of throwing a rock or twig onto the place where someone was killed: Schneeweis, *Wenden*, 100–101; Geiger, "Die Behandlung," 163; Felix Liebrecht, *Zur Volkskunde* (Heilbronn, 1879), 282–283.

Edward Tripp of Yale University Press pointed out to me that, considered from this perspective, it makes sense that Anubis, the Egyptian god of tombs and embalming, would be represented with the head of a jackal. Jackals would in fact "preside" over the disposal of the dead, given the opportunity.

For an account of coffins designed to prevent bears from breaking in and eating the corpses, see Milovan Gavazzi, "The Dugout Coffin in Central Bosnia," *Man* 53, 202 (1953): 129.

For burial methods designed to protect the coffin from wolves, see Philip Tilney, "Supernatural Prophylaxes in a Bulgarian Peasant Funeral," *Journal of Popular Culture* 4, 1 (1970): 222, 223.

80. Vukanovic "The Vampire" (1960), 49; Trigg, *Gypsy Demons*, 155.

81. Burkhart, "Vampirglaube," 243.

82. Lambertz in *Wörterbuch der Mythologie*, 490.

83. Bargheer, *Eigenweide*, 84. I have in my files a newspaper account of an event of this sort: "A hand protruding from an incline near the Harbor Freeway led to the discovery of the badly decomposed body of an adult male . . ." (*Los Angeles Times*).

84. Meyer, *Mythologie*, 96.

85. Glaister and Rentoul, *Medical Jurisprudence*, 119–120.

86. Murgoci, "The Vampire in Roumania," 332.

87. See Burkhart, citing Schneeweis, *Serbokroatische Volkskunde*, 239, n. 141. Also, Löwenstimm, *Aberglaube*, 93–103; Friedrich Haase, *Volksglaube und Brauchtum der Ostslaven* (Hildesheim/New York: Georg Olms Verlag, 1980), 329; reprint of 1939 edition; Zelenin, *Russische (ostslavische) Volkskunde*, 329. Also, Geiger, "Die Behandlung" (Switzerland): disposal of bodies in water, 153, 155–156.

88. See, for example, Haase, *Volksglaube*, 302; E. Cabej, "Sitten und Gebräuche der Albaner," *Revue internationale des études balkaniques* (1934–35): 224; Vakarelski, *Bulgarische Volkskunde*, 303, 309; G. Lemke, *Volksthümliches in Ostpreussen* (Mohrungen, 1884), vol. 1, 56.

89. *Grettir's Saga*, trans. Denton Fox and Herman Pálsson (University of Toronto Press, 1974), 72; Vakarelski, *Bulgarische Volkskunde*, 307; Lemke, *Volksthümliches*, vol. 3, 51.

90. *Grettir's Saga*, 72, for rocks; Zelenin, *Russische (ostslavische) Volkskunde*, 327, for brush.

91. P. V. Glob gives numerous examples of this in *The Bog People*. See also Pauli, *Keltischer Volksglaube*, 174–179; Schneeweis, *Wenden*, 102; Geiger, "Die Behandlung," 158. Dieck (*Die europäischen Moorleichenfunde*, 50–127) catalogues the methods of holding down the bodies.

92. Hock, *Die Vampyrsagen*, 42; Tetzner, *Die Volkssagen*, 461.

93. Meyer, *Mythologie*, 96.

94. Reiter in *Wörterbuch der Mythologie*, 201.

95. Schneeweis, *Serbokroatische Volkskunde*, 88, 104; Krauss, *Slavische Volksforschungen*, 127–128; Vukanovic, "The Vampire" (1958), 22; Trigg, *Gypsy Demons*, 152; Burkhart, "Vampirglaube," 220.

96. Beitl, *Deutsches Volkstum*, 45.

97. Reiter, *Wörterbuch*, 201.

98. Jan Perkowski, "The Romanian Folkloric Vampire," *East European Quarterly* 16, 3 (September 1982): 313.

99. Árpád Csiszár, "A hazajáró lélek," *A nyieregyházi Jósa András Muzeum Évkönyve*, 8–9 (1965–66): 159–96; summary in German: 199–201; see 200.

100. Balassa and Ortutay, *Ungarische Volkskunde*, 673. See also Vakarelski, *Bulgarische Volkskunde*, 305; Schneeweis, *Serbokroatische Volkskunde*, 88; and Adolf Schullerus, *Siebenbürgisch-sächsische Volkskunde im Umriss* (Leipzig, 1926), 125.

101. Dömötör, *Volksglaube*, 251–252.

102. For death figure with scythe: Vakarelski, *Bulgarische Volkskunde*, 311; with sickle: Haase, *Volksglaube*, 301.

103. Burkhart, "Vampirglaube," 215, 229. See also Schneeweis, *Serbokroatische Volkskunde*, 11.

104. Schneeweis, *Wenden*, 85.

105. Trigg, *Gypsy Demons*, 152.

106. Stith Thompson, *Motif-Index of Folk-Literature* (Helsinki, 1932), vol. 2, 380, E442: "Ghost laid by piercing grave with stake." See also Sebestyén Károly, "Speerhölzer und Kreuze auf dem Széklerboden," *Anzeiger der ethnographischen Abteilung des ungarischen National-Museums* (1905), vol. 2, 99; Burkhart, "Vampirglaube," 243; Ernö Kunt, *Volkskunst ungarischer Dorffriedhöfe* (Budapest: Corvina Kiadó, 1983), p. 40; translation into German by Valér Nagy.

107. Krauss, *Slavische Volksforschungen*, 127. In some areas thorns are put into the grave (see Schott, *Walachische Maerchen*, 198).

108. Strackerjan, *Aberglaube*, 154.

109. *Los Angeles Times*, Nov. 21, 1978.

110. Pauli, *Keltischer Volksglaube*, 174–179; Schneeweis, *Serbokroatische Volkskunde*, 106; Naumann, *Primitive Gemeinschaftskultur*, 105; Mannhardt, "Über Vampyrismus," 269; Karl Brunner, *Ostdeutsche Volkskunde* (Leipzig, 1925), 195; Fischer, "Bog Bodies of Denmark," 178, 182, 192.

111. Burkhart, "Vampirglaube," 223.

112. Erhard Eylmann, *Die Eingeborenen der Kolonie Südaustralien* (Berlin, 1908), 232.

113. Beitl, *Deutsches Volkstum*, 187; Schneeweis, *Serbokroatische Volkskunde*, 88; Vakarelski, *Bulgarische Volkskunde*, 303.

114. Hellwald, *Die Welt der Slawen*, 370; Schneeweis, *Serbokroatische Volkskunde*, 10; Vakarelski, *Bulgarische Volkskunde*, 303.

115. Wuttke, *Der deutsche Volksaberglaube*, 222.

116. Aribert Schroeder, *Vampirismus* (Frankfurt, 1973), 45–46. The words used here may very well refer to the sound created by the splitting open of the swollen body cavity.

117. J. A. E. Köhler, *Volksbrauch, Aberglauben, Sagen und andere alte Überlieferungen im Voigtland* (Leipzig, 1867), 257–258. See also Zelenin, *Russiche (ostslavishe) Volkskunde*, 329; Löwenstimm, *Aberglaube*, 98ff.

118. Zopf (*Dissertatio*, 11–12) cites an essay, published in 1732, in which it is remarked that it is in fact not abnormal for a corpse to bleed this way.

119. J. J. M. de Groot, *The Religious System of China* (The Hague, 1892–1910), vol. 1, 32.

120. Not just in Europe: "It is, according to the Chinese, by no means a rare thing in their country for corpses to sit up on their death-bed and strike terror and fright into the hearts of their mourning kinsfolk" (de Groot, *Religious System*, vol. 5, 750). A Chinese acquaintance from Peking also mentioned this belief to me in conversation. See also Westermarck, *Ritual and Belief*, 449.

121. Blum and Blum, *The Dangerous Hour*, 71.

122. The Turks being not only the bugbears of the Greeks but also the westernmost culture that did not necessarily use chairs. "Sitting up like a Turk," then, could mean sitting with legs straight out. Murgoçi cites the expression, p. 119; also, Raymond T. McNally, *A Clutch of Vampires* (Greenwich, Conn.: New York Graphic Society, 1974), 191.

123. Lawson, *Modern Greek Folklore*, 377. The following etymologies are all Lawson's.

124. Danforth, *Death Rituals*, 52.

125. Evans, *The Chemistry of Death*, 10–11. See also R. L. Airth and G. E. Foerster, "Some Aspects of Fungal Bioluminescence," *Journal of Cellular and Comparative Physiology* 56 (1960): 173–182.

126. See, for example, Trigg, *Gypsy Demons*, 156.

127. Markus Köhbach, "Ein Fall von Vampirismus bei den Osmanen," *Balkan Studies* 20 (1979): 89.

128. Evans, *Chemistry of Death*, 84.

129. Ralston, *Songs of the Russian People*, 409; Zelenin, *Russische (ostslavische) Volkskunde*, 329–330; Haase, *Volksglaube*, 329; Löwenstimm, *Aberglaube*, 102. Such alcoholic vampires were blamed for droughts, having continued beyond death their habit of drinking everything in sight.

130. Hock, *Die Vampyrsagen*, 1; Burkhart, "Vampirglaube," 250; Wilhelm Hertz, *Der Werwolf* (Stuttgart, 1862), 126; Richard Andree, *Ethnographische Parallelen und Vergleiche* (Stuttgart, 1878), 81.

131. Trigg has an informative discussion of these: *Gypsy Demons*, 145, 178–179.

132. *Mercure galant*, quoted in Hock, *Die Vampyrsagen*, 34.

133. See "Stana" in section I. Also Arnold Paole in Sturm and Völker, *Von denen Vampiren*, 451.

134. Burkhart, "Vampirglaube," 221; Perkowski, "Romanian Folkloric Vampire," 316; Wuttke, *Der Deutsche Volksaberglaube*, 221–222; Richard Beitl, *Deutsche Volkskunde* (Berlin, 1933), 188; Mannhardt, "Über Vampyrismus," 261–262.

Clinical Vampirism: Blending Myth and Reality

More or less independent of the mainstream scholarship devoted to the vampire, we find a steady stream of essays reflecting a psychiatric interest in the subject. Disturbed patients who exhibited a penchant for drinking blood, either their own—that activity termed autovampirism—or that of their victims—sometimes referred to as clinical vampirism—presented a problem for psychiatrists. What was the meaning of such behavior? How could it be explained? And what, if any, treatment might be effective for such individuals? In marked contrast with Barber's "literal" explanation of the vampire, we find Dr. Philip D. Jaffé, a psychiatrist and faculty member of psychology and education sciences at the University of Geneva in Switzerland, and Frank DiCataldo, an expert on juvenile delinquency, affiliated with the Bridgewater State Hospital in Bridgewater, Massachusetts, who offer quite a different picture of reputed vampires that figure prominently in a number of documented clinical and legal cases.

It may be legitimately asked whether or not "clinical" vampires have much to do with the vampire of tradition. One could argue, for instance, that the label "vampire" is only a convenient metaphor for a form of mental pathology which includes the ingestion of blood. On the other hand, it might also be contended that whatever the underlying causes of the mental pathology might be, they could in fact be related to the underlying ultimate origins of the folkloristic vampire.

Whatever the actual relationship between clinical vampirism and the folkloristic vampire might be, there can be no question that the psychiatric approach to the vampire is well established and is likely to continue for decades to come. Those favorably disposed towards such an approach may wish to read Donald R. Morse, "The Stressful Kiss: A Biopsychosocial Evaluation of the Origins, Evolution, and Societal Significance of Vampirism," Stress Medicine 9 (1993): 181–199; and Richard M. Gottlieb, "The Legend of the European Vampire: Object Loss and Corporeal Preservation," Psychoanalytic Study of the Child 49 (1994): 465–480.

Reprinted from the *Bulletin of the American Academy of Psychiatry and the Law* 22 (1994): 533–544. Copyright © 1994 American Academy of Psychiatry and the Law. Reprinted with permission.

143

In the modern age, vampires have become media stars. Published in 1897, *Dracula* by Bram Stoker[1] made the word *vampire* a household term. More recently, the vampire trilogy by Anne Rice[2] became a bestseller. On the silver screen, W. Murnau's *Nosferatu* (Prana Films, Berlin, 1992) remains a classic, and a new Dracula movie is periodically released to please today's audiences. This enduring fascination with vampires evolved from beliefs and superstitions dating back to medieval Europe and to humankind's most archaic myths. Curiously, while providing inspiration for the arts, their legacy is also found in the rare clinical condition of vampirism, which groups some of the most shocking pathologic behaviors observed in humanity. In this article, we review the clinical aspects of overt vampiristic behavior and its various definitions and describe its relationship to more established psychiatric disorders. The original case study of a "modern vampire" will help illustrate how myth and reality can blend and solidify in dramatic fashion. But first, by way of introduction, we review the vampire myth to which clinical vampirism owes its existence.

Mythological Precursors to the Modern Vampire

Records of vampirelike figures exist in several ancient religions. Commonly mentioned are the Vajra deities of Tibet represented as blood drinkers, the Atharva Veda and the Baital-Pachisi in ancient Indian literature, and Mexico's Ciuateteo, who was associated with women in Mexico having died during their first labor. Summers[3] describes what is perhaps the first pictorial evidence of the vampire, an Assyrian bowl showing a man copulating with a female vampire whose head has been severed. He also reports on Babylonian, Semite, and Egyptian beliefs involving a dead person that continues to live in its original body and feeds off the living. Similar ancient beliefs are traced to ancient European, Chinese, Polynesian, and African cultures, and most refer to demonic female figures and fused relationships between the living and the dead, expressed through blood rituals as well as sexualized and aggressive exchanges. Current manifestations of these ancient beliefs still are found in voodooism and associated practices in the Caribbean and in Latin America. In Catholicism, wine continues to symbolize Christ's blood and is consumed by priests during mass.[4]

The modern vampire media myth probably originated in Scandinavia and the British Isles, but it most firmly took hold in medieval central and eastern Europe. It owes as etymology to Slavic languages (e.g., *upir* in Bulgarian, *vopyr* in Russian, *vapir* in Serbian, *vampir* in Hungarian). Periodic vampire scares agitated these regions and their superstitious inhabitants late into the nineteenth century. A prevalent belief involved a person who had died leaving his tomb at night to attack his victims, often friends and relatives, to suck their blood to retain his own immortality. The vampire then returned to his coffin before sunrise or risked paralysis and total helplessness.

Some superstitions give the vampire the power of metamorphosis, the ability to transform into animal form (most frequently a butterfly or a bat)[5] or into vapor and mist. In addition, because the vampire is "dead" and soulless, it has no reflection. Those who the vampire attacks are generally in a trance and are almost sensually embraced while their blood is sucked. Summers[6] also relates more cannibalistic practices, whereby the vampire bites the victim's abdomen and sometimes extracts and eats the heart. The victim eventually dies and, unless proper measures are taken, will in turn become a vampire. Other ways to join the "undead," depending on local tradition, are to commit suicide, practice black magic, be cursed by parents or the Church, be a werewolf, or even be an unlucky corpse in Greece on the way to the cemetery and have a bird or cat cross in front of the procession. Jones[7] reports that in Dalmatia vampires were divided in two categories: innocent and guilty, respectively called Denac and Orko. Some of the prerequisites to becoming an Orko vampire were working on Sunday, smoking on a religious holiday, and incestuous relations with a female ascendant, in particular, a grandmother.

To counter vampires, schemes ranging from the crude to the elaborate were designed to identify potential vampires and to eliminate them from the world of the living. Garlic and the crucifix were considered effective apotropaics (i.e., protective measures against evil). Identifying vampires in many ways paralleled witch-hunting techniques. Telltale signs indicating a possible vampire were unusual birthmarks, infants born with teeth, red-haired and sometimes blue-eyed children, tall and gaunt people, and epilepsy. Tombs often were opened to see if the cadaver had moved, if it had fresh cheeks, open eyes, and if the hair and nails were still growing. Similar rituals were performed in Connecticut in the eighteenth and nineteenth centuries.[8]

Suspected vampires or suspicious corpses faced a variety of measures. These ranged from symbolic exorcism to brutal mutilation. In Bulgaria a sorcerer armed with a saint's picture would drive the vampire into a bottle, which was then thrown into a fire.[9] Elsewhere, the suspected vampire would be put to death, and some of its blood or flesh consumed. If already buried, the cadaver was unearthed and the head severed and placed between the feet. If necessary the heart was also boiled in oil and dissolved in vinegar. The most popular response was to impale the vampire on a wooden stake with a single blow through the heart. Sometimes a priest was called on to shoot the vampire with silver bullets.

The image of the vampire also owes much of its notoriety to reality. A companion in arms of Joan of Arc, Gilles de Rais, in the fifteenth century, and the Hungarian countess Erzsebet Bathory, two centuries later, are famous for having murdered up to six hundred children to obtain their blood. Dracula, Bram Stoker's literary creation, was probably inspired by Vlad, a Walachian nobleman in the fifteenth century whose cruelty earned him two epithets "Tepes" (i.e., "the Impaler") and Count "Dracul" (i.e., "dragon" or "devil").

Several authors suggest that the "undead" quality of vampires may have resulted from inadequate or premature burial during times of plague.[10] Many people were perhaps mistakenly buried alive while suffering from catatonic stupor and hysterical states.[11] Barber[12] offers elements of forensic pathology to understand the combined effects of premature burials and human tissue decomposition (e.g., cadavers may change position and hair and nails may appear to continue to grow). There is also an explanation based on the porphyrias, genetic disorders that produce reddening of the eyes, skin, and teeth; receding of the upper lip; cracking of the skin; and bleeding in sunlight.[13]

These reality-based speculations cannot fully account for the vampire myth, which is too psychologically complex and deeply embedded in ancient powerful beliefs and symbols. Indeed, Wilgowicz[14] points out that Dracula is only the "typical figure of a large family with entangled branches." In a sense, the more modern and media-inspiring image of the vampire masks fundamental aspects of the underlying myths and archetypes, the very ones that may allow for a more significant understanding of the rare clinical condition of vampirism. Indeed, today's human beings who are described as vampires owe this label primarily to overt behavior. Yet, closer examination reveals the power of the more ancient vampire myths and the process by which they are transposed into modern manifestations.

Clinical Vampirism: Overview and Definitions

Both clinical and forensic psychologists and psychiatrists have described cases that involve acts that are strongly reminiscent of some aspect of the mythical vampire's behavior. Clinical definitions of vampirism reviewed in the literature place the emphasis on overt vampiristic behavior.

In the broadest definition, Bourguignon[15] proposes to call "vampirisms . . . all sexual or aggressive acts—whether or not there is blood suction—committed on a deceased or a dying person." This view tends to cover a variety of behaviors that the author himself identifies: necrophilia, necrosadism, necrophagia, sadonecrophilia, and vampirism. The case of Antoine Léger, who in 1824 drank his victim's blood but also raped, murdered, mutilated, and partially devoured a young girl, is summarized by Bourguignon to illustrate an instance of polyvampirism.

A more recent case fitting this broad definition of vampirism is described in detail in the psychiatric literature.[16] In 1978, during a two-day rampage in the Mayenne region of France, a thirty-nine-year-old man attempted to rape a preadolescent girl, also biting her deeply in the neck, murdered an elderly man, whose blood he drank and whose leg he partially devoured, killed a cow by bleeding it to death, murdered a married couple of farmers, and almost succeeded in doing the same with their farm hand. Arrested on the third day, he also admitted to strangling his wife almost a year before and disguising her death as a drowning.

Vandenbergh and Kelly[17] propose a definition that excludes overt necrophilic activity and emphasizes a libidinal component. They see clinical vampirism "as the act of drawing blood from an object (usually a love object) and receiving resultant sexual excitement and pleasure." In this view, the sucking or drinking of blood from the wound is often an important part of the act but not an essential one. They report on a case of a young man serving a prison sentence who came to the attention of prison authorities after several inmates were caught stealing iron tablets and expressed a fear of developing anemia. The investigation showed that the young man had been trading sexual favors with these inmates in return for the opportunity to suck their blood.

Hemphill and Zabow[18] attempt to define vampirism closely to the Dracula myth as a recognizable, although rare, clinical entity characterized by periodic compulsive blood-drinking, affinity with the dead, and uncertain identity. Relying on the modern vampire myth, they reject associated features such as desecrating graves, violating corpses, eating human flesh, or having sexual intercourse with the living. Their clinical sample expressed no interest in sex, and blood ingestion represented a compulsive behavior that brought mental relief to the participant without any ability to psychologically comprehend the experience or ascribe it any meaning.

A fourth definition involves autovampiristic behavior. This condition is distinguished from self-mutilating behaviors, intentional suicide attempts, dramatic gestures in the context of treatment of borderline patients, and manipulative self-harm that may take place for secondary gain in prisons.

Vandenbergh and Kelly[19] discuss the case of a twenty-eight-year-old man

147

who at puberty began masturbating and taking erotic satisfaction at the sight of his own blood flowing. With practice he was able to direct blood spurts from his neck artery to his mouth. McCully[20] describes autovampiristic behavior in a young man that strikingly resembles the previous case. Although there is no conclusive evidence, we believe that the same patient is described in both publications.

Bourguignon[21] introduces an important distinction within autovampiristic behaviors by relating the case of a young woman hospitalized during her fourth pregnancy following repeated vomiting of considerable amounts of blood. She apparently enjoyed these hemorrhages and the sight of her blood. She also voluntarily disconnected transfusion equipment, let her blood drip, and stated she would prefer to drink it. At first no investigation was able to determine the source of the bleeding. Finally a mouth examination by a specialist revealed several bleeding wounds at the base of the tongue. Treating staff inferred that she sucked these wounds, swallowed the blood, and then vomited. Apparently sometimes she just would keep the blood in her mouth before rejecting it, because subsequent analyses revealed that gastric juices were not always present. She eventually developed severe anemia and died two years later. An autopsy revealed a stomach bloated with blood. A psychological feature of critical diagnostic importance was the patient's mythomania. It is likely that this patient suffered from the rare syndrome of Lasthénie de Ferjol,[22] described exclusively in female patients, often paramedical staff, who bleed themselves surreptitiously and wrap themselves in a web of nontruths. In addition to hiding their instrumental involvement in the condition, they also make up stories regarding important aspects of their lives.

Regardless of which definition is adopted or, for that matter, if they are all adopted, overt vampiristic and autovampiristic behaviors are rare phenomena. Relying on figures of a thesis by Desrosières, Bourguignon tallies fifty-three cases, all but one, men having acted out almost exclusively on deceased women various blends of necrophilic vampirism.[23] Prins[24] conducted an informal inquiry into the incidence of vampirism in Great Britain by contacting mainly forensic mental health specialists. Seven cases were reported, one of which was a third-hand account. Hemphill and Zabow[25] report on four cases of vampirism, which they view as an all-male phenomenon as opposed to autovampirism, which is a gender-blind but predominantly female behavior.

Cases of clinical vampirism are sufficiently rare to warrant a full description of a "modern vampire" with whom both authors were directly involved at a maximum-security forensic hospital in the United States. The case of Jeremy also illustrates many of the nosological difficulties associated with this pathologic behavior. This aspect will be discussed in the last section of this paper.

The Case of a "Modern Vampire"

In addition to the authors' personal knowledge of the case, biographic information also was drawn from hospital records. Other sources include a journalist's report of an interview with the patient[26] and a review of portions of the trial transcript in which the patient's mother was a principal witness.

Jeremy, currently thirty-five years old, was raised in a seemingly ordinary middle-class family. His father worked as an electrical engineer, and his mother was a mathematics teacher. He has a brother, two years younger, whom he felt his mother favored over him. He harbors an intense hatred toward her and believes that her testimony at the trial sealed his conviction for the murder of his paternal grandmother. He often has alleged that his mother was physically abusive during his childhood. Descriptions of the abuse vary over time and are colored by delusional thinking. For instance, he believes that she belonged to a witchcraft club, when in fact she taught astrology on the side. During the club's occult séances, Jeremy claims that blood was drawn from him. He has openly expressed his wish to kill his mother and fantasizes about her death. He has written her letters seething with hatred from prison and the maximum security hospital where he now serves his sentence.

Jeremy first demonstrated his fascination with blood at age five when he was hospitalized with pneumonia. While convalescing, he drew pictures of hypodermic needles dripping blood and buttocks with open wounds oozing blood. In school, his preoccupation expanded to include drawings of goblins, bats, witches, and scenes of violent deaths from gunshot wounds. To this day, he paints vampires ravaging helpless females. He also became an avid reader of witchcraft literature and horror novels, including most of the classics.

His mother testified that when he was thirteen years old he started killing small animals, such as cats, squirrels, fish, and birds, and ate them. He also became nocturnal and wandered the streets of his hometown.

By adolescence he was using illicit drugs on a daily basis and was arrested for shoplifting and vandalism. At fifteen years of age, he was caught stealing a case of tear gas from the local police station. This led to the first of several court-ordered hospitalizations. After his discharge, he began showing signs of psychosis. He developed the delusion that a transmitter in his head was

149

controlled by someone in outer space. He felt something was wrong with his head and built and wore a cardboard pyramid in the hope it would somehow protect and heal him. He was in and out of treatment until age seventeen, when he disclosed to a therapist that he was thinking of killing his father.

After a two-week hospitalization, he returned home. However, his family was alarmed when he began keeping an ax at his bedside. They installed locks for their bedrooms. They even slept in shifts so that one family member would be awake at all times. Eventually Jeremy's mother obtained a court order to remove him from the home. He moved into his own apartment and then traveled to Florida.

He called his parents from Florida, telling them that vampires were trying to kill him. A year later, at age nineteen, he returned home and lived with his family again. His mental condition deteriorated rapidly. He was unable to sleep, became withdrawn, and neglected his hygiene. He reported hearing voices for the first time. These voices warned him to beware of his family and friends, because they were vampires. His interest in consuming animal and human flesh was rekindled. He killed several cats and removed their brains to see if he could learn how to correct his own brain, which he believed was dysfunctional. He also reportedly drank horse blood.

His obsession with the ingestion of blood, especially human blood, seems to come from his belief that he could become a vampire and escape the torment of voices in his head and be granted eternal life. Initially he obtained human blood through accidental circumstances. Later, in psychiatric hospitals, he cut elderly and infirm patients with small staples and also traded sex for blood. He also bought a hand gun with the intention of shooting someone to draw blood.

After another court-ordered hospitalization for killing, dissecting, and eating a cat, he was released into the custody of his now-divorced father. Auditory hallucinations kept warning him that some people were vampires. They ridiculed him because he had never killed anyone and told him that to become a vampire he must kill and drink someone's blood. Furthermore, he believed that his grandmother used an ice pick to steal his blood while he slept. That she was an invalid and in a wheelchair did not shake him from his belief. He also believed that she was trying to poison him. A few days later, he murdered her.

Jeremy's verbatim account of the murder, documented in the court-ordered forensic mental health evaluation, reveals his psychotic state of mind:

> So it was raining one day, and I washed out of this job interview so then I took
> out a gun and painted the bullets gold. I asked my grandmother if she wanted

anything done and she said she wanted me to do the laundry. I did the laundry and asked her if she wanted anything else done. She said 'no.' So I put on my suit and shot her. I thought she wanted to die. When I pulled the gun on her I was surprised. She said 'no, no, don't do that.' But it was too late. Once I pulled the gun on her, I had to do it. I shot her in the heart, and she was wiggling and screaming at me. Then I shot her three more times real fast. Then I started saying a bunch of weird things to her real fast. I whispered in her ear something about the devil, something I had read in a witchcraft book once. I gave her the last rites and said a small short prayer.

The coroner's report indicates the victim also was stabbed, but Jeremy has always denied this. Currently he denies drinking her blood, but at one point he admitted trying to suck her wounds but gave up because she was "too old."

He dragged the corpse off the sofa and into a bedroom where he poured dry gas on it. He ignited the corpse, which eventually led to the whole house catching fire. He then disposed of the gun in a nearby river, picked up his father, and drove him to his house. He was with his father when the police called to report the tragedy. Jeremy and his father drove to what remained of the torched house. He tried to enter it to retrieve a box, telling the police it contained tax returns. The box already had been confiscated by the police and contained among other things gold-painted bullets. The next day he went to the police station and forcibly tried to recover the box. A struggle ensued, and he was arrested and charged with assault and battery on a police officer. He confessed to the murder the following day.

His trial showcased a battle of mental health experts. Jeremy's lawyer pleaded not guilty by reason of insanity and introduced four expert witnesses who testified that he suffered from paranoid schizophrenia. The prosecution, in an attempt to get a murder conviction, introduced their own expert, who testified that Jeremy suffered from a borderline personality disorder and was criminally responsible. The jury convicted Jeremy of second-degree murder, which carries a life sentence, and returned a concurrent lengthy sentence for arson.

He was sentenced to a maximum-security prison and managed rather well for three years on antipsychotic medication. After stopping medication, he developed the delusion that a prison officer was stealing his spinal fluid. He also believed that the left side of his body was dying, and that by consuming human flesh or spinal fluid he could reverse the process. He bought a shank from the prison underground for protection and shortly after almost killed the prison officer he feared.

Jeremy was charged with attempted murder but this time was found not guilty by reason of insanity. He was committed to a maximum-security forensic hospital and has remained there for the past three years. Considerable therapeutic effort has brought behavioral stability. However, he still remains invested in a portion of his delusion of being a vampire needing to consume human blood and flesh. There are no plans to discharge him from this hospital in the near future.

Jeremy underwent a complete psychological assessment in 1992, and records of test results dating back to 1978, before the killing of his grandmother, also are available. Overall, Jeremy's intellectual functioning falls in the average range according to Wechsler's classification, with verbal IQ slightly superior to performance IQ. The analysis of projective records reveals a subtle transformation between the two assessments.[27] From the 1978 records, a clinical picture of psychotic dimensions emerges with some salient psychopathic traits in the background. However, fourteen years later, his presentation is rather psychopathic with some elements attesting to an underlying psychosis. This apparent contradiction will in part orient the discussion in the following section.

The Relationship to Psychopathology

The relationship of vampirism to psychopathology is complicated by the low incidence of this behavior. Some authors, such as Benezech and associates, citing the psychological complexity of their cases, describe associated symptomatology and refrain from any further speculation.[28] Others, including McCully, theorize from the perspective of individual depth psychology,[29] but their analysis offers little possibility of generalizing to other cases. Yet, as descriptions of vampirism cases have accumulated, inferences about psychopathology may be drawn. The reader will recognize Jeremy's symptoms in several of the following categories.

Kayton[30] considers that the vampire myth gives "a unique phenomenological view of schizophrenia," and indeed overt vampiristic delusions have been associated most notably with this disorder. The connection is particularly salient in the more gruesome cases involving cannibalistic and necrosadistic behavior that resemble the content of schizophrenic delusional material acted out. These cases generally present massive disorganized oral sadistic regressions, depersonalization, confused sexuality, multiple concurrent delusions, and thought disorder in content and form. Psychodynamic explanations draw attention to Karl Abraham's biting oral stage, during which the infant uses his teeth with a vengeance, to Melanie Klein's description of children's aggressive fantasies,[31] and to W. R. D. Fairbairn's notion of intense oral sadistic libidinal needs formed in response to actual maternal deprivation.[32]

Despite the speculative nature of this theoretic approach and regardless of whether early psychological and/or physical abuse actually took place, it is interesting to note that schizophrenics often manifest persecutory delusions of incorporation, introjection, devouring, and destruction. Lacking the capacity for symbolic thought, the ingestion of blood and/or body parts may be a way for the schizophrenic to literally replenish himself. This feature may also be a more regressed manifestation of peculiar dietary habits sometimes exhibited by some schizophrenics. Another consideration is the lack of any stable sense of self. Some schizophrenics may well succumb to extremely concrete forms of testing their very existence such as cutting through the skin to determine that blood flows and merging with and living off dead or dying victims. According to Kayton,[33] other aspects often observed in schizophrenic patients and related more directly to the vampire myth are a preoccupation with mirrors (another sign of profound identity disturbance) and reversal of the day-night cycle.

The psychodynamics of vampirism are quite different for the cases featuring psychopathic and perverse personality traits. As defined by Cleckley and later by Hare,[34] psychopathy is a personality disorder characterized by grandiosity, egocentricity, manipulativeness, dominance, shallow affect, poor interpersonal bonding, and lack of empathy, anxiety, and guilt. Among the most contrasting elements with schizophrenics displaying overt vampirism are that psychopathic and perverse personalities carry out more integrated and organized behavior and reality testing appears mostly intact.

Bourguignon,[35] emphasizing the strong libidinal component in vampiristic behavior, labels it a perversion. The perverse aspects can be observed in few cases of vampirism, specifically when the subject apparently draws sexual satisfaction from drinking a live victim's blood. Here, the subject's history may be the key to understanding the fixation on blood and its idiosyncratic meaning.

Within the psychopathic clinical cases, depending on the actual circumstances of the vampirism, the strong desire to control the victim may be the most important feature. This aspect may account for the popularity of sadomasochistic scenarios involving aspects of vampirism. In mainstream sexuality, love bites between amorous partners may be highly symbolic remnants of vampire sensuality. However, in the case of necrophilic and necrosadistic vampirism, even when, for example, cadavers are sexually violated, the link between vampirism and perversion is not clearly established. In this we disagree with Bourguignon,[36] and our review of published cases of clinical vampirism suggests that as far as vampirism is concerned sexual behavior appears almost completely subordinated to a destructive and sadistic drive barely more elaborate than what is observed in the more gruesome schizophrenic vampirism. The cases of Jeffrey Dahmer, the Wisconsin multiple murderer of the early 1990s, and Sergeant Bertrand in the mid-1850s in France illustrate this predominance despite sexual acting out.[37]

When vampirism is embedded in a psychopathic personality disorder, the potential for extremely dangerous behavior seems compounded. The cases presented by Hemphill and Zabow[38] fall into this category. In cases of vampirism within psychopathy, subjects frequently present the common salient childhood impulse control difficulties, are undersocialized, and demonstrate an early tendency to violate limits and rules. More often than not, a history of animal abuse including mutilations is elicited. These features tend to persist into adulthood: lack of empathy towards others becomes glaring, and criminalization can occur. The acquisition of physical force and the propensity to act out on innocent victims without the capacity to foresee and without concern for unpleasant consequences create the conditions for lethal behavior.

Whereas clinical vampirism would seem to maintain strong nosological ties to schizophrenia, Jeremy's case indicates connections with various diagnostic categories. Indeed, a striking feature of unusual forensic cases involving extreme behavior is that they are almost literally situated at what Prins[39] calls the "boundaries of psychiatric disorder." As such, clinical vampirism is one of the few pathologic manifestations that blends myth and reality in dramatic fashion and contains a hodgepodge of nosological elements, including schizophrenic, psychopathic, and perverse features. Unfortunately, there has been scant literature on the question of violence in psychopaths who also suffer from psychosis. In fact, there is considerable historical resistance within most diagnostic systems to juxtapose psychosis and psychopathy. A notable exception has been the contributions of Meloy[40] and Meloy and Gacono.[41] The association of schizophrenic and psychopathic features seems particularly relevant with regard to clinical vampirism.

Conclusions

One of the inherent aspects of all myths is that new versions succeed one another, with the most recent reflecting transpositions of the earlier ones. By virtue of its universality, the vampire myth does not escape this evolution.

Earliest mythology has associated vampires with female figures representing potential destruction and children in a state of dependency and helplessness. Wilgowicz[42] points to affinities between the Dracula-inspired vampire myth, on the one hand, and childbirth, on the other. Birth implies opening the eyes and sunlight entering. Symbolically, birth also buries the umbilical and blood-sharing relationship between mother and fetus. The modern, Dracula-based vampire myth insists on blood ties in a macabre sense, i.e., suction of the victim's blood, but also in a relational and familial as well as sexual sense, i.e., victims were generally family members.

We believe contemporary psychoanalysis and psychology have generated new versions of the vampire myth. Jones[43] relies on traditional psychoanalytic theory to analyze the vampire myth from the living's perspective. Love, hate, guilt, libidinal urges, sadistic drives, and incestuous feelings towards important figures who died form the psychological web that contributed to the creation and fear of vampires. However, when the myth blends with reality, as in Jeremy's case, complementary explanations are needed. In this view, maternal figures provide affective nourishment essential for the child's successful development, but under unfavorable circumstances, children also can experience depletion and a form of psychological vampirization.[44]

Vampiristic behavior thus no longer represents the outward expression of vitiated intrapsychic drives, but acquires a strong dyadic and relational quality, albeit irremediably disturbed. Vampirism and vampirization are the two poles of this extremely close, literally blood-tied relationship. Clinical vampirism represents the most dramatic manifestation of perhaps the most archaic relationship running amok. Vampiristic behaviors that very frequently involve a fascination with the dead or actually killing represent in our view a hopeless attempt to extricate from an archaic relationship with parental figures, even though the victims are rarely the parents themselves.

Notes

This article is an expanded version of a presentation made at the XIXth International Congress of the International Academy of Law and Mental Health, Lisbon, Portugal, June 1993.

1. B. Stoker, *Dracula* (Oxford: Oxford University Press, 1897).

2. A. Rice, *The Vampire Lestat* (New York: Ballantine, 1986); A. Rice, *The Queen of the Damned* (New York: Ballantine, 1989); A. Rice, *Interview with a Vampire* (New York: Ballantine, 1991).

3. M. Summers, *The Vampire* (New York: University Books, 1960).

4. In 785, King Charlemagne of France was compelled to legislate against the literal interpretation of transubstantiation.

5. The association with bats seems to have been most popularized in movies. However, in 1762, the French naturalist Buffon named a bat variety *Vampyrus sanguisangus.*

6. Summers, *The Vampire.*

7. E. Jones, *On the Nightmare* (London: Hogarth Press, 1931).

8. "New Englanders 'Killed' Corpses, Experts Say," *New York Times*, Oct. 31, 1993, p. 36.

9. L. Kayton, "The Relationship of the Vampire Legend to Schizophrenia," *Journal of Youth and Adolescence* 1, 4 (1972): 313–314.

10. H. Prins, *Bizarre Behaviours: Boundaries of Psychiatric Disorder* (London: Routledge, 1990).

11. Kayton, "Relationship of the Vampire to Schizophrenia."

12. P. Barber, *Vampires, Burial and Death: Folklore and Reality* (London: Yale University Press, 1988).

13. Prins, *Bizarre Behaviours*; H. Prins, "Vampirism: A Clinical Condition," *British Journal of Psychiatry* 146 (1985): 666–668.

14. P. Wilgowicz, *Le Vampirisme: De la Dame Blanche au Golem* (Meyzieu, France: Césura, 1991), 8.

15. A. Bourguignon, "Situation du vampirisme et l'autovampirisme," *Annales Medico-Psychologiques* (Paris) 135, 2 (1977): 181–196.

16. G. Fellion, J. P. Duflot, P. Anglade, and J. Fraillon, "Du fantasme à la réalité: A propos d'un passage à l'acte criminel et cannibalique," *Annales Medico-Psychologiques* (Paris) 138, 5 (1980): 596–602; M. Benezech, M. Bourgeois, J. Villeger, and B. Etchegaray, "Cannibalisme et vampirisme chez un schizophrène multimeurtrier," *Bordeaux médical* 13 (1980): 1261–1265; and M. Benezech, M. Bourgeois, D. Boukhabza, and J. Yesavage, "Cannibalism and Vampirism in Paranoid Schizophrenia," *Journal of Clinical Psychiatry* 42, 7 (1981): 290.

17. R. L. Vandenbergh and J. F. Kelly, "Vampirism: A Review with New Observations," *Archives of General Psychiatry* 2 (1964): 543–547.

18. R. E. Hemphill and T. Zabow, "Clinical Vampirism: A Presentation of Three Cases and a Reevaluation of Haigh, the 'Acid-Bath Murderer,' " *South African Medical Journal* 63 (1983): 278–281.

19. Vandenbergh and Kelly, "Vampirism."

20. R. S. McCully, "Vampirism: Historical Perspective, and Underlying Process in Relation to a Case of Auto-Vampirism," *Journal of Nervous and Mental Disease* 139, 5 (1964): 440–452.

21. Bourguignon, "Situation du vampirisme et de l'autovampirisme."

22. The Lasthénie de Ferjol syndrome, named after the heroine of Barbey d'Aurevilly's novel, *Une histoire sans nom*, was first described by J. Bernard, Y. Najean, N. Alby, and J. D. Rain ("Les anémies hypochromes dues à des hémorragies volontairement provoquées: Syndrome de Lasthénie de Ferjol," *Presse médicale* 75 [1967]: 2087–2090). C. Burguin and J. Feillard present a more recent case

(" 'Histoire sans nom': A propos de la mythomanie," *Évolution psychiatrique* 51 (1986): 187–204).

23. P. Desrosières, "A propos d'un cas de nécrophilie, place du corps dans les preversions: Nécrophilie, nécrosadisme et vampirisme," doctoral dissertation (#37), University of Paris–Créteil, France, 1974; Bourguignon, "Situation du vampirisme et de l'autovampirisme."

24. Prins, *Bizarre Behaviours;* Prins, "Vampirism"; H. Prins, "Vampirism—Legendary or Clinical Phenomenon?" *Medicine, Science and the Law* 24, 4 (1984): 283–293.

25. Hemphill and Zabow, "Clinical Vampirism."

26. C. Page, *Blood Lust: Conversations with Real Vampires* (New York: Harper Collins, 1991).

27. P. D. Jaffé, F. DiCataldo, and C. Tschopp, "A Late Night Story: Rorschach Records of a Vampire," paper presented at the XIVth International Rorschach Congress and Projective Methods, Lisbon, Portugal, July 1993.

28. Benezech, Bourgeois, Villeger, and Etchegaray, "Cannibalisme et vampirisme."

29. McCully, "Vampirism."

30. Kayton, "The Relationship of the Vampire Legend to Schizophrenia."

31. Discussing the primitive use of the body to express aggressive fantasies, Rivière graphically lists the child's physical armamentarium: "Limbs shall trample, kick, and hit; lips, fingers and hands shall suck, twist, pinch; teeth shall bite, gnaw, mangle and cut; mouth shall devour, swallow and kill (annihilate); eyes kill by a look, pierce and penetrate; breath and mouth hurt by noise . . . " (J. Rivière, "On the Genesis of Psychical Conflict in Early Infancy," *International Journal of Psychoanalysis* 17 [1936]: 407).

32. W. R. D. Fairbairn, *An Object-Relations Theory of the Personality* (New York: Basic Books, 1952).

33. Kayton, "The Relationship of the Vampire Legend to Schizophrenia."

34. H. Cleckly, *The Mask of Sanity,* 5th ed. (St. Louis, Mo.: Mosby, 1976); R. Hare, *Psychopathy: Theory and Research* (New York: Wiley, 1970); R. Hare, "Twenty Years' Experience with the Cleckley Psychopath," in *Unmasking the Psychopath,* ed. W. Reid, D. Dorr, J. Walker, and J. Bonner (New York: Norton, 1986).

35. Bourguignon, "Situation du vampirisme et de l'autovampirisme."

36. Ibid.

37. In his own written rebuttal to views expressed at his trial by a famous forensic psychiatrist, Sergeant Bertrand exclaims: "Oui! Destructive monomania has always been stronger in me than erotic monomania, it is undeniable, and I believe that I would never have taken any chances to rape a cadaver had I not been able to destroy it afterwards. Therefore destruction wins over sexuality, whatever is said, and nobody is able to prove the contrary; I know better than anyone what was going on in me" (Bourguignon, "Situation du vampirisme et de l'autovampirisme").

38. Hemphill and Zabow, "Clinical Vampirism."

39. Prins, *Bizarre Behaviours.*

40. J. R. Meloy, *The Psychopathic Mind: Origins, Dynamics, and Treatment* (Northvale, N.J.: Aronson, 1988).

41. J. R. Meloy and C. Gacono, "A Psychotic (Sexual) Psychopath: 'I Just Had a Violent Thought . . . ,' " *Journal of Personality Assessment* 58 (1992): 480–493.

42. Wilgowitz, *Le Vampirisme*, 8.

43. Jones, *On the Nightmare.*

44. M. Yvonneau, "Matricide et vampirisme," *Évolution psychiatrique* 55 (1990): 567–577.

The Vampire as Bloodthirsty Revenant: A Psychoanalytic Post Mortem

The use of the word myth *to refer to stories of the vampire is anathema to the professional folklorist. For the folklorist,* myth *is a technical term referring to sacred narratives explaining how the world or humankind came to be in their present form. Because encounters with vampires, real or imagined, have nothing whatever to do with the creation of the world or humankind, they do not qualify as bona fide myths. Nor are such stories "folktales," which are fictional, as indicated by an opening formula (e.g., "Once upon a time"), signalling that what follows is not to be taken as literal, historical truth. Vampire accounts are what folklorists call legends, that is, stories told as true and set in the postcreation world. They might conceivably also be classified as memorates, which are personal narratives of encounters with a supernatural creature, also told as true. When such personal narratives become the property of an entire community, they would be considered legends rather than memorates. Most nonfolklorists, however, tend to use the word* myth *to refer to any story which is thought to be fallacious or untrue. Now that we have established that stories of vampires are legends (or memorates), at least from a folklorist's point of view, what else can we say about the vampire? Too often folklorists are prone to worry unduly about classification, and they utterly fail to offer much in the way of interpretation. Instead, the task of the interpretation of folklore falls by default to anthropologists, historians, literary critics, and psychiatrists.*

The final essay in this volume is an attempt by a folklorist with a confessed Freudian bias to interpret the vampire as a creature of legend. Whether or not it constitutes any advance in our understanding of this remarkable nightmarish figment of the human imagination is for the reader to judge.

In accordance with a pronounced penchant for the ritual number three, Western folklorists are prone to divide cultural materials into a tripartite classificatory scheme: elite culture, mass or popular culture, and folklore. Sometimes these admittedly somewhat arbitrary categories are mutually exclusive. That is, there are surely literary creations which have no analogs or parallels in either popular culture or folklore. By the same token there may be instances of popular culture (e.g., comic books, television programs, motion pictures, and the like) which are totally independent of both elite or high culture and folklore. In the same way, there may be folklore which is orally transmitted from person to person, from generation to generation, which has never served as the inspiration for either popular or elite culture.

Elite culture and popular culture, however, are more similar to one another than either is to folklore. Indeed, sometimes the line of demarcation between high culture and popular culture is very subjective. What makes a particular example from a popular-culture genre, such as a detective story, a tale of science fiction, a cowboy/outlaw Western adventure, or a silhouette romance, qualify as so-called high culture? In any event, both high and popular cultures are fixed in print or locked into videotape or film. In marked contrast, there are *always* multiple versions of folklore, versions which exhibit variation from one to another. A literary novel or a television program cannot change over time. They are necessarily the same for each new generation. True, the perception or reception of them can vary with succeeding sequences of audiences, but the texts themselves cannot change. Folklore, on the other hand, is constantly in a state of flux. No two versions of an item of folklore will be verbatim identical. Multiple existence (in more than one time and/or place) and variation are the hallmark criteria of folklore or oral tradition. In the majority of cases, there is another important distinguishing characteristic, namely, authorship. In most instances, the author of a literary work is known and so also are the authors of works in popular culture. We know who the creators of *Star Trek* and *Tarzan* are. The creators of folklore, however, are almost always anonymous.

The vampire (Motif E 251. Vampire. Corpse which comes from grave at night and sucks blood) is an example of a subject or topic which is found in all three levels of culture. There are literary treatments of the vampire in countless novels (and some *with* counts!), short stories and poems (see Marigny 1985; Carter 1989; Frost 1989); and there are depictions of the vampire in popular culture, for example, television ("Dark Shadows") and innumerable films (see Riccardo 1983; Melton 1994:719–774); and there are plenty of documentations of the vampire figure in folklore. Whereas we know who the authors of the literary renderings of the vampire are and whereas films involving vampires provide credits indicating who the writers of the screenplay are, in contrast, we have absolutely no idea who the individual or individuals might have been who created the initial folkloristic figure of the vampire. We do not even know for certain where in the world the vampire first appeared. One thing we do know, however, is that the original source of both literary and popular cultural representations of the vampire came from folklore, not the other way round. Bram Stoker's *Dracula* of 1897 may well have influenced the literary works and films which appeared after that date, but Bram Stoker, an Irishman by birth, did not invent the Transylvanian vampire. That figure existed long before Stoker wrote his famous novel (see Florescu 1985–86; and Ryan 1993).

Because the vast bulk of vampire scholarship has tended to concentrate upon literary and popular cultural renderings of this curious and enigmatic creature, by design I shall limit my consideration of this figure to the folklore of the vampire. Actually, the vampire has attracted the attention of many folklorists of the past. Jacob Grimm in a posthumously published note to his *Deutsche Mythologie* defined vampires as "dead men come back, who suck blood" (Grimm 1966:1586). Other nineteenth-century folklorists writing about vampires include Mannhardt (1859), Hanush (1859), Krauss (1892a, 1892b), and Afanas'ev (1976). Twentieth-century folkloristic discussions have been penned by Polívka (1901), Vukanović (1957–59), Burkhart (1966), Oinas (1978, 1982), and Perkowski (1976, 1989, 1992a, 1992b). There are also substantial surveys of vampire beliefs and legends in individual countries, for example, Bulgaria (Popov 1983; Beynen 1988), Czechoslovakia (Wollman 1920–23), Greece (du Boulay 1982), Romania (Weslowski 1910; Murgoci 1926; Nixon 1979; Cremene 1981; Perkowski 1982; Senn 1982), Russia (Jaworskij 1898; Afanas'ev 1976), and Serbia (Durham 1923; Djordjevic 1953). In Poland, a vampire questionnaire was issued, suggesting that belief in vampires persisted in that country into the twentieth century (Fischer 1927).

Widespread as the vampire is throughout eastern Europe, it is not true, as has been claimed, that "belief in vampires is found all over the world" (Anon. 1950:1154). This statement in the *Standard Dictionary of Folklore, Mythology and Legend* is demonstrably false. The vampire is *not* universal by any means. Native Americans do not have vampires. Nor do most of the indigenous peoples of Oceania have vampires. Fear of the dead is one thing; vampires in particular are quite another. (For that matter, there is not one single myth, legend, or folktale which is universal in the sense of being known by *all* human populations, past and present, as even the most cursory inspection of the six-volume *Motif-Index of Folk-Literature* clearly attests.) According to the encyclopedic *Vampire Book* (1994), a vampire "is a reanimated corpse that rises from the grave to suck the blood of living people and thus retain a semblance of life" or "a peculiar kind of revenant, a dead person who had returned to life and continued a form of existence through drinking the blood of the living" (Melton 1994:xxii, 629). Vampire discussions frequently include apotropaic measures to ward off vampire attacks (see Krauss 1892b; Jellinek 1904:323) as well as descriptions of time-tested techniques effective in killing them once and for all, for example, by driving a stake through their hearts or their navels (Murgoci 1926:328) or by decapitation (Wollman 1923:143).

In reviewing what is known about the vampire, we may mention the term itself. What is the meaning or significance, if any, of the word *vampire?* One theory proposes a Turkish origin for the term (Naylor 1983:95; Wilson 1985:577), but there seems to be consensus that the source of the word is the Slavic *vampir* (Bielfeldt 1971; Naylor 1983; Wilson 1985; Perkowski 1989:32–33). As for the possible semantic significance of *vampire*, one theory, supported by the great nineteenth-century Russian folklorist A. N. Afanas'ev, suggests that the term derives from the Greek root *pī*, meaning "to drink" (Afanas'ev 1976:164; see also Marigny 1986:168; and Buck 1949:331). Although one modern researcher finds this theory "attractive," he refers to problems with it (Naylor 1983:97). I shall argue later that this theory is extremely plausible.

The attempts to interpret the basic meaning of the vampire figure may for the sake of convenience be divided into two broad categories: literal-historical and metaphoric-symbolic. The literal-historical approach is exemplified by the prolific writings of Montague Summers, who seems to have believed that there are in fact actual vampires. In his words, "For the hauntings of a Vampire, three things are necessary: the Vampire, the Devil, and the Permission of Almighty God." Summers is not sure whether it is the Devil who energizes the corpse or whether the deceased reappears by himself through "some dispensation of Divine Providence." Each case must be decided individually on its own merits. Can the Devil really do this? Summers' unequivocal answer: "There is no doubt the Demon can do this" (1995:174). A host of parapsychological essays on the vampire argue in a similar vein (Riccardo 1983:91–99). Yet another instance of the "literal" approach is represented by those psychologists who contend that the vampire legend is based upon clinical cases of mentally disturbed individuals who drink the blood of their victims (see Vanden Bergh and Kelly 1964; Prins 1984, 1985; Jaffé and DiCataldo 1994; and Bourguignon 1997). A more reasoned illustration of the literal-historical approach is Paul Barber's 1988 *Vampires, Burial, and Death*, in which he seeks to demonstrate that all the alleged physical characteristics of the vampire correspond to the physiological reality of corpses in the process of decomposition. For Barber, folklore consists of history encumbered by a legendary overlay, and the task he sets himself is to deconstruct that overlay to find the kernel of historical truth contained therein (1987:3; 1988:152). It is the folk's empirical observation of corpses, he contends, that has led to the creation of the vampire imago. For example, since the tongue of a corpse may protrude and since blood may seep from its open mouth, observers wrongly assumed that the vampire must attack his victims "with teeth or tongue and suck their blood" (1988:157, 195–196). Barber's sophisticated reliance on forensic pathology makes his discussion plausible, but it falls well short of offering a satisfactory explanation of what is almost certainly fantasy, not reality.

Before discussing a possible metaphoric-symbolic interpretation of the vampire, I should like to mention two specific characteristics of the vampire which I believe any persuasive theory of the vampire must account for. Because descriptions of the vampire in various cultures abound, I shall not review all aspects of the creature here (see Summers 1995, 1996; Melton 1994).

The first characteristic is the vampire's invariable return to attack "those who on earth have been his nearest and dearest" (Nixon 1979:18; see also Schierup 1986:179). There is even a Greek idiom, "The vampire hunts its own kindred" (du Boulay 1982:232) or, in an earlier rendering, the vampire "feeds on his own" (Bent 1886:397), which supports the notion that the vampire is connected somehow with family dynamics. Twitchell, in his essay "The Vampire Myth" (the reader is reminded that narratives about vampires are *legends*, stories told as true and set in postcreation time, *not myths*, which are sacred narratives explaining how the world and humankind came into being), even goes so far as to comment, "The most startling part of the folkloric vampire is that he must first attack members of his own family" (1980:86).

The second curious characteristic requiring an explanation is the belief that the vampire sometimes drinks milk rather than blood. Ernest Jones in his pioneering essay on the vampire notes this feature when he comments: "The German Alp sucks the nipples of men and children, and withdraws milk from women and cows more often than blood. The Drud also sucks the breasts of children, while the Southern Slav Mora sucks blood or milk indifferently" (1971: 119). In Romania, we are told that vampires on St. George's Eve "take milk away from nursing mothers" (Murgoci 1926:332).

These two features of vampires—the attempt to attack close family members and the reported efforts of the vampire to drink milk rather than blood—are at first glance somewhat puzzling. But surely the most perplexing question to be explained is, Why do vampires need to suck the blood (or milk) of the living to facilitate a kind of life after death? Why, in sum, is the vampire a "bloodthirsty revenant"?

To answer this fundamental question, we need to place the vampire phenomenon in a wider theoretical framework. That structural framework, apparently common to Indo-European and Semitic worldview in antiquity, involves a set of bisecting humoral binary oppositions: hot and cold, and wet and dry. To this very day, folk disease theory depends upon combinations of these distinctions; for example, diseases (and cures) are classified as being "hot" or "cold." The word *sick* in English—about which, by the way, the OED claims, "Relationship to other Teutonic roots is uncertain, and no outside cognates have been traced"—is very likely a derivative of the Latin *siccus*, meaning "dry" (cf. *sec* in French). In classical Greek thought, we are told that "the Greeks conceived the living as 'wet' and the dead as 'dry' " (Lloyd 1964:101). Perhaps the best articulation of the principle that liquid is life and drying is dying was made by Richard Broxton Onians in his brilliant tour de force entitled *The Origins of European Thought about the Body, the Mind, the Soul, the World, Time, and Fate*, first published in 1951. According to Onians, life is perceived as a process whereby liquid gradually diminishes until the final desiccation, which is death (1973:214–215). I myself have earlier observed that it is possible to argue by analogy. Indo-European peoples could easily see the evolution, or more aptly the devolution, of grapes into raisins, plums into prunes, and so on, with this *secular* transition marked by the appearance of wrinkles. So as older men and women became wrinkled with the onset of advancing age, these wrinkles could perfectly logically be interpreted as the consequences of a drying-out process (Dundes 1980:102–103). In this context we can understand why the replenishment of liquid lost, as a means of rejuvenation, is such a common theme, with manifestations as varied as the search for the fountain of youth and the application of ointments and oils to aging skin.

Closer to the vampire issue, we can also appreciate the specifics of various death and burial practices. In modern Greece, we find the custom of "breaking vessels filled with water on the tombs of departed friends" (Onians 1973:272; see also Sartori 1908). Politis, the founder of Greek folkloristics, in an essay on this custom, comments that "the water held by these broken vessels was an offering to the dead" and that "it refreshes the departed" (1894:35, 41). He reports further, "In Crete a jar full of water is deposited at the grave, where it is left for forty days, the belief being that during all that time the departed soul wanders over the haunts where it lived, and returns every evening to drink of the water provided" (1894:37). Some have argued that the broken vessel is a symbol of the deceased and that "the pouring out of the water symbolizes the vanishing soul and the dead body will fall to pieces like the broken crock. Others say that they pour out the water 'in order to allay the burning thirst of the dead man' " (Onians 1973:275). The antiquity of this ritual is confirmed by the Babylonian custom whereby the nearest kinsman of the deceased was obliged to serve as "pourer of water" at the grave or tomb. Hence a Babylonian curse: "May God deprive him of an heir and a pourer of water" (Onians 1973:285).

All this helps explain why the dead are perceived as being thirsty. Ever since Bellucci's 1909 essay, "Sul bisogno di dissetarsi attribuito all'anima dei morti," and Deonna's equally excellent 1939 discussion, "La soif des morts," this folkloristic conception of the thirsty dead has been amply documented. (There is also Sartori's 1908 cross-cultural survey, "Das Wasser im Toten-gebrauche.") So the vampire as a thirsty dead corpse fits very well into the standard Indo-European and Semitic worldview paradigm.

From this, we can now understand why the dead are so anxious to obtain liquid refreshment to become re-fleshed. But why the sucking act (which in the literary forms of the vampire was metamorphosed into biting)? To answer this question (as well as the associated question of why the very conception of life should be tied to liquid), we must have recourse to psychology.

The majority of psychological analyses of the vampire have concentrated almost exclusively on literary versions of this creature, with special emphasis on Bram Stoker's 1897 novel *Dracula*. (For useful reviews of this massive literature, see Margaret L. Shanahan's extensive entry, "Psychological Perspectives on Vampire Mythology," in *The Vampire Book* [in Melton 1994: 492–501], and the section "Psychoanalytical Approaches" in Leatherdale's *Dracula: The Novel & the Legend* [1985:160–175] and Gelder 1994.) There are also several clinical studies of patients exhibiting what is adjudged to be vampirelike behavior (see Yvonneau 1990; and Gottlieb 1991, 1994). Psychological or psychoanalytic studies of the folkloristic vampire proper are many fewer in number. Let us begin with Freud.

One of the sources cited by Freud in his much maligned *Totem and Taboo* was an 1898 treatise by Rudolf Kleinpaul entitled *Die Lebendigen und die Toten in Volksglauben, Religion und Sage*. In that treatise which Freud praised, there is an entire section devoted to the vampire (1898:119–129). In summarizing Kleinpaul's discussion, Freud stated, "Kleinpaul believes that originally . . . the dead were all vampires, who bore ill-will towards the living, and strove to harm them and deprive them of life" (Freud 1938:853). This prompted Freud to inquire: Why do the "beloved dead" become "demons"? Is it just that the soul of the dead "envies the living" and wants to be reunited with them? His answer depended upon two premises. First, Freud contended that there is inevitably ambivalence towards the deceased loved one, that is, feelings of *both* love and hate. The latter may have involved an actual wish, albeit perhaps an unconscious one, for the death of the beloved person (1938:854). When the person dies, the survivor not surprisingly feels some guilt (for having at some point wished for the death). In some cases, the survivor may feel anger that he or she has been abandoned by the deceased. The second premise, according to Freud, is that feelings of guilt and anger on the part of the survivor are *projected* onto the deceased. In other words, "I feel anger towards the deceased" is transformed through projection into "the deceased feels anger towards me, the survivor." "Even though," said Freud, "the survivor will deny that he has ever entertained hostile impulses towards the beloved dead," the result is nonetheless the survivor's fear of being injured by a vengeful "hostile demon" (1938:855).

Freud's explanation of vampires is more fully articulated by his loyal disciple and biographer Ernest Jones, whose essay on the vampire was originally published in German in 1912, just one year before *Totem and Taboo* was published. Jones also interprets the vampire in terms of projection. The living survivors' ambivalent feelings of both love and hate (e.g., towards parents) are supposedly projected onto the deceased so that it is the corpse who feels both love and hate towards the living (1971:99–100). That is why, according to Jones, vampires frequently return to visit their nearest relatives, for example, wives, husbands, or children. Jones also suggests that the vampire belief complex involves a form of regression to an infantile "sadistic-masochistic phase of development" (1971:110). As the infant may express anger towards a parent through biting, so, through projection combined with *lex talionis*, the adult fears that the dead parent will retaliate by returning to bite him or her (1971:112). Jones, like Freud, believed that the "hostile 'death-wishes' nourished by the child against the disturbing parent or other rival" are, after the actual death of this parent, translated through projection to a guilty conscience and a fear that the dead parental figure will return to exact vengeance (1971:112). The mixture of love and hate towards the parental figures is symbolized by sucking (love) and biting (hate), actions taken by vampires towards the living (1971:121).

The sadistic component of vampirism was noted by many writers, for example, Krafft-Ebing in his *Psychopathia Sexualis* (1953:129) and Havelock Ellis in his *Studies in the Psychology of Sex* (1928:126). But the specific hypothesis relating oral sadism to infantile conditioning came from psychoanalysis. Karl Abraham in his important 1924 paper, "The Influence of Oral Erotism on Character-Formation," described a shift from sucking to biting in the so-called oral phase of infantile development. In Abraham's words, ". . . the irruption of teeth . . . causes a considerable part of the pleasure in sucking to be replaced by pleasure in biting" (1953:396), and in that same paper, Abraham actually speaks of "regression from the oral-sadistic to the sucking stage," which has an element of cruelty in it as well, "which makes them [such individuals] something like *vampires* to other people" (1953:401, my emphasis). Abraham's astute observation of oral phases was echoed by psychoanalyst Melanie Klein, who confirmed that "normally the infant's pleasure in sucking is succeeded by pleasure in biting" (1960:179). It is this line of reasoning which led ineluctably to such statements as "The vampire becomes a projection of oral sadism left over from the early infant-mother relationship" (Henderson 1976:610; see also Kayton 1972:310).

Melanie Klein, however, went further than her mentor Karl Abraham. It was she who postulated the critical importance of the maternal breast. She contended that an infant may, because of either overindulgence or deprivation of the maternal breast, direct aggressive impulses at that breast, its initial contact point with the mother (1960:185–186). Henderson's rendering of this situation is: "When mothering is not available at the right moment or is intruded when the infant is not reaching out for it, the breast becomes hateful and persecutory" (1976:610). Klein readily admits that this idea of an infant "trying to destroy its mother" presents a "horrifying not to say an unbelievable picture to our minds" (1960:187). The possible linkage between the "drying up of the breast" and vampirism is proposed by Copjec, who claims, "Most visual images of vampirism center on the female breast" (1991:34 n. 16).

From a folkloristic perspective, we can see that, with the principle of *lex talionis*, the infant-child may fear retaliation for such aggressive impulses and that such retaliation by the parents might take the form of sucking or biting. Folklore fantasy is full of swallowing monsters who threaten to eat up children, while the "vagina dentata" (Motif F 547.1.1; see Otero 1996) could represent for males the maternal teeth threatening to bite (off) their male projection, just as male infants sought to bite (off) the projecting breast of the mother. In any event, the nursing mother confronted with oral sadistic sucking or biting on the part of a frustrated or angry infant may withdraw her breast from the infant's mouth, a perfectly reasonable course of action under the circumstances. This withdrawal of the breast would, from the infant's point of view, constitute a form of "object loss." In other words, sucking (and/or biting) the breast leads to object loss, meaning the withdrawal of the maternal breast (which in infantile logic appears to be inexhaustible: every time the infant wishes nourishment, the breast seems to be magically full again). Object loss, in general, is related to so-called separation anxiety on the part of infants, an anxiety-provoking situation which is articulated in such games as peek-a-boo and later hide-and-seek, where the "lost" object is in every case "found" and the separation anxiety alleviated (Frankiel 1993).

Now if we understand that the death of a loved one is also a form of object loss, in the psychological sense, and if there is guilt on the part of the living as having caused that death (e.g., through wishful thinking at some point), then it is possible that through projective inversion that the lost object (the deceased loved one) will return to take revenge by means of sucking or biting. This, I maintain, is precisely what we have in the folkloristic figure of the bloodsucking revenant known as the vampire.

There is another aspect of the vampire phenomenon that needs elucidation and concerns the conception of death itself. It is once again Ernest Jones who provides the critical clue. In his brilliant 1924 essay, "Psycho-Analysis and Anthropology," delivered as an address to the British Royal Anthropological Institute in February of that year, Jones suggested that death is "a reversal of the birth act leading to a return to the pre-natal existence within the maternal womb" (1951:137–138). The tomb-womb symbolic equation is now pretty much taken for granted. Freud in a footnote in his *Interpretation of Dreams* went so far as to propose that "the profoundest unconscious reason for a belief in a life after death" is "a projection into the future of this mysterious life before birth." Freud also claimed that the dread of being buried alive stems from the same prenatal experience (1938:395 n. 1). As one analyst phrases the issue, "The symbolism is obvious: Earth equals mother; coffin equals womb. The vampire is, thus, born anew each night and begins anew its search for sustaining lifeblood from another" (Henderson 1976:618).

The tomb-womb equation explains why bodies are so often buried in the fetal position. It is not to save space or work for grave-diggers, but rather to allow the corpse to assume a comfortable if not comforting position. (This also gives a rationale for why adults in pain or distress often try to sleep in the curled-up fetal position [Jones 1951:144 n. 4]). If death beliefs assume a rebirth, says Jones, then "rebirth" is really "debirth" (1951:139 n. 1). What has all this to do with vampires? I submit that, if a vampire wants to be reborn, it must do so in regressive terms, and as a newborn babe gains sustenance through sucking at its mother's breast, so a "newborn" vampire must do likewise, albeit in symbolic guise. Jones himself, in his groundbreaking essay on the vampire, quotes striking evidence supporting this hypothesis. He cites, for example, folklorist Friedrich Krauss: "Among the Southern Slavs it is believed when a Mara (there called Mora) once tastes a man's blood she falls in love with him and can never more leave him. . . . she is particularly fond of sucking children's breasts" (1971:126). But despite all his insights and brilliance, here Jones unfortunately goes astray. He explains these "phantasies" as being symbols of "semen" (1971:119), an all too typical instance of the excessively male-biased interpretations so often found among early Freudians. As Stevenson points out in his 1988 *PMLA* essay on the sexuality of *Dracula*, Jones is confused. If blood is semen, how could a male vampire obtain "semen" from sucking blood *from women* (1988:146)? But Stevenson in turn is also confused when he perceives that Dracula's attack on Mina seems to be a mother engaged in breast-feeding. In this climactic and startling episode in the novel, Dracula, one may recall, forces Mina to suck *his* breast. "What is going on!" Stevenson asks, "Fellatio? Lactation? It seems the vampire is sexually capable of anything" (1988:146). Bierman calls it "a thinly disguised primal scene in oral terms" (1972:194).

The answer at this point should be obvious. The fact that the vampire sucks milk from children's breasts, for example, could easily be construed as a perfect reversal of the initial infantile prototype. Instead of infants sucking from adult breasts, adults suckle from children's breasts. We know very well from our own Judeo-Christian eschatological cosmology that heaven, the promised land after death, offers "milk and honey," an old-fashioned form of sweetened milk offered to infants. The idiom of "a land flowing with milk and honey" as a metaphor for abundance occurs no fewer than twenty-one times in the Bible (Beck and Smedley 1971:167). And what are we to make of the phrase "and the hills shall flow with milk" (Joel 3:18)? The only hills that flow with milk are maternal breasts. So the idea of a blissful death involving a regression to a postnatal paradise including lots of milk and honey is seemingly consonant with Judeo-Christian worldview.

Now we can better understand why the dead are thirsty. The life-giving liquid can be water, blood, or milk, among other choices. This is why the vampire is said to "suck" fluids from its victims. Sucking is the initial infantile response to the maternal breast, which according to Melanie Klein is the infant's "first object relation" (1957:3). Biting comes later (as it does in literary versions of the vampire plot) with a marked increase in oral sadism. As we've noted, the infant's teeth are its first weapon against the maternal breast. Just as the infant may want to suck the living (breast) dry, so the deceased is imagined as wanting to return to suck the living dry. Just as an infant appears to have an insatiable appetite or thirst for milk, so the vampire constantly has to seek more liquid refreshment or sustenance. However, whereas the maternal breast to the infant seems to be a magical, inexhaustible source of nutriment, the living victims of vampires are not. When they lose their vital fluids, they themselves become vampires in need of liquid replacement. Whether this is simply a folk recognition of the communicable nature of infectious diseases, or whether it is merely an affirmation of the principle of "limited good" (Foster 1965), the end result is the same. In the latter case, if there is a finite amount of liquid "good," the vampire's gain is automatically the victim's loss. More important, by sucking on the victim, the vampire may be said to *merge* with the victim (Kayton 1972:310), which would constitute a veritable replication of the prototypic infantile breast-feeding scenario. The victim then becomes a vampire, that is, also regresses to an oral sadistic infantile level.

I believe the theory of vampires here proposed has the advantage of explaining a good many puzzling details about the vampire belief complex. We can now understand why vampires are thirsty: they are thirsty because all the dead in the Indo-European and Semitic world are considered to be thirsty, not just vampires. They are thirsty because death is debirth; the transit to the other world is the reverse of the birth process, that is, the movement through the birth canal. To be reborn, the deceased must undo death, that is, be born again. If death is truly debirth, then reversing the death process would be equivalent to rebirth. It is almost mathematical. Death is the negation of life, but the negation of death is once again life. Minus a minus equals a plus! Being born again leads to a symbolic reinstatement of the initial nurturing process, that is, the reestablishment of the first object relationship: sucking the maternal breast. But as the dead are angry (at being dead—or so the living suppose), the sucking is quite vicious; the dead suck their victims to death. We can now also understand why the vampire attacks members of its own immediate family, and also why the vampire is said to sometimes attack cows and goats, obvious milk-giving substitutes for the original maternal breast. We can now better appreciate the various apotropaic measures employed to prevent vampires from carrying out their nefarious actions. Burning a corpse, like cremation, completes the desiccating process (see Čajkanović 1974). Once *all* the liquid is removed, the corpse is permanently dead. Decapitation is also effective because, if the deceased has no mouth, it cannot possibly mount an oral attack on the breast. Driving a stake through the purported vampire's heart is not an attempt to pinion the corpse by impalement, but rather an efficacious means of draining the last remaining liquid (blood) from it, which like burning or cremation completes the desiccating death of the only partly deceased.

The oral erotic basis of vampirism would also help explain why this belief complex can so easily serve as a convenient metaphor for adult sexuality ranging from "normal" oedipal heterosexuality (in many literary texts, the vampire typically attacks a member of the opposite sex) to homosexuality (Dyer 1988) and lesbianism (Case 1991; see also Melton 1994:301–302, 362–366; and Gordon and Hollinger 1997). The latter forms of sexuality, after all, often do involve oral-genital sucking activity. For that matter, even kissing is essentially an act of sucking, not to mention the "love-bite" (Morse 1993:193).

Finally, it is my contention that it is the underlying oral erotic basis of the vampire belief complex which partly explains the endless fascination of this enigmatic creature. In prudish Victorian times, the Bram Stoker novel provided a much-needed outlet for repressed sexuality (see Bentley 1972; Stevenson 1988), but even in the twentieth century, the vampire of popular culture and literature serves a similar function. The fear of being attacked by a vampire—at night, in one's own bedroom—can be construed as a form of wishful thinking. The vampire in the grave is analogous to a sleeping parent. It is an incarnate expression of a child's ambivalence towards his or her parent of the opposite sex. While the initial sucking of the breast can be an expression of love, too much sucking (or certainly biting) can be an act of aggression. The vampire, though overtly carrying out an aggressive act, also approximates the original life-giving and partly erotic breast-feeding relationship. That is why the vampire is both feared and regarded as fascinating, even to young children watching vampire movies on television or vampires in animated cartoons.

In conclusion, we can now argue that the theory of the origin of the word *vampire*, which suggested that the term comes from a root *pī*, meaning "to drink," makes perfectly good sense. Drinking, or rather sucking, is an essential sine qua non of vampirism. And this is so even if one cannot accept the proposed infantile origin of this remarkable living legend, which will never die as long as it can continue to renew itself with future generations yet unborn.

References

Abraham, K. 1953. "The Influence of Oral Erotism on Character-Formation." In Karl Abraham, *Selected Papers on Psychoanalysis*, 393–406. New York: Basic Books.

Afanas'ev, A. N. 1976. "Poetic Views of the Slavs Regarding Nature." In *Vampires of the Slavs*, ed. Jan L. Perkowski, 160–170. Cambridge: Slavica Publishers.

Anon. 1950. "Vampire." In *Standard Dictionary of Folklore, Mythology, and Legend*, ed. Maria Leach, 1154. New York: Funk & Wagnalls.

Barber, P. 1987. "Forensic Pathology and the European Vampire." *Journal of Folklore Research* 24:1–32. (See also herein, pp. 109–142.)

Barber, P. 1988. *Vampires, Burial, and Death: Folklore and Reality*. New Haven: Yale University Press.

Beck, B. F., and D. Smedley. 1971. *Honey and Your Health*. New York: Bantam.

Bellucci, G. 1909. "Sul bisogno di dissetarsi attribuito all'anima dei morti." *Archivio per l'antropologia e le etnololgia* 39:211–229.

Bent, J. T. 1886. "On Insular Greek Customs." *Journal of the Anthropological Institute* 15:391–403.

Bentley, C. F. 1972. "The Monster in the Bedroom: Sexual Symbolism in Bram Stoker's *Dracula*" *Literature and Psychology* 22:27–34.

Beynen, G .K. 1988. "The Vampire in Bulgarian Folklore." *Vtori Mezhdunaroken Kongres po bulgarestika*, 456–465. Sofia.

Bielfeldt, H. K. 1971. "Die Wortgeschichte von Deutsch *Vampir* und *Vamp*." In *Serta Slavica in Memoriam Aloisii Schmaus*, 42–47. Munich: Rudolf Trofenik.

Bierman, J. 1972. "Dracula: Prolonged Childhood Illness and the Oral Triad." *American Imago* 29:186–198.

Bourguignon, A. 1997. "Vampirism and Autovampirism." In *Sexual Dynamics of Anti-Social Behavior*, ed. Louis B. Schlesinger and Eugene Revitch, 271–293. 2nd ed. Springfield: Charles C. Thomas.

Buck, C. D. 1949. *A Dictionary of Selected Synonyms in the Principal Indo-European Languages*. Chicago: University of Chicago Press.

Burkhart, D. 1966. "Vampirglaube und Vampirsage auf dem Balkan." In Alois Schmaus, ed., *Beiträge zur Südosteuropa-Forschung*, ed. Alois Schmaus, 211–252. Munich: Rudolf Trofenik.

Čajkanović, V. 1974. "The Killing of a Vampire." *Folklore Forum* 7: 260–271. (See also herein, pp. 72–84.)

Carter, M. L. 1989. *The Vampire in Literature: A Bibliography*. Ann Arbor: UMI Research Press.

Case, S.-E. 1991. "Tracking the Vampire." *Differences: A Journal of Feminist Cultural Studies* 3(2): 1–20.

Chotjewitz, P. O. 1968. "Der Vampir: Theorie und Kritik einer Mythe." *Merkur* 8:708–719.

Copjec, J. 1991. "Vampires, Breast-Feeding, and Anxiety." *October* 58:25–43.

Cremene, A. 1981. *La Mythologie du vampire en Roumanie*. Monaco: Éditions du Rocher.

Deonna, W. 1939. "Croyances Funeraires: La soif des morts; le mort musicien." *Revue de l'histoire des religions* 119:53–81.

Djordjević, T. R. 1953. ["Vampires in the Folk Beliefs of Our People"]. (in Serbian). *Recueil Serbe d'ethnographie* 66:149–219.

du Boulay, J. 1982. "The Greek Vampire: A Study of Cyclic Symbolism in Marriage and Death." *Man* 17:219–238. (See also herein, pp. 85–108.)

Dundes, A. 1980. *Interpreting Folklore*. Bloomington: Indiana University Press.

Durham, E. 1923. "Of Magic, Witches and Vampires in the Balkans." *Man* 23: 189–192.

Dyer, R. 1988. "Children of the Night: Vampirism as Homosexuality, Homosexuality as Vampirism." In *Sweet Dreams: Sexuality, Gender, and Popular Fiction*, ed. Susannah Radstone, 47–72. London: Lawrence & Wishart.

Ellis, H. 1928. *Studies in the Psychology of Sex*. Vol. 3. Philadelphia: F. A. Davis.

Fischer, A. 1927. "Upior, strzgon czy wieszczy?" *Lud* 26:84.

Florescu, R. 1985–86. "The Dracula Search in Retrospect." *New England Social Studies Bulletin* 43:25–50.

Foster, G. 1965. "Peasant Society and the Image of Limited Good." *American Anthropologist* 67:293–315.

Frankiel, R. V. 1993. "Hide-and-Seek in the Playroom: On Object Loss and Transference in Child Treatment." *Psychoanalytic Review* 80:341–359.

Freud, S. 1938. *The Basic Writings of Sigmund Freud*. New York: Modern Library.

Frost, B. J. 1989. *The Monster with A Thousand Faces: Guises of the Vampire in Myth and Literature*. Bowling Green: Bowling Green State University Popular Press.

Gelder, K. 1994. *Reading the Vampire*. London: Routledge.

Gordon, J., and V. Hollinger, eds. 1997. *Blood Read: The Vampire as Metaphor in Contemporary Culture*. Philadelphia: University of Pennsylvania Press.

Gottlieb, R. M. 1991. "The European Vampire: Applied Psychoanalysis and Applied Legend." *Folklore Forum* 24:39–61.

Gottlieb, R. M. 1994. "The Legend of the European Vampire: Object Loss and Corporeal Preservation." *Psychoanalytic Study of the Child* 49:465–480.

Grimm, J. 1966. *Teutonic Mythology*. Vol. 4. New York: Dover.

Hanush, J. J. 1859. "Die Vampyre." *Zeitschrift für Deutsche Mythologie und Sittenkunde* 4:198–201.

Henderson, D. J. 1976. "Exorcism, Possession, and the Dracula Cult: A Synopsis of Object-Relations Psychology." *Bulletin of the Menninger Clinic* 40:603–628.

Jaffé, P. D., and F. DiCataldo. 1994. "Clinical Vampirism: Blending Myth and Reality." *Bulletin of the American Academy of Psychiatry and the Law* 22:533–544. (See also herein, pp. 143–158.)

Jaworskij, J. 1898. Südrussiche Vampyre. *Zeitschrift des Vereins für Volkskunde* 8: 331–335.

Jellinek, A. L. 1904. "Zur Vampyrsage." *Zeitschrift des Vereins für Volkskunde* 14: 322–328.

Jones, E. 1951. "Psycho-Analysis and Anthropology." In Ernest Jones, *Essays in Applied Psychoanalysis*, 114–144. Vol. 2 of *Essays in Folklore, Anthropology and Religion*. London: Hogarth Press.

Jones, E. 1971. *On the Nightmare*. New York: Liveright.

Kayton, L. 1972. "The Relationship of the Vampire Legend to Schizophrenia." *Journal of Youth and Adolescence* 1:303–314.

Klein, M. 1957. *Envy and Gratitude: A Study of Unconscious Sources*. New York: Basic Books.

Klein, M. 1960. *The Psychoanalysis of Children*. New York: Grove Press.

Kleinpaul, R. 1898. *Die Lebendigen und die Toten in Volksglauben, Religion und Sage*. Leipzig: G. J. Göschen.

Krafft-Ebing, R. v. 1953. *Psychopathia Sexualis*. New York: Pioneer Publications.

Krauss, F. S. 1892a. "Vampyre in südslawischen Volksglauben." *Globus* 61:325–328.

Krauss, F. S. 1892b. "Südslawische Schutzmittel gegen Vampyre." *Globus* 62:203–204. (See translation herein, pp. 67–71.)

Leatherdale, C. 1985. *Dracula: The Novel & the Legend*. Wellingborough: Aquarian Press.

Lloyd, G. E. R. 1964. "The Hot and the Cold, the Dry and the Wet in Greek Philosophy." *Journal of Hellenic Studies* 84:92–106.

Mannhardt, W. 1859. "Über Vampyrismus." *Zeitschrift für Deutsche Mythologie und Sittenkunde* 4:259–282.

Marigny, J. 1985. *Le Vampire dans la littérature anglo-saxonne*. 2 vols. Paris: Didier Érudition.

Marigny, J. 1986. "La tradition légendaire du vampire en Europe." *Les Cahiers du G.E.R.F.* 1:165–186.

173

Melton, J. G. 1994. *The Vampire Book: The Encyclopedia of the Undead.* Detroit: Visible Ink Press.

Morse, D. R. 1993. "The Stressful Kiss: A Biopsychosocial Evaluation of the Origins, Evolution, and Societal Significance of Vampirism." *Stress Medicine* 9: 181–199.

Murgoci, A. 1926. "The Vampire in Roumania." *Folklore* 86:320–349. (See also herein, pp. 12–34.)

Naylor, K. E. 1983. "The Source of the Word 'Vampir' in Slavic." *Southeastern Europe* 10:93–98.

Nixon, D. 1979. "Vampire Lore and Alleged Cases." *Miorita* 6:14–28.

Oinas, F. 1978. "Heretics as Vampires and Demons in Russia." *Slavic and East European Journal* 22:433–441.

Oinas, F. 1982. "East European Vampires & Dracula." *Journal of Popular Culture* 16:108–116. (See also herein in part, pp. 47–56.)

Onians, R. B. 1973. *The Origins of European Thought.* New York: Arno Press.

Otero, S. 1996. " 'Fearing Our Mothers': An Overview of the Psychoanalytic Theories Concerning the Vagina Dentata Motif F 547.1.1." *American Journal of Psychoanalysis* 56:269–288.

Perkowski, J. L. 1976. *Vampires of the Slavs.* Cambridge: Slavica Publishers.

Perkowski, J. L. 1982. "The Romanian Folkloric Vampire." *East European Quarterly* 16:311–322. (See also herein, pp. 35–46.)

Perkowski, J. L. 1989. *The Darkling: A Treatise on Slavic Vampirism.* Columbus, Ohio: Slavica Publishers.

Perkowski, J. L. 1992a. *Cats, Bats, and Vampires.* New York: Dracula Press.

Perkowski, J. L. 1992b. *Daemon Contamination in Balkan Vampire Lore.* New York: Dracula Press.

Politis, N. G. 1894. "On the Breaking of Vessels as Funeral Rite in Modern Greece." *Journal of the Royal Anthropological Institute* 23:28–41.

Polívka, G. 1901. "Über das Wort 'Vampyr'." *Zeitschrift für österreichische Volkskunde* 7:185.

Popov, Rachko. 1983. "Vampirut v bulgarskite narodni viarvaniia." (The Vampire in Bulgarian Folk Beliefs). *Vekove* 9:36–43.

Prins, H. 1984. "Vampirism—Legendary or Clinical Phenomenon." *Medicine, Science and the Law* 24:283–293.

Prins, H. 1885. "Vampirism—a Clinical Condition." *British Journal of Psychiatry* 146:666–668.

Riccardo, M. V. 1983. *Vampires Unearthed: The Complete Multimedia Vampire & Dracula Bibliography.* New York: Garland.

Ryan, J. S. 1993. "The Vampire before and after Stoker's *Dracula*." *Contemporary Legend* 3:145–154.

Sartori, P. 1908. "Das Wasser im Totengebrauche." *Zeitschrift des Vereins für Volkskunde* 18:353–378.

Schierup, C.-U. 1986. "Why Are Vampires Still Alive? Wallachian Immigrants in Scandinavia." *Ethnos* 51:173–198.

Senn, H. A. 1982. *Were-Wolf and Vampire in Romania*. Boulder: East European Quarterly.

Shanahan, M. L. 1985. "Psychoanalytical Approaches." In C. Leatherdale, *Dracula: The Novel & the Legend*, 160–175. Wellingborough: Aquarian Press.

Shanahan, M. L. 1994. "Psychological Perspectives on Vampire Mythology." In *The Vampire Book: The Encyclopedia of the Undead*, ed. J. G. Melton, 492–501. Detroit: Visible Ink Press.

Stevenson, J. A. 1988. "A Vampire in the Mirror: The Sexuality of Dracula." *PMLA* 103:139–149.

Summers, M. 1995. *The Vampire*. London: Senate.

Summers, M. 1996. *The Vampire in Europe*. London: Bracken Books.

Thompson, S. 1955–1958. *The Motif-Index of Folk-Literature*. 6 vols. Bloomington: Indiana University Press.

Twitchell, J. 1980. "The Vampire Myth." *American Imago* 37:83–92.

Vanden Bergh, R. L., and J. F. Kelly. 1964. "Vampirism: A Review with New Observations." *Archives of General Psychiatry* 11:543–547.

Vukanović, T. P. 1957–59. "The Vampire." *Journal of the Gypsy Lore Society* 36:125–131; 37:21–31, 111–118; 38:44–55.

Weslowski, E. 1910. "Die Vampirsage im rumänischen Volksglauben." *Zeitschrift für österreichische Volkskunde* 16:209–216.

Wilson, K. M. 1985. "The History of the Word 'Vampire'." *Journal of the History of Ideas* 46:577–583. (See also herein, pp. 3–11.)

Wollmann, F. 1920–23. "Vampyrické pověsti v oblasti středo-Evropské." *Narodopisný věstnik československsky* 14(1):1–16; 14(2): 1–57; 15(1):1–58; 16:80–96, 133–149; 18:133–161.

Yvonneau, M. 1990. "Matricide et vampirisme." *L'Evolution Psychiatrique* 55:575–585.

Selected Bibliography
Index

A Selected Bibliography: Suggestions for Further Reading on the Vampire

√ Barber, Paul. *Vampires, Burial, and Death: Folklore and Reality*. New Haven: Yale University Press, 1988. 236pp. A scholarly, thoroughly researched treatise proposing a new interpretation of the vampire as deriving from the empirical observation of the characteristics of corpses in decay.

Burkhart, Dagmar. Vampirglaube und Vampirsage auf dem Balkan. In *Beiträge zur Südosteuropa-Forschung*, Alois Schmaus, ed., 211–252. Munich: Rudolf Trofenik, 1966. A solid substantial overview of vampire traditions in the Balkans.

Carter, Margaret L. *The Vampire in Literature: A Critical Bibliography*. Ann Arbor: UMI Research Press, 1989. 135pp. A useful compilation of sources relating to literary, not folkloristic, vampires.

Dresser, Norine. *American Vampires: Fans, Victims, Practitioners*. New York: Vintage Books, 1989. 255pp. A folklorist's popularly written overview of the presence of the vampire in modern American culture with attention to the impact of the vampire on the mass media.

Frost, Brian J. *The Monster with A Thousand Faces: Guises of the Vampire in Myth and Literature*. Bowling Green, Ohio: Bowling Green State University Popular Press, 1989. 152pp. The first part consists of an inventory of the forms of the vampire, the second part, "The Vampire in Weird Literature" (36–124), reviews the numerous literary depictions of the creature.

Jones, Ernest. *On the Nightmare*. New York: Liveright, 1971. 374pp. This book, first published in English in 1931, includes an important fourth chapter, "The Vampire" (98–130), which offers the first in-depth psychoanalytic interpretation of the vampire.

Leatherdale, Clive. *Dracula: The Novel and the Legend*. Wellingborough: The Aquarian Press, 1985. 256pp. Although concentrating on Bram Stoker's *Dracula*, the author does, nevertheless, discuss some of the various modern theoretical approaches to the vampire.

Marigny, Jean. *Le Vampire dans la littérature anglo-saxonne*. 2 vols. Paris: Didier Érudition, 1985. 880pp. An extensive, published doctoral dissertation, originally written in 1983 at the University of Grenoble, which offers a truly comprehensive survey of literary treatments of the vampire in English.

√ McNally, Raymond T., and Radu Florescu. *In Search of Dracula: The History of Dracula and Vampires*. Rev. ed. Boston: Houghton Mifflin, 1994. 297pp. Of all the books centering on Bram Stoker's *Dracula* (rather than on the vampire per se), this is one of the most authoritative.

√ Melton, J. Gordon. *The Vampire Book: The Encyclopedia of the Undead*. Detroit: Visible Ink Press, 1994. 852pp. Among the various dictionaries and encyclopedias devoted to the vampire, this is one of the most comprehensive, with entries covering most aspects of the creature; these entries are accompanied by useful bibliographic references.

Perkowski, Jan L. *Vampires of the Slavs*. Cambridge, Mass.: Slavica Publishers, 1976. 294pp. A selection of thirteen essays make up this edited volume, half of which were translated from Russian, French, and other languages. Among the highlights: Dom Augustin Calmet's "Vampires of Hungary, Bohemia, Moravia, and Silesia" (76–135); A. N. Afanas'ev's "Poetic Views of the Slavs Regarding Nature" (160–179); and T. P. Vukanović's valuable study of Gypsy vampire traditions (201–234).

Perkowski, Jan L. *The Darkling: A Treatise on Slavic Vampirism*. Columbus, Ohio: Slavica Publishers, 1989. 169pp. A series of essays constitutes this book by one of the leading students of the vampire, covering among other subjects the confusion of the vampire with other creatures (e.g., the werewolf) and including discussions of Dracula and English literary vampires.

Riccardo, Martin V. *Vampires Unearthed: The Complete Multimedia and Dracula Bibliography*. New York: Garland, 1983. 135pp. This bibliographic aid covers novels, poems, plays, movies, comic books, and such topics as vampire bats, vampire jokes, and vampire cookbooks. It also lists magazines and even clubs concerned with vampires.

Summers, Montague. *The Vampire*. London: Senate, 1995. 356pp. Originally published in 1928 with the title *The Vampire: His Kith and Kin*, this erudite classic survey of vampires, written by a true believer, is still well worth reading.

Summers, Montague. *The Vampire in Europe*. London: Bracken Books, 1996. 330pp. Originally published in 1929, this survey, more limited than *The Vampire*, still offers excellent coverage of Europe, with its five chapters devoted to ancient Greece and Rome; England and Ireland; Hungary and Czechoslovakia; modern Greece; and finally Russia, Romania, and Bulgaria.

Index

181

CPSIA information can be obtained at www.ICGtesting.com
Printed in the USA
269806BV00004B/25/P